SCRAPE THE BARREL

KARLEY BRENNA

Scrape the Barrel

Copyright © 2024 by Karley Brenna

All rights reserved.

No part of this book may be reproduced in any form or by any electronic or mechanical means, including information storage and retrieval systems, without written permission from the author, except for the use of brief quotations in a book review.

This is a work of fiction. Any names, characters, places, brands, media, and incidents are either the products of the author's imagination and used in a fictitious manner. Any resemblance to actual people, places, or events is purely coincidental and fictional.

Do not copy, loan, sell, or redistribute.

Paperback ISBN: 979-8-9888184-3-4

Edited by: Bobbi Maclaren

Cover: Dirty Girl Designs by Ali Clemons

*To the moms who feel alone, like you're holding the world on your shoulders just to see their smiles—we see you.
You are loved.*

IMPORTANT NOTE

Dear reader,

Within these pages, heavy topics that may be sensitive to some readers are discussed. They are listed below, but please keep in mind that some may contain spoilers to what unfolds in this book. As always, I do my best to handle these topics with the care they deserve.

-Discussion of body image issues

-Mention of a cesarean delivery

-Brief mention of drunk driving (not by either of the MCs)

-Indication of potential sexual assault

-Losing a significant other and child in a car accident (not from the MCs)

-On page panic attacks

-Anxiety representation and on page panic attacks

-Missing pet

-Domestic abuse

-On page violence

-Explicit content and strong language

-Surprise pregnancy (epilogue)

"Courage is being scared to death and saddling up anyway."
– John Wayne

1

SAGE

This morning couldn't be more hectic if it tried.

Avery, my five year old daughter, had forgotten her coloring pencils at home—but that was just the beginning. To prevent the meltdown of the century, I'd turned around after we got to the parking lot of Bell Buckle Brews, but halfway home, we got stuck on the road waiting for elk to cross. After what felt like forever, I'd put the pedal to the metal—without actually speeding—and ran inside once we made it home, grabbed her things, and jogged back out to the car. But naturally, on my way back, I tripped on the stick she'd been playing with the day before and fell on my ass, resulting in the colored pencils flying all over the lawn. After plucking the pencils out of the overgrown grass, inadvertently adding a few plucked green blades to the bag, we'd rushed back to the cafe only thirty minutes before opening, which made everything else fall behind.

The pastries weren't in the oven, the dishes weren't cleaned the night before thanks to my lovely coworker Gemma, so I had to scrub like my life literally depended on it because my position at this cafe depended on it. I couldn't afford to lose my job over some dirty dishes. Because yes, I would be the one blamed for Gemma not doing her closing duties the night before. That was just how it worked here.

Typically, my mornings went smoothly. Avery and I were always on top of things. We had our routine down. If it was a school day, Avery would get her things together in her backpack on her own while I prepped her lunch, then I'd drop her off on the way to work. But with it being the middle of summer, she didn't have school, and I didn't have a babysitter to watch her, so she came to my job with me every day. The same went for winter break, spring vacation, or any other holiday during the school year.

If she wasn't at school, she was with me.

Bell Buckle was a small town on the north eastern side of Idaho with a population of only a couple hundred people, which made it difficult to find anyone with the time to watch an almost six year old girl. I also had a hard time trusting people, so if someone did come up with the ability to watch her while I was at work, I'd typically let them down easy. I was probably causing more problems for myself by doing that, but with how our life was only mere years ago, I wouldn't risk it if I felt off about someone.

Having Avery under my wing here made me feel better, even though it did make work difficult. There was typically only one employee working in the cafe at a time, other than the small overlap when shifts switched. With Bell Buckle being small and all, we didn't have so much foot traffic to where one person couldn't handle it all.

But today was one of those days where I wished someone was here to help.

It didn't even have to be my friend and coworker, Penny.

I'd take anyone.

Even Gemma.

"Mama, can I have something to eat?" Avery asked, coming out from the back of the cafe through the swinging door.

"Can you give me five minutes and I'll bring something back to you?" I asked as I pulled a breakfast sandwich out of the warmer with tongs and poured coffee into a mug at the same time. Some of the dark liquid splashed over the rim, adding to the multitude of other spills on the counter I kept telling myself I'd clean up when I had a minute.

If I got a minute.

Of course, the one day I was late had to be the busiest morning all summer.

Avery let out a huff and went back through the door to where her small table was set up with activities to keep her busy throughout the day. She got moody when she was hungry.

I set the sandwich and coffee on the counter beside the register. "Eight dollars and twenty-three cents, please."

Eric, one of the local ranchers, handed over a ten dollar bill. "Thanks, Sage. Keep the change."

"Thanks. Have a good day, alright?"

He grabbed his items off the counter. "Same to you."

Eric walked over to one of the tables and sat down, pulling the curled up newspaper out of the back pocket of his jeans. I heaved a breath, then turned to throw Avery's sandwich together before another customer came up to order.

"Hey, Sage. Refill?" Jeff, another local, asked from where he was seated by the window at the front of the cafe.

"Coming!" I called to him. I put more beans in the machine to brew as I grabbed Avery's sandwich and slipped through the door to the back.

"Here you go, Aves," I said, setting it down on a napkin in front of her.

She set her coloring pencil down and grabbed for the sandwich. "Thanks, Mama."

"You're welcome. I'm going back out there for a bit."

"Wait. Do you like my picture?" she asked, holding the paper up with her free hand.

I quickly studied the stick figures in the field of flowers, giving a nod. "I love it."

"Should I add anything else, do you think?"

"Needs more flowers. I'll check on you in a little, okay?"

"Okay," she mumbled through a mouthful of food.

I pushed through the swinging door with my shoulder, grabbing the decanter of coffee off the machine before turning. Right as I pivoted, my arm smacked right into a hard chest, causing the handle to slip out of my hand. It fell to the floor with a crash, shards of glass and drops of coffee spraying everywhere.

"Shit, I'm so sorry," I said to whoever I'd run into.

I didn't bother to look at who it was before grabbing a towel off the counter and bending to mop up the coffee.

"Be careful of the glass," the man warned as he crouched beside me, another rag in his calloused hand.

"I know how to—" I cursed as one of the shards of glass sliced my finger.

He grabbed my hand, pulling it closer to him to look at the cut.

"You should clean this up so it doesn't get infected. I'll take care of the mess."

I finally looked up into hazel eyes rimmed by dark lashes. I'd never seen the guy in my life. He was all man, his dirty blonde hair curling at the nape of his neck under his tan cowboy hat. He had to be new in town or just passing through. In a town so small, everyone knew everyone, and I'd know if I'd seen this man before.

"Ma'am?"

Blinking, I looked down at my finger. "It's not that bad."

"Even the tiniest cuts can get infected," he stated with my hand still gently gripped in his.

I pulled my hand away, brushing my finger on my apron. I internally cursed at the blood that smeared the fabric. That'd be a pain to get out.

"I can't have a customer clean this," I said, grabbing the towel again. If he cut himself, it'd be on me. Though, with hands as thick-skinned as his, I doubted anything could pierce the flesh.

"It's not a problem."

I focused on soaking up the coffee with the rag. "It's a liability thing."

I needed something to put the glass in so I could clean the rest of the mess. I stood at the same time he did, our foreheads banging into one another. I squeezed my eyes shut for a second as he steadied me with rough hands on my shoulders.

"Should someone this clumsy really be working in a coffee shop?" he asked, his voice sounding accusatory. As if I was the problem here.

I straightened, narrowing my eyes at him. "I am *not* clumsy."

He pursed his lips, his eyes shooting to the mess on the floor and then back to me. "You've hit me twice in the last two minutes."

"*Hit* you?" Was he *serious*?

"What else would you call it?"

I grabbed an empty coffee cup off the counter, bending back down to gently pick up the glass on the ground. My head pulsed where we'd bumped into each other, and my finger was still bleeding, which had to be a sanitary issue, but I couldn't care less right now.

The man's boots shifted in my peripheral as I plucked the shards, then disappeared for a second until they came back into view.

"If you won't take care of it, then at least let me," he started.

I looked up at him from where I was still crouched. "I'm fine."

He took a step back, holding his hands up, one of them gripping a wad of paper towels. "Alright."

I was so over today.

My eyes fell to the stain of coffee on his shirt and another curse rolled off my tongue. I tried to keep the swear words to a minimum around Avery, but today was *not* my day.

Heaving a sigh, I stood again, taking the paper towels from his raised hand. I pressed my finger into the wad, the cut stinging slightly. "I appreciate you trying to help, but I assure you I can take care of it. You're not supposed to be behind the counter anyway."

His gaze darted to the door I'd come out of, then back to me. "I wasn't sure if anyone was working here."

"So your plan was to check in the back?" I asked, looking down at my finger to see how bad the cut was.

Thankfully, it didn't look like it needed stitches.

"Yeah," he admitted.

"Well, the door wouldn't be unlocked if there wasn't someone working here," I said, hating the anger in my tone.

He slowly nodded, like he knew that.

"I'm sorry about your shirt," I blurted.

He looked down like he was just now realizing there was coffee on it. "No biggie."

I turned to the sink, running my finger under the water. The bleeding was slowing, but I didn't want coffee or other bacteria sitting in the wound.

"You can have a coffee on the house," I said over my shoulder, my focus on my finger as I rinsed it clean.

When I didn't get a response, I looked in his direction, but he wasn't there.

My eyes raked over the rest of the cafe, but he was gone.

I shouldn't have been so irritated with him. It truly wasn't his fault. I was typically able to keep my calm, but after everything that had already happened today and it barely being nine a.m., my self control snapped.

"Mama, can I have a—"

"Avery, don't come out here! I have to clean this glass," I hurriedly said before she could slip out from behind the door. "I'll let you know when you can come out."

"Okay." The door swung back shut.

My chest rose with the deep inhale I took in an attempt to calm myself even the slightest, placing both hands on the metal countertop beside the sink.

Only four more hours, and then I could go home and crawl under the soft covers of my bed before I had to do it all over again tomorrow.

2

Callan

"Just get a coffee at the cafe," I muttered to myself as I headed toward my truck, repeating the words my brother had said to me over the phone only an hour ago. "It's quick and easy."

I had run out of coffee at home, which I never let happen, so I'd headed to my parents' house at Bottom of the Buckle Ranch without it. Figuring I'd just pour myself a cup there, I'd come to find, to my utter disappointment, that their coffee machine broke this morning.

Go figure.

So I'd called Lennon, my oldest brother, and he'd suggested Bell Buckle Brews. I stayed the hell away from cafes because the coffee was too damn fancy. Americano, espresso, latte, cappuccino, a fucking puppacino. All I wanted was black. Plain black coffee. Not some fancy shit with foamed up milk and syrups.

I loved my mom and little sister, Lettie, but even their hazelnut and caramel creamers made my nose sting.

I'm all for sweets, but drinking it in the form of coffee? That's where they lost me.

Today was the first and last day I'd braved the coffee shop. It wasn't the woman's—Sage, according to her nametag—fault, but I didn't want to be bombarded by chaos before I'd had any sort of caffeine. Though, her green eyes had been bright enough to pull me out of my exhaustion for a moment, her soft, pink lips a distraction from the craving of rich coffee.

Regardless of that, by nature, I was the nicest out of my four siblings, but that was only *after* coffee.

I was also typically a pretty patient person—I had to be with my job of teaching kids and teens how to ride horses. But it wasn't even nine a.m., and I'd already been put through the ringer in a wild horse chase of trying to find a cup of joe, so when I'd stood behind the register for all of two minutes waiting for an employee, I took it into my own hands to go find them.

For all I knew, they were in the back smoking or something.

Then Sage had rammed into me, shattered an entire decanter of coffee, bumped heads with me, and refused to clean her cut, and my nice guy attitude snapped. I felt bad, and honestly, I should have walked back in there and apologized, but instead, my hand grabbed the handle of my truck and yanked open the door.

I drove in the direction of the small grocery store in town, hoping that they had coffee machines in stock. I wasn't in the mood to drive back to my house with a new bag of coffee beans, make a cup, then head back to my parents' ranch for work, so I was buying them a new machine.

A few minutes later, I pulled into the parking lot and pulled the keys out of the ignition with a bit too much force. I sat back against the seat, inhaling deeply to steady my racing heart.

It wasn't the lack of coffee making me this irritable. It was being out in town.

I didn't just overthink fancy coffee orders, I overthought everything. Every person in every store, if I should wave the guy ahead at the stop sign or go first, how easily accessible the parking lot was at any place.

Being home and on my parents' ranch was where I felt most content, so I didn't see the point in leaving either place often. Aside from groceries, the occasional visit to the bar, and diesel for my truck, I had no desire to be out in town. I loved helping my mom with events for her horse rescue, Bottom of the Buckle, but that was about as far as my social skills took me.

This may not be a popular opinion, but kids were easy to talk to, which is what made me love teaching them to ride. Every kid was always so overjoyed to sit on a horse, and I loved being the one to elicit those smiles on their faces.

On the contrary, attempting to make an adult smile was like pulling teeth, which was probably why my other brother, Reed, was so closed-off from everyone. Sure, I was caring and would do anything for those that I loved, but that held an expectation for me to be charismatic, too.

So often, I'd swallow down the anxiety that would crawl up my chest, land like a rock in my throat, and beat the hell out of my heart.

Smile and wave, isn't that what they say?

It was basically my life motto at this point.

"Just one more store and you can go home," I told myself before opening the truck door and heading inside the market.

"Good morning, Callan," the lady behind the counter greeted as I tugged at the bottom of my shirt. It didn't need fixing—my hands just needed something to do.

As small towns go, everyone knows everyone, but not me. With my rare appearance in town and mindset of *get in and get out*, I didn't memorize people's faces. But people memorized mine, being a Bronson and all.

"Good morning," I said back, to be polite. "Do you have any coffee machines by chance?"

The gray-haired woman nodded, the end of her short ponytail getting caught on her shoulder with the movement. "We actually have a few of the Keurig Elites if that's what you're looking for."

What the fuck was a Keurig?

"Yep, that's the one. Which aisle is it down?" I asked.

"I'll show you." She came around the counter, leading me down an aisle that smelled similar to the cafe. "Right here." She pointed to the boxes on the bottom row.

I bent, picking one up.

"Do you have pods for it?" she asked.

Pods?

"Uh, no," I replied. What the fuck was a *pod*?

"I personally like this flavor," she said as she reached for a bright blue box on the shelf.

"That'll work."

"Did you have any other shopping to do?"

"Nope, just this." *Please just get me out of here.*

She turned, heading back to the register. My thumb fiddled with the bottom corner of the box as I followed. She scanned the two products, then read off the total. After paying, I balanced the two items in my hands, thanked her, and headed for my truck.

"A Keurig?" a familiar voice asked from behind me as I was setting the boxes on the passenger seat in my truck.

I turned to see Lennon standing there in his Tumbleweed Feed shirt. He owned the feed store a few blocks down the road, having just officially taken over the building from the leasing company a few months ago.

"Don't ask."

Lennon set an elbow on the side of my truck bed. "I take it you skipped the cafe?"

"Long story." I wasn't in the mood to explain.

He lifted a chin toward the passenger side of the truck. "That for your place? I've never pegged you for a fancy coffee kind of guy."

"It's for Mom and Dad's place. Theirs broke this morning." Lennon tried to hide his smile, but was terribly unsuccessful.

"What?" I asked.

"Just get it on recording when Dad sees the machine sitting in the kitchen. I'm begging."

I rolled my eyes, closing the passenger door. "I've got to get to work."

He hit the side of my truck bed twice, stepping away. "See you tonight?"

I furrowed my brow in confusion. "Tonight?"

"You promised dinner with me and Oakley, remember?"

"Right. Yeah. I'll be there."

Lennon headed inside the grocery store as I rounded the truck to get in on the driver's side to head toward my parents' ranch. They lived on the outskirts of town on a massive property where they raised a decent number of cattle, grew hay, and ran their horse rescue. The volunteers helped majorly with the rescue load, but my dad was always out on the ranch taking care of things. With me and Reed almost always on the property for work, mine being the riding lessons and Reed being a farrier, we were typically the ones assisting him with various ranch chores.

I liked helping in general, but ask me to do anything on the ranch and I'd do it with a smile on my face.

About twenty minutes later, I was pulling up the long driveway to Bottom of the Buckle Ranch and killing the engine on my truck. The pressure in my chest eased with the feeling of being home, even though I was only out for barely an hour.

Reed was bent over his horse's hoof by the red barn while our dad was stuffing something in his saddle bag.

I got out, coming around the other side of my truck to grab the two boxes.

"Damn horse threw another shoe again," Reed grumbled from where he was hunched over.

"Might say something about the farrier," Dad teased him.

Reed shot him a glare as I closed the passenger door with my shoulder. "He's clumsy. Keeps stepping on his other foot and yanking it off."

"Morning, guys," I said to the two of them.

Dad turned, his eyes dropping to the boxes in my hands. "What's that?"

"New coffee machine," I replied.

His eyes narrowed, inspecting the picture on the side. "Where's the pot?"

I looked down at the side of the box, seeing the picture for the first time. "Good question."

"It's one of those fancy coffee machines," Reed stated. "It doesn't have a pot."

"Then how the fuck do you make coffee out of it?" Dad asked.

Reed dropped the horse's leg gently, standing to his full height with a frown. "Pods."

"*Pods?*" Dad said it like he was trying the word out on his tongue.

"I thought the same thing," I told him.

"Even I know what a coffee pod is," Reed snided with an eye roll.

"I'm going to go set this up and see if I can figure it out," I said. "I'll be back out for my lesson in thirty minutes."

They went back to their tasks, Dad heading inside the barn while Reed dug through his bag on the ground beside him. I headed inside the old farmhouse my parents had renovated, hoping that this machine would be easier to set up than it looked.

3

Sage

I glanced at the clock, counting down the minutes until Gemma came in for the lunch hour so I could head home with Avery. As much as I disliked Gemma's work ethic and attitude, I'd feel relieved when she walked through that door. After the morning rush had slowed down, I'd cleaned as best I could and made sure to wrap my finger after putting antibiotic ointment on the cut.

It stung, but it would heal.

The cowbell strung above the door sounded and I looked up to see Lennon Bronson walking in. The man was a tall glass of water with his dirty blonde hair and baseball cap, but we'd always just been friendly to each other. He was dating one of my favorite customers who also happened to be his employee at the feed store. He and Oakley were perfect for each other, which made my mind wander to wishing I'd find my perfect person one day, too.

The last man in my life was far from it.

"How's your day, Sage?" Lennon asked, approaching the counter.

I sighed, my shoulders drooping a bit as I let my defenses drop. I didn't have to be my usual fake, cheery self to him. He wasn't just some random customer, he was a friend.

"Do you really want to know?" My mind grew exhausted just thinking of having to rehash the day's events.

He chuckled, flashing a half smile. "From the sound of it, guess I don't."

Avery strided through the back door, a drawing in her hand as her eyes landed on Lennon. "Mr. Bronson! Do you wanna see my horse?"

"Is that even a question? Of course, I do." He leaned toward her as she stepped up on the stool behind the counter, setting her drawing on the metal surface.

"I don't know what to name him," she said.

He picked up the paper like he was deep in thought, pressing his lips into a thin line. "Hmm. What are our options?"

She pushed her dark brunette hair out of her face, the color courtesy of her dad. Mine was more of an ash brown.

"Sparkle, Boots, and Pigeon," she listed with confidence.

He arched a brow at the last one, peering over the top of the paper at her. "Pigeon?"

She nodded. "I think Boots is my favorite, though."

He set the paper back down in front of her. "Boots it is."

"Okay!" She pulled her pink colored pencil out of her pocket, doing her best to write the name on the paper above the brown horse. "Mama, how do you spell Boots?"

I pulled out my notepad and pen from the front of my apron, writing the word down as I said each letter out loud, then handed it to her.

"You ever get around to bringing her to the ranch?" Lennon asked me, as Avery spelled the word out loud to herself while she wrote it.

"To the ranch?" I asked.

"For those riding lessons I told you about a few months ago. My brother would be more than willing to teach her to ride."

I glanced down at the drawing as Avery slashed the "t," gnawing on my bottom lip. Amidst the chaos of raising a five-year-old on my own, I'd completely forgotten about his offer. She'd been begging me for a horse when Lennon offered for her to come ride at the ranch. Avery was obsessed with horses and would have a blast, but it'd be hard to find time in our schedule. At least with school being out, it was manageable, but I didn't want to deflate her once summer ended if the lessons slowed down.

"Sage?" Lennon interrupted my thoughts.

I gave him a tight-lipped smile. "I'll bring her by when I can."

He dipped his chin in a nod, pleased with my answer. Even though Lennon didn't have kids of his own, he could see how draining it was to be at the top of my game every day. He wanted to give me the break he so desperately saw that I needed.

That's what happened when you had a kid. While your feelings still mattered, you'd do anything to never let your kid see the storm, and that meant no days off.

"I most likely won't be there, but one of my brothers will. Just let them know I sent you," he said.

"Does it matter what day?" I didn't want to be rude and stop by without an appointment or anything, but with the cafe and Avery, my schedule was never set in stone. It was hard to plan much of anything.

"Nope. Cal's almost always there."

"Cal?" I'd never heard that brother's name before. I knew Lettie, Reed, and Beckham Bronson, but I assumed that was it. I'd lived here for three years, so I figured I'd met all the Bronsons.

"Callan. He's about a year older than you, teaches lessons at our parents' ranch, looks most like me than my other brothers..." He listed the traits like a little light bulb would go off over my head at any minute.

I shook my head, absentmindedly running my fingers through Avery's hair as she added flowers to her drawing. "Doesn't ring a bell."

As if on cue, the cowbell rang above the door as Gemma walked in.

I glanced at the clock out of habit, seeing that she was ten minutes late. She always was, but I'd learned my lesson the last time when she bit my head off for even opening my mouth about a schedule. I'd been late to pick up Avery from school that day, and I blamed myself for it, even though it was nowhere near my fault.

"You're here," I said with what had to be my hundredth forced smile of the day.

"I'm here," she repeated dryly, coming around the counter to head through the back door.

I patted Avery's shoulder, looking down at her. "Why don't you grab your stuff and we can head home?"

"Okay, Mama." She finished off her flower on the paper, leaving the drawing behind as she went to grab her backpack. Though it was summer, she still brought it with her so she had snacks, various toys, and extra drawing supplies to keep her busy throughout my shift.

"Well, just look for the guy that's the complete opposite of Reed, and you'll find him," Lennon said, going back to the Callan topic.

"I'll be sure to tell Reed you said that," I teased with a smile. "Did you want anything before I leave?"

He shook his head. "Just wanted to check in, see how things were going. You've seemed..."

"Stressed?" I filled in.

His face fell. "Stressed."

"I'm a single mom to a five-year-old with no babysitter and a full-time job. What's not to be stressed about?" I didn't mean it literally, yet it was literal in every sense of the word, and I hated the way his eyes changed, sympathy for my situation apparent in them. "I'm okay, Len. Really. Thank you for checking in."

"Oakley would have my ass if I didn't," he said, and he was right, she would. We'd grown to be great friends since she moved into town months ago. "Do you need the address?"

"I honestly don't remember where I put the paper you wrote it on, so that'd be great." I never lost so many things until I had Avery, then mom-brain kicked in and I was overly forgetful.

I slid him the notepad and pen from beside Avery's drawing and he wrote the address down.

"Tell Oakley I said hi and that I'll text her once I get a free moment." Would I ever have a free moment, though?

"I will." He set the pen on the pad, tapped the counter twice, then headed for the door. "See you later, Sage."

"See you," I replied as he disappeared out the door.

"Ready," Avery said as she came to my side with her backpack slung over her shoulders.

"Let me just tell Gemma we're leaving."

I peeked my head through the back door to find Gemma sitting at the table by the refrigerator. "I'm heading out."

She didn't bother to look up from her phone as she teetered on the back two legs of the chair. "You think your kid can clean up her mess?"

My eyes moved to Avery's small table shoved against the wall, a breakfast bar wrapper and a colored pencil sitting on top. I briefly closed my eyes and inhaled a calming breath, though it did little to ease the frustration I felt toward Gemma. I grabbed the wrapper in a fist, shoving it in the pocket of my jeans, then picked up the single colored pencil.

Without a word, I headed back out to Avery, not bothering to put the pencil in her backpack as I grabbed her hand and headed out of the cafe to my car. Once we approached the trunk, I unlocked the doors and slid Avery's backpack off before she got in the car to buckle herself into her booster seat.

Setting the pink backpack on the passenger seat along with the pencil, I shut my driver door and turned the key in the ignition. We lived in town, so the drive home was short. I pulled into the driveway that led up to the beige home—everything about it was bland, from the paint to the layout. But I couldn't complain when our landlord left us alone and allowed pets.

Avery's buckle clicked and she was out in seconds, running up to the door. Sliding out of the driver's side with Avery's backpack in hand, I headed up the concrete pathway to the house, fitting the key in the lock and opening the door.

"Do you want to watch a movie?" I asked as she walked inside. I didn't have the energy for much else, and while I was well aware that people shamed screen time, sometimes a mother just needed a minute. And a glass of wine. I was *definitely* pouring myself a glass of wine.

"Frozen?" she asked, not bothering to close the door behind us like I'd reminded her countless times to do so her cat wouldn't run out.

Kicking the door shut, I set her backpack on the hook in the front entry. "Sounds good to me. Want to change into some comfy clothes and we can turn it on?"

She tossed her hair over her shoulder as she turned to me. "Are you getting in comfy clothes, too?"

I set my phone and pocket-sized wallet on the ivory kitchen counter. "How could I watch a movie without being comfy?"

I turned and put my hands out like I was going to tickle her, but before I could reach her, she erupted in a fit of giggles and darted down the hall. "I'm gonna catch you!" I called as I prowled down the hall.

"No, you're not!" she squealed before shutting her bedroom door.

The smile on my face stuck as I dressed in gray sweatpants and an oversized black t-shirt. It was my first genuine smile of the day. Though it was summer, I loved my sweatpants no matter the temperature outside.

I beat Avery back to the kitchen so I poured the glass of wine I'd been craving since I'd first made it to work this morning. My phone buzzed on the counter as I set the bottle back in the fridge. Glancing over at it, I saw it was the same unknown number that'd been calling me for a few days now. I knew the area code by heart, having grown up in Portland, but there was only one person from my hometown who would be trying to reach me, and a call from them wasn't possible.

"I'm ready!" Avery announced as she zoomed by the doorway to the kitchen, straight into the living room.

"Be right there, Aves," I called to her.

I set the glass on the counter, my hand trembling on instinct as I attempted to take a steadying breath. On impulse, my fingers came up to my necklace, fiddling with the charm dangling from it. My grandmother had given it to me as a little girl, and I wore it every day since. The piece of jewelry had become a comfort piece to wear, my hand always finding it when the nerves set in.

What if it was him?

What if he was out and trying to find me? Trying to find Avery?

My fingers shook around the rose gold jewelry. I had to breathe or it would get worse.

In through my nose, out through my mouth.

I counted to ten.

To thirty.

To whatever number it would take to make those thoughts fit back into the box they were supposed to stay trapped in.

Everything was fine.

He was still in prison for another couple years.

I had nothing to worry about.

Once I mentally hit the sixties, I grabbed my wine, heading out to the living room. Opting for our favorite sherpa blanket off the back of the couch, I tossed it over my legs, pulling Avery closer to my side with our cat, Pudding, on her lap.

We were safe here.

We had to be.

4

CALLAN

I grabbed the green bean casserole out of Lennon's oven and set the dish on a hot pad next to the chicken breasts and brown sugar roasted carrots on the counter. Lennon and Oakley had made the sides while I worked on the chicken, but I'd offered to finish off the dinner when the timer had gone off mid-conversation in the living room.

The two of them moved to the dining room table after Oakley refilled her glass of wine and Lennon grabbed the bowl of roasted carrots. I balanced the other two dishes as I followed behind.

"Want another beer?" Lennon asked after setting the bowl down.

"Sure, thanks." I double checked the table, making sure each setting had the proper utensils and a napkin.

Taking a seat on the opposite side of Oakley, I situated my napkin on my lap as Lennon came back in with our beverages.

"It looks delicious," Oakley observed, eyeing the green bean casserole.

"A favorite of yours, too?" I asked.

She nodded. "I could eat it at every meal. I hate how some people wait until Thanksgiving to indulge."

I let out a small chuckle as she reached for the serving spoon. "I feel the same way."

"I hate green beans," Lennon stated.

"So you've reminded us four times now," Oakley remarked as she piled a heaping portion onto her plate.

"They're just so bland—" he started.

"That's why you add the crispy onions," Oakley and I said in unison, since we'd had to tell him every time he brought it up.

We all served ourselves, then dug in.

"So, I'll just get it out, then. Oakley is co-owner of the store now," Lennon announced, breaking the silence at the table.

My eyebrows practically shot six inches in the air. "Really?"

Lennon nodded as Oakley's cheeks flushed. "Having her as just my employee was a bit...difficult."

I cleared my throat, grabbing for my beer. I didn't want to know what they did in that office of theirs. "Congrats, you guys."

"Thanks, Cal. We work really well together," she said.

A smirk bloomed on Lennon's mouth after he finished chewing. "At work and at home."

"I love you guys, but I really don't think I can keep my food down hearing about your sex life." Especially because I didn't have one of my own.

"Well, I got you another client," Lennon told me, blissfully changing the subject.

"Do I know them?" I asked.

"Since you don't go anywhere but your usual spots, no, you don't. At least, she doesn't know you. You need to get out more, Cal," he said.

"I do get out."

His eyes pinned me in my seat as his brows lowered. "Our parents' ranch and the bar don't count."

"Those aren't the only places I go," I defended as Oakley took a sip of wine, watching us.

Lennon set his napkin on the table, leaning back in his chair. "The grocery store doesn't count, either."

I shoved the remaining carrots around on my plate with a sigh. "I know." It was no secret that I was a homebody. I loved my job and my family, so I kept my focus on those two things. Was that such a problem? I was content.

"Maybe you'll think she's cute," Lennon said, jumping back to the new client he roped in for me.

"She is pretty cute. Her daughter is adorable, too," Oakley agreed.

I looked at the two of them. "Another lovestruck mom?"

Lennon's eyes narrowed as he crossed his arms, somewhat defensively. *Interesting.* "No."

Oakley looked between the two of us, sensing Lennon was getting umbrageous. "She's really sweet. I think you'll like her."

"Look, guys, I'm not really looking to date, but thanks for thinking of me." I hadn't dated since my ex, and I wasn't planning on changing that. Being given an ultimatum to choose between your girlfriend or your family will make you lay off dating for a while, that's for sure.

We finished our dinner and chatted for a bit before I stood, gathering the dishes from the table and bringing them to the kitchen. I turned the faucet to hot and began scrubbing.

"You don't have to clean up," Lennon said, coming into the kitchen with the empty beer bottles to toss them in the recycling.

"It's alright." I liked cleaning. It helped keep my mind occupied when all it wanted to do was wander.

Lennon leaned back against the counter beside the sink, crossing his arms. After I scrubbed the remaining dishes clean, I turned off the water and faced him while I dried my hands on a rag.

"What?" I could tell he had something on his mind.

"Go easy on her," he said.

"Oakley?"

He frowned. We both knew he wasn't talking about Oakley. "The client I set you up with. She'll be by sometime this week. She's nice, so I expect you to treat her the same."

"I'm always nice." It was true—I was. I got it from our mom. Where my other brothers had their reasons for being the way they were, I was always the nice one, offering to help the moment I saw someone needed it. We all would. That's how we were raised. But my brothers thought of me as soft for how I went about it.

"I'm going to head home," I told him. I had an early lesson tomorrow and was already tired from the shit show of the day I'd had.

"Text me when you get home."

"I will." Grabbing my cowboy hat off the counter, I slipped it on, heading for the front door. I peeked in the living room on my way, seeing Oakley on the couch with her wine. "Goodnight, Oakley."

She twisted on the cushion, looking over the back at me. "Goodnight, Cal. Drive safe."

"Will do." I headed out the door, the summer air warming my arms from the AC inside their house. Sliding behind the wheel of my 2018 Ram 3500, I headed home. The backroads were dark, as usual, the moon and stars lighting up the fields that stretched for miles in every direction.

I would always take more clients, even if my schedule was already packed, but the way Lennon got almost protective over this woman made me think he was recruiting her for all the wrong reasons. I didn't need to be set up with anyone, let alone a mother. There were enough single, and married, moms that flirted with me while I instructed their children how to ride. Sure, she could be different, but I knew what came with the territory, and I wasn't sure if I was ready.

SCRAPE THE BARREL

Not after what happened all those years ago.
But maybe this woman would be different.
I doubted it.

5

SAGE

My SUV bumped along the dirt road as it trudged up the driveway to Bottom of the Buckle Ranch. Avery couldn't sit still in the back seat, going on and on about how she hoped one of the horses here looked like Boots, the one in her drawing.

I wasn't sure what Callan looked like, but I recognized Bailey, Lettie's fiancé, right away as I came to a stop in front of the white barn.

Avery was already unbuckled and out the door by the time I had my seat belt halfway off. To say she was excited was an understatement.

"Bailey! I get to ride a horse today!" she exclaimed to him as she ran in his direction.

I got out, not bothering to lock my car behind me.

Bailey offered me a smile as he turned his attention to Avery, who came skidding to a stop in front of him in her pink cowgirl boots. "A horse, huh?"

She nodded quickly. "Yeah. Do you think I can ride your horse?"

He took the piece of straw out of his mouth, flicking it to the ground. "Nova's a little too advanced for you, Aves, but I'm sure Callan has the perfect horse just for you."

"Just for me?" Avery asked as I came to a stop a few feet behind her, taking in the ranch. It was beautiful out here, with three barns, multiple arenas, and pastures that stretched for miles. The bright green grass swayed in the slight wind like waves in an ocean. The sound filled the air, the pine trees swaying at the tips where they towered over the land.

Where was this when I was having a terrible day? One breath of this air and I'd forget all about the stress. It smelled like pine and oak mixed with the scent of the various animals around the ranch. The Idaho breeze was calming, relaxing my stiff body instantly.

"Hmm, it might be. Can you keep a secret?" Bailey asked Avery, crouching to her height.

She nodded again, and he leaned closer. "I think he might put you on Lettie's horse."

Avery's face lit up. "Really?"

Bailey nodded with a wink, then stood, ruffling her hair as he faced me. "Callan will be out in a minute, he's just finishing up with a student."

"Thanks, Bailey," I said.

I glanced behind me at the white farmhouse, then heard boots scuffling on the dirt. I turned to find Avery running toward the fence lining one of the pastures.

"Avery!" I called out, hurrying after her.

"Yes, Mama?" she asked like she hadn't just run away from me.

"You can't run off like that. We don't know this place."

"We don't bite," a male voice said to my right.

I turned to find a man wearing a tan cowboy hat, light wash jeans, and a gray t-shirt that hugged his body. The same man that I spilled coffee all over in the cafe. If he recognized me, he didn't give any indication.

He stood about five feet away with a hand casually slung over the fence. His eyes moved to Avery. "You ready for your lesson?"

Avery spun so fast that her hair whipped out behind her. She beamed up at him from where she stood next to me. "Yes! I'm so excited."

"You're Callan?" I asked, feeling a little dumbstruck. My hair was in a ponytail, my plaid shirt hanging open to reveal my white tank top underneath. I'd chosen sneakers and flared jeans to complete the outfit, but now I felt like I looked a little homeless compared to him. Not that he was wearing anything fancy, but at first glance, he was definitely the kind of good-looking that could get away with wearing anything and he'd still be striking.

He nodded, holding a hand out for me to shake it. "My apologies, I thought you knew. Callan Bronson."

I shook it. "Sage McKinley."

"Pretty name," Callan remarked as I let go of his hand. It may have just been the sun, but I swore his cheeks turned a pinkish hue. "And you are?" he asked, turning to Avery.

"Avery," she supplied eagerly.

He brushed his hands on his jeans, almost like he was nervous. "Avery. Just as pretty a name as your mother's. Ready to get started?"

She nodded and he waved her along as he turned to head for the barn. Avery practically skipped alongside him. I stayed a few feet back, crossing my arms as I watched the two of them ahead of me.

His dirty blonde hair curled just below his hat, showing off his tan neck. His biceps were that perfect size—just enough to stretch the sleeves of his shirt.

I hoped he didn't look at me the way I was studying him right now. I looked like I just rolled out of bed and decided to show up. I cursed myself for not putting on any makeup. But why did it matter? I wasn't here to impress anyone.

"Can I know what color the horse is?" Avery asked as they entered the barn.

"I could tell you, but that would spoil the surprise," Callan said as he grabbed a halter off the hook by the door.

"I hope it looks like Boots," Avery murmured, more to herself than to Callan.

"Who's Boots?" he asked as they made their way down the aisle.

"My horse I drew. I hope I can have a horse just like him someday."

My heart sank. I wished I could give Avery everything she wanted right when she wanted it. Call it spoiled, but my mom-heart hated not being able to give her everything she dreamed of. She was obsessed with horses, always drawing them or playing with her horse figurines. I'd make it happen for her one day, I just didn't know when that one day would come.

"With determination like that, I think it'll happen," Callan told her.

Avery came to a stop beside him outside of a stall. "Can I show you my drawing next time? I forgot to bring it with me."

"I'd love that." He unlatched the door and slid it open while I stood across the aisle, giving them their space. I liked seeing Avery be independent, but I also didn't want to get in their way.

"This is Lettie's horse, Red. He's a little old, but he loves taking kids around the arena, so I think he'd be perfect for you today. What do you think?" He looked down at her to see her eyes practically bulging out of her head in the shape of two hearts as she stared up at the massive animal. The horse had a dark, rich coat that faded to a lighter shade throughout his body, but his head and legs were a deep red.

"He's so pretty! Yes, I'd love to ride him!" She paused, moving her gaze up to Callan. "You don't think Lettie will be mad, right?"

Callan's little sister, Lettie, came into Bell Buckle Brews frequently enough that she and Avery knew each other pretty well now.

"She won't be mad, I promise. Then when you see her next, you can tell her all about your ride." Callan took a step into the stall, the horse letting out a snort as he lowered his head slightly, like he knew what to do without Callan asking.

He slipped the rope halter over his nose and situated the knot, then patted Red's neck. "You want to lead him out?" he asked Avery.

"Can I?" she questioned, seeming a bit unsure of herself.

"Of course. He's really sweet. I know he seems big and scary, but he's a big softie on the inside." He gave the horse a pat just above his shoulder for emphasis.

I couldn't help the smile from pulling at my lips. Callan was already showing that he was good with kids, but I guess he had to be when he worked with them daily.

He held the lead rope out to Avery and she grabbed it gently. "Do I just walk?"

He nodded. "I'll walk beside you so you know where to go."

They both stepped out of the stall and I stayed put, waiting for them to pass with the horse. I kept a good ten feet back from Red's rear as we made our way down the aisle. Avery was talking Callan's ear off, glancing over her shoulder at Red every few steps. She even shot me a smile when her eyes caught on me. I gave her a thumbs up in return.

After they came around a corner, Callan helped Avery clip Red into cross ties, the horse standing patiently as they hooked a rope onto either side of his halter. They got to work saddling him together. Avery did her best to take in every bit of information, listening intently to every instruction he gave her.

Once Red was all tacked up, Avery picked out a helmet and we headed out to the arena. I stayed on the outside, leaning against the fence as I watched them.

Callan brought a mounting block over, holding Avery's hand to help her up the steps. He didn't seem annoyed at having to walk her through every step. If anything, it seemed like he was more than happy about it.

Avery's butt plopped in the saddle and Callan got to work adjusting her stirrups. "Mama, look!"

I smiled at her, tears welling in my eyes at seeing my little girl on a horse for the first time. "I see, Aves! You look so good up there."

"Like a cowgirl?" she asked as Cal came around the horse to work on the other stirrup.

"Like my little cowgirl." Seeing my baby doing something she always wanted to do pulled my heart right out of my chest and set in directly in the palm of my hand. Avery was my entire world. I'd do anything to see that smile on her face every day.

***

About an hour later, after Callan had led Avery around the arena a few times, we headed back into the barn to untack Red. Avery was telling Callan all about her friends at school and how they'd be so jealous when they heard she got to ride a horse. Even as he put his hands under her armpits, lifting her out of the saddle, she kept rambling on.

To say Avery was ecstatic about her ride was an understatement.

I stood off to the side, watching them as Callan worked to take the saddle off the red roan horse, setting it on the stand by the cross ties.

"You want to brush the dirt off of him?" he asked Avery.

"Can I?"

"Of course. He'll love it." Callan dug through a black bucket, then pulled out a pink brush, handing it to her. "Stroke from front to back all over. I'll be right here if you need help."

Avery got to work brushing the horse as he stood there patiently, clearly loving the attention. Callan came over to stand beside me, leaning on his hands folded behind him against the wall.

"Thank you for this," I said, not taking my gaze off of Avery as she hummed to herself.

"She's a natural."

Out of the corner of my eye, I saw him facing me, so I glanced over at him, then back to Avery. He was studying me, and I had the biggest feeling he was recalling the coffee incident.

"I'm sorry about the coffee. I didn't mean to come off as rude in any way, I was just having a bad day and—"

"It's all good, Sage," he interrupted before I could ramble myself into a hole. "I didn't think you spilled it on me on purpose. After all, I was the one behind the counter when I shouldn't have been."

I turned to face him as Avery reached as high as she could to try to brush the horse's back. "Regardless, I shouldn't have been so...short-tempered."

He pushed off the wall, grabbing a mounting block from beside him, and brought it over to Avery. He helped her step up onto it so she could reach Red's back easier, then returned to his spot next to me, leaning back against the wall, like him helping her was second nature.

That did something to my insides and I hated it.

"We all have bad days sometimes," Callan said, jumping right back into the conversation with ease. "I wasn't at my best either, so I apologize for that as well."

My fingers played with the hem of my flannel as I looked down at my shoes, not sure what to say to him.

"How's your finger?"

I glanced at the bandage wrapped around the cut. "It's healing quickly. Nothing more than a scrape, really."

He dipped his chin. "Good. Do you have a day that works best for you to bring her back?"

My eyes jumped to his. "I can't afford lessons."

He shook his head, his brow furrowing slightly under the brim of his hat. "It's on me."

"I can't not pay you for riding lessons, Callan." There was no way I'd allow that.

His eyes moved back and forth between mine slowly like he was thinking of a way around this. "How about you bring pastries, and I consider that your payment."

I let out a disbelieving scoff. "A seventy-dollar riding lesson is not equal to a three-dollar pastry."

"Then bring some for the volunteers. They'd love it." A lot of people in town volunteered for Bottom of the Buckle Horse Rescue. His parents had started it well before their children were born and kept it going all these years, saving countless horses' lives. If you lived in Bell Buckle, you knew about the rescue.

"And your family," I decided.

He nodded once, turning his attention back on Avery. "And my family."

"Mondays work best for me, but I can make other days work, too." Bell Buckle Brews was closed on Mondays, so I typically used the day to catch up on chores or yard work, but all of that could be set aside to bring Avery out here for an hour or two.

"How about we play it by ear?"

"I'm sure Avery will take advantage of that. She'd be here every day if I let her."

"All done!" Avery announced as she stepped down from the mounting block.

Callan pushed off the wall, closing the few steps to her and taking the brush from her. "Did you get *all* the dirt?"

She nodded, confidence shining in her response. "Every teeny tiny speck."

He leaned close to Red's face, wrapping an arm under his chin to scratch the opposite cheek. "That true, Red?" he asked in a whisper.

The horse pawed his foot in response.

"See? Even he knows it," Avery declared.

Callan took a step back, nodding like he was contemplating if it was true. "Okay, I'll take your guys' word for it. Do you want to help me put him out in the pasture?"

"Yes, please."

Callan unhooked the cross ties and handed the lead rope to Avery. The two of them walked side by side down the aisle of the barn again, the horse's hooves clomping on the matts as they headed outside and I followed behind.

Once we were at the gate to the pasture, Callan took the lead rope from Avery. "Sometimes they get a little excited about being out here, so I'll take his halter off. Why don't you stand by the fence right here?" He motioned to the spot.

Avery nodded and came to stand a few feet from Callan, her pink boots kicking up dust. She watched as Callan opened the gate to the pasture, then undid the knot on the rope halter. As soon as it was free, Red took off at a gallop into the field, making his presence known to all the other horses with a whinny.

Callan latched the gate as Avery watched the horse join the others.

"Thank you for letting me ride him, Mr. Bronson," Avery said as she turned to Callan.

"Of course, Avery. And you can call me Callan, okay?"

"Okay," she responded.

"What day do you want to come back?" I asked Avery, leaving it up to her.

Her jaw dropped as she gasped, like she couldn't contain her excitement at the thought of coming back. "I get to ride again?"

I nodded.

She squealed and charged me, wrapping her arms around my waist. I stumbled back a step, a light laugh escaping me. "Tomorrow!" she shouted, her voice muffled against my lightweight flannel.

"We have to go to the cafe tomorrow, but how about the next day?"

Avery looked up at me. "Yes!" She turned to Callan, her arms still wrapped around me. "Can we come the day after tomorrow?"

I knew that giving her the option would lead to this, but he didn't seem to mind at all.

He smiled at her and it was like everything in the universe stopped and narrowed down on that look alone. "That sounds perfect to me."

It sounded perfect to me, too.

6

Callan

Lennon sat in the wood chair beside me, his legs kicked out in front of him as he sipped his whiskey. I'd opted for a cold beer—perfect for this warm night. We'd been on my porch for about twenty minutes now. Lennon told me all about his day at work and how a pipe broke in the bathroom, flooding the back of Tumbleweed Feed.

"Sage came by today with Avery," I told Len after he was done ranting.

His gaze moved from the field to me. "No shit?"

I took a sip from the long neck, hoping the cool liquid would keep my cheeks from heating at the thought of Sage and her ponytail. "You sound surprised."

He propped an elbow on the arm of the chair. "I just didn't expect her to come."

That got my attention. "Why?"

He shrugged. "I've known Sage for quite some time now, given she's usually at the cafe in the mornings, and typically, she never seems to let the stress get to her. But lately, she's seemed a bit...frazzled?"

Frazzled? What the fuck was that supposed to mean?

"Maybe she's got something going on at home," I guessed.

Lennon frowned at me. "With Avery? I don't know about that."

"Doesn't she have a husband or something?" I asked, though after our conversation at dinner, I knew it was a foolish thing to ask. Lennon wouldn't try to set me up with a married woman.

Lennon's look deepened, his brows pulling lower. "Did you see a damn ring on her finger?"

"No." And yeah, I'd admit, I looked. Just because I wasn't really wanting a relationship right now didn't mean I couldn't be curious.

He looked back out at the field. "I don't know the story there."

"Maybe it's just the stress of being a single mom, then." Because I was guessing she didn't have a boyfriend, either. Though I couldn't say for sure. Someone as pretty as Sage was bound to have a man in her life.

He shook his head. "She's had it pretty under control as long as I've known her."

"Every day is different, Len. Especially with a child. If teaching lessons has taught me anything, it's that kids fluctuate day to day. They're growing, physically and mentally, which means they can be moody."

Len arched a brow, swirling his whiskey in his glass. "Moody, huh? That's what you got from Avery?"

"No. Moody was the last thing I got from Avery. She was so damn excited, she couldn't stop talking." A smile pulled at the corners of my mouth at the memory. That girl was the spitting image of her mother.

"Avery's a little chatterbox, that's for sure."

It was adorable.

I shook the thoughts from my head. They were just clients. Every kid was adorable.

But Avery had that little spark to her, and if I had to guess, it was her mom that kept that spark lit. You didn't see so much joy in life without being unconditionally loved. I'd seen it on Sage's face as she watched Avery ride today. She was so happy for her, but through it, worry still shone on her face. I just couldn't tell if it was worry for Avery on the horse, or something else.

"I offered her more lessons," I told Len.

He looked shocked as he turned to me again. "For free?"

"Well, I tried. Sage insisted she had to do something in return for them, so I told her to bring pastries for the ranch."

Lennon's jaw fell a little. "The whole damn ranch?"

"It was the only agreement she'd take." And I wouldn't say no. Not if it meant seeing Avery that happy again. I didn't know them, but something told me they needed this.

It was also a small excuse to see Sage again, too.

"Cal, you never offer lessons for free," he stated.

"Your point is?" I knew where he was going with this, and I didn't want to hear it.

"You like her."

I scoffed, sitting back in the chair and swigging my beer. "I've only met her twice now. I can't like her."

"So you did go to the cafe the other day," he said, putting the pieces together on his own.

"I did."

"Why didn't you get a coffee, then?"

I sighed. Did I really have to relive this to my older brother?

"We bumped into each other. Twice. She spilled coffee, cut her finger. It was a whole thing. But regardless, I don't like her."

He arched a brow.

"Obviously, I *like* her, but not in the way you're insinuating." Now that Lennon had a girlfriend, he thought he could be everyone's matchmaker, and I was not about to be his next target.

"We'll see."

I rolled my eyes.

It wasn't going to go anywhere between me and Sage, and the sooner Lennon got off his high horse and understood that her daughter was just my student, the better off we'd all be.

I didn't need my family trying to play matchmaker on me, too.

7

SAGE

The lids on the Tupperware full of baked goods couldn't keep the sweet smell from wafting into the car as we drove to the Bronsons' ranch.

"Do I get to have one, too?" Avery asked from the back seat.

I adjusted my grip on the steering wheel as I turned down their driveway. "You've already had two."

"What's one more?" she chimed.

"You don't want a tummy ache while you're riding, do you?" Because I knew what came after she overindulged in my pastries. This wouldn't be the first time.

"Well, no. But it's only one more."

And that one more would turn into three more the second I turned my back. Avery had an even bigger sweet tooth than me, and my baking-to-relieve-stress problem was not helping.

If anything, Callan letting me bring these for the ranch was a good thing, because then it'd keep them off my kitchen table. Regardless if he had said yes or no, they were going to be made anyway.

Baking was the thing I did to calm my nerves. The precise measurements and aroma that came from a warm croissant or fresh scone grounded me when nothing else would. Sure, I could light a candle and get a similar scent throughout the house, but it wasn't the same. It was the process of baking that did it for me.

I pulled the car up to the white barn, taking the key out of the ignition and getting out along with Avery. I rounded the vehicle, opening the passenger door to grab the Tupperware on the seat. There were a total of three. I wasn't sure how many to make as I didn't know how many volunteers or ranch hands they had here, but I figured it was better to be safe than sorry and make more.

Cowboys were always hungry, anyway.

"Here, let me help you," Callan's deep voice offered from behind me.

I turned, coming face to face with him, the Tupperware touching both our chests. "Thank you."

He set a hand under the bottom one, his fingers grazing mine as he grabbed them from me, our eyes latched onto each other. The hazel of his irises was so rich, with flecks of amber and gold exploding around his pupils. It was like a galaxy, and I was lost in it.

"My mama brought these for you," Avery interrupted.

I swallowed as Callan cleared his throat, both our gazes dropping to Avery beside us. "Well, for everyone," I corrected.

"Were you her taste tester?" he asked Avery.

She nodded, her hair bouncing over her shoulders. "I always am."

"And what's the verdict?"

"Dee-licious," she answered with confidence.

The corner of Callan's mouth ticked up. "That's what I like to hear."

He headed inside the barn, Avery skipping beside him as I followed. After setting the pastries down on a table by the tack room, he turned to her with his hands on his hips. "You remember everything from our last lesson?"

"I listened super close so I would," Avery confirmed.

"Do you remember what the first step is?" he asked her, raising a brow.

She nodded. "Halter!"

He flashed a smile and nodded his head in the direction of the hooks. "Why don't you go grab one and meet me by Red's stall?"

"Can I pick the color?"

He dropped his hands to his sides. "Of course you can. Any color you want."

She hurried to the hooks as Callan faced me.

"Do you want me to bring one of these over to the volunteers?" I asked him.

He shook his head. "Bailey will take care of it."

"I'll take care of what?" Bailey questioned from down the aisle, his head poking out from a stall that was propped open with a wheelbarrow in the entrance. "Hey, Sage!"

I waved. "Hey, Bailey."

Callan looked over his shoulder at him. "When you're done, can you bring one of these containers over to the rescue barn?" Each of the three barns served its purpose here on the ranch, as I'd come to learn during our last visit. The green barn was for rescues, the white barn for personal horses, and the red barn for quarantine intakes. Whenever they brought home new horses, they separated them for a period of time before mixing them with the others to be sure they weren't sick. I knew that part because Avery liked to talk everyone's ears off in the cafe, especially about horses. She was always asking questions about the rescue.

"Sure can," Bailey said before ducking back into the stall to continue his chores.

Callan's gaze moved back to where Avery was standing moments ago, but now she'd disappeared. "Guess she beat us over there."

He began walking down the aisle and I fell in step beside him as we headed for Red's stall. Avery was already there, patting Red's nose where he had his muzzle stuck out of the little window.

"You don't have to bring them again if it's too much trouble," Callan said as we walked, his spurs clanking with each step.

"It's okay. I like baking."

"If it's ever too much work, don't feel bad skipping a day, okay?"

My eyes fell to the matts under our feet. "You think I have too much on my plate."

"I didn't say that."

"You didn't have to."

He stopped, his hand slightly closing around my elbow to get me to pause before he dropped it. "I don't know you very well, Sage, but I think you're doing great. Hell, I could never raise a child on my own."

I crossed my arms. "How do you know I'm alone?"

"Well, I just—I thought—" he stuttered.

I let out a sigh, dropping my arms. "I'm sorry. I'm not meaning to be rude." My hand came up to my necklace on instinct. "I'm really appreciative of what you're doing for Avery."

"It's not just for her."

My brows furrowed as my fingers paused on the charm. "What?"

His hand grabbed at the back of his neck as he gave me a sympathetic look. "It just seems like you could use a break."

"Everyone can use a break, Callan, but you don't need to be the one to give it to me. You don't owe me anything." Ugh, what was my problem? He was being so nice, and I was being a total bitch. I should just take what he was offering and appreciate it.

"I know." He dropped his hand. "But if you'll let me, I'd like to try. At least for an hour during her lessons."

I pursed my lips together, glancing over at Avery, then back to Callan. "Okay."

I didn't want people to see me as incapable of handling Avery on my own, but why was I getting defensive over someone offering to give me a much-needed break? There was no crime in taking a step back from your child for an hour.

"If you want to go up to the house, you can. Or stay down here. Whichever. But she's in good hands."

By the way he said it, he meant it. "I know. Thank you."

"We'll be done in an hour." Callan took a second longer to study me, then turned to head for Avery, immediately falling into his casual, cool self with her.

After watching them put the halter on Red, I headed back out to my car to grab my romance novel from the center console. Closing the door, I looked around to find a place to read and settled on the chair sitting by the white barn. Instead of leaving it where it was, I picked it up and moved it closer to the pasture so I could look out at the horses grazing in the field as I got lost in the pages of my book.

An hour wasn't bad.

This was nice.

I feared I could get used to it.

Twenty minutes later, footsteps approached as I finished the last paragraph in the chapter I was reading. I looked up, expecting to see Callan or Avery, but found Callan's mother standing there instead.

"Good book?" she asked, glancing at the paperback.

I nodded, closing it. "It is." I wouldn't get into the nitty gritty of the smut I'd just read. That was not a conversation I wanted to have with Charlotte Bronson.

"I was wondering if I could ask you a favor," she started.

I stood from the chair, gripping the book in front of me. "What's that?"

"We have a meeting for the horse rescue tomorrow night, and I know it's last minute, but I'd love if you could bring some pastries for everyone. If it's too much to ask—"

"No, I can do it." With tonight to prep and tomorrow to bake, I could hurry to get it done. Thankfully, I had the day off, otherwise it wouldn't be possible. "How many are you thinking? And what time is the meeting?"

"Enough for about fifty people," she answered with a slight wince. "Is that too many?"

I shook my head. "Not at all." I'd be up all night, but I didn't want to turn her down.

"Great. It's at six p.m. You don't have to stay for the meeting if you need to be home. I can always have someone drop by and grab them, too. I know finding someone to watch Avery can be difficult. If you want, you can even bring her, if that's easier."

Bringing Avery to a meeting for a rescue was the last place she needed to be. She'd sneak around eating all the sweets, and then she'd be up all night. "I'm sure she can have a playdate for a few hours. Don't worry about having someone pick them up."

Charlotte nodded. "It's at the library in town. We rented out the event space in the back. Call me when you get there, and I'll send one of my boys out to help."

My fingers brushed along the pages of the book as I gave her a closed-lip smile. "Sounds good."

She grinned back, patting my arm. "Thanks, Sage. I really appreciate it."

"Of course." It'd be a tight timeline, but I'd do my best to pull it off. I had to figure out what to make, account for baking times, be sure I had extras in case any were a bad batch, and prep any fillings tonight. There was a lot that went into catering for that big of a group, but I could do it.

I'd done a lot harder things in life and came out just fine. This wasn't impossible.

***

I was wrong.

I was currently in the act of kicking myself for agreeing to make enough baked goods for fifty people, plus extras *just in case*. Why did I need to stress myself out more? I should have made the recipe for fifty, but instead I upped it to seventy-five, and that was for each item. What if people wanted more than one? What if some of them burned?

It would've been fine if I'd stuck with one item, but then I'd decided I wanted to make a variety for people to choose from, so I'd dug through my recipe book to pick out two other sweets. It took a bit to multiply the ingredients for the size of the batch I needed to make, then I got to work prepping what could be made last night. That included chopping, deseeding, and pulling out what would fit on the counter so I didn't have to dig through our tiny pantry in the middle of cooking. I thanked myself for that this morning before I dove in.

On top of baking this many pastries for that many people with this short of a timeframe, I had made arrangements for Avery to go to her friend's house, so I didn't have to worry about her at the meeting. After all, an almost six-year-old didn't belong in a horse rescue meeting. I'd spend more time stressing over where she was and what she was doing while my focus needed to be on this.

With the amount of people going to this get-together, it could be a big deal for my future if I ever wanted to get out of Bell Buckle Brews. I didn't mind working there, but having my own baking business wouldn't be bad either. Making my own hours and managing my own clients—it would be perfect.

It'd definitely give me the flexibility I needed for Avery's school hours.

So this had to be flawless. A lot was riding on these cherry turnovers, white chocolate cranberry scones, and blueberry tarts. On the bright side, my house smelled absolutely amazing.

The timer on the counter rang out and I yanked my oven mitts on as I blew a stray strand of hair out of my eyes. Opening the oven door, I was met with a blast of heat as I pulled out the last batch of cherry turnovers.

After turning the oven off, I moved the pastries to a metal rack and rushed to my bedroom while they cooled. My time management was on par with baking, but when it came to myself, I left little time to get ready.

Glancing at the clock, I opted to skip the shower and do a light makeup look instead. I dusted bronzer over my eyelids, slapped on a single coat of mascara, let my cheeks shine with their natural blush, and took my hair out of the ponytail it'd been dying to come free from all day.

I ran a brush through my hair and sprayed some dry shampoo in it, then headed for my closet. I didn't have much to choose from outside of work and casual attire, so I sifted through my few sundresses, landing on a short blush pink one. Little roses popped all over the material.

I slipped out of my clothes and tugged on the dress, giving myself a second to glance in the mirror to make sure I looked presentable, then headed back out to the kitchen to start boxing up the pastries.

As I was in the middle of doing that, my phone rang on the edge of the counter, but I didn't have time to stop and talk to whoever was calling. They'd have to wait a minute for me to call them back once I was in my car.

Finishing up with the boxing, I took three trips to and from my car, trusting my balancing techniques far too much with each tall stack that I could barely see around.

I was just about to get in when I remembered my phone in the kitchen. Running back inside to get it, I tapped at the screen on my walk back out, but it wouldn't light up.

It was my luck that my phone decided to die right before the meeting.

I'd have to hope everything was okay with Avery, but even if something was wrong, her friend's mother knew where I was.

Finally settling in behind the wheel, I shifted the car into reverse and headed toward the town library.

Soon, people's bellies would be full with my baked goods and the stress would all be worth it. But for now, I'd continue to overthink that everything probably came out terrible and I'd overdone it.

Heaving a sigh, I let my muscles relax a fraction on the drive.

Just a few more hours.

8

CALLAN

"Can you put the tablecloth on for me?" Mom asked as she rushed behind me with centerpieces piled in her hands.

She went all out for these meetings. Bottom of the Buckle Horse Rescue was her life's passion, after all. She treated it like another one of her children, and honestly, I couldn't blame her. If I ran a nonprofit that changed literal lives, I'd treat it like my most prized possession, too.

"Yep." I grabbed the folded up tablecloth, unraveling it to lay it over the surface. It was brown and ivory with bits of color weaved through the southwestern pattern. Horses galloped across the edges, dust kicked up in their wake. It was my mother's favorite—I knew because she used it at almost every event for the rescue.

I liked helping my mom, whether it was in the house or with the rescue. She'd just direct me what to do, and I'd do it. I didn't have to put so much thought into it like how I did with the riding lessons for kids. One wrong move with them and they could get seriously injured. Though the risk was higher than other hobbies children could partake in, the reward was well worth it.

That's why I'd wanted to become an instructor—to see the smile on their faces when they'd overcome their fears or reach a goal they'd set.

From the ground, riding a horse seemed so simple, but once you got on, you realized how many buttons those beasts had. My job was to teach them how to respect that power and yield to the animal, creating a bond rather than a leadership role.

You couldn't beat horses into submission and expect them to respect you. You had to be gentle, quiet, and speak their language. They were prey animals at heart.

After I had the cloth laid out and the crinkles flattened to my best ability, Mom came back with the last few centerpieces, setting them out with even space in between.

The room we were renting in the back of the library looked like those meeting rooms you saw in skyscrapers, but instead of one long table in the middle, the room was wide enough to hold four of them. Three were being used for attendees to sit at, and the fourth was for the hors d'oeuvres—which was the table I was currently helping set up.

"Can I get your help with these?" Mom asked, coming up beside me with a thick stack of papers.

I grabbed them from her. "Sure. Where would you like them?"

"One for each chair, please."

Her brunette hair was frizzing at the edges like it typically did after a long day, and to say this day was long for her was an understatement. I wished she wouldn't stress so much about these types of events, but stressing was in her nature. She'd been scrabbling around all day to make sure everything was here before we had to set up. Lettie had taken a few trips back and forth from the ranch when she'd realized she'd forgotten something. Summertime last year, our parents gave more responsibility to Lettie with the rescue, and ever since, she'd killed it with every event we had. The passion my mom had for the nonprofit ran just as strong through Lettie. She was here tonight, running around setting things up, barely having a moment to spare. Mom had put her in charge of the agenda, so she was nervous about the PowerPoint she had spent hours working on. She'd clicked through it about a dozen times on the projector while we set up.

I got to work setting the papers out in front of each chair, not paying any mind to what was written on them. It was most likely an agenda and some dates throughout the end of the year for events we'd be holding for the rescue, like the annual parade we did at the fair. The date was fast approaching, so I'm sure it'd be a topic of discussion tonight.

I'd planned to stay for the meeting so I could help my mother clean up afterward with the other various volunteers that were currently helping us set up, so I'd hear about it anyway.

The door to the room opened, the creak echoing throughout the space. I glanced toward the entrance, but then did a double take when I saw who it was.

Sage McKinley.

In a fucking dress.

My foot caught on something and I cursed, reaching out to steady myself on the chair. A few of the papers slipped from my hand, but I regained my grip before the entire stack could go down.

I bent to retrieve the fallen parchment while mentally scolding myself.

Sage was wearing a short pink sundress with little roses on it that landed right at her mid-thigh—which should be illegal, by the way, because Sage looked too fucking good. I would have noticed the rest of her, aside from her legs, if there hadn't been a tower of reusable containers covering half her body.

I stood, setting the papers on the table, then weaved my way through the row.

"Let me help you with those," I offered as I approached, not waiting for her response to take them from her.

"Thank you," she said, heaving a breath.

Turning around, I made my way over to the table along the wall. After setting them down, I found her behind me, looking out over the room.

"This is all for the rescue?" she asked.

I nodded. "My mom is one of those go-big-or-go-home type of women."

"I see that." Sage scanned the room, her eyes coming to a stop on me. They caught on my tan cowboy hat for a moment before she cleared her throat. "I'll just go grab the rest."

"I can help." Without the Tupperware covering the other half of her, I had to fight to keep my eyes from trailing down. It wasn't wrong for me to think she was beautiful—if anything, it was a compliment. Beauty, raw in its form, stood before me, and I could do nothing but admire it. Admire her.

She accepted the offer with a small nod, her long hair catching on the spaghetti straps of her dress, before she turned and headed back for the door. I quickened my stride to get there before her, grabbing the handle to hold it open. Before she slipped out, she gave a quick wave to Lettie, who'd finally spotted her from the front of the room.

"Thank you." Sage walked by, and we strode through the library in silence before heading out the entrance.

The outside air was still warm, the sun just beginning to set. There was a pink tinge to the sky, creating the most eerily beautiful hint of rose over the landscape.

"They're in the trunk," she said as we came up to her SUV. She felt around for the latch by the license plate, then pulled. The trunk swung open to reveal about a dozen Tupperware, all filled with pastries.

"Wow. That's…"

"A lot," she filled in. "I know. I wasn't sure exactly what to make, so I figured an assortment would be good. Your mom said there'd be about fifty people, so I made extra in case people wanted more than one of each."

I turned my attention from the trunk to her, seeing that she was eyeing the boxes like she was just now realizing she may have gone overboard. But she didn't. It was cute that she was worried people might want seconds. That alone showed her empathy like a badge.

My eyes landed on a splotch of flour dusting her cheekbone and I wiped my hand on my jeans in one small movement to stop myself from reaching out to her. I hadn't noticed it inside, likely because I was distracted by her in this dress. "You've got, uh," I started, raising my hand toward her face. She looked at me, waiting for me to continue. "Here." Slowly, I brought my thumb to her cheek, wiping the white powder away.

Like an idiot, my thumb hovered there, swiping again for good measure. My other fingers brushed her hair, moving a few strands with the movement. Her skin was soft. She was like the delicate wildflowers that bloomed around the ranch in the spring, reaching toward the sun with their vibrance, aching to have their beauty seen by even one pair of eyes.

I saw hers.

Her cheeks flushed, but her eyes stayed glued to mine, and fuck, I hadn't looked at someone like this in so long. *Really* looked at them. It was like I could see all of her just in her eyes;

pain, beauty, happiness—it was all right there, laid out like a map.

But why pain?

Sage seemed so...pure. Like she could do no wrong, and yet she held this worry like it was a part of her.

It shouldn't be, and the side of me that wanted to fix everything for everyone screamed at me to get it out of her, and make the only thing that shined on that beautiful face joy.

Lowering my hand to wipe it on my black vest, I cleared my throat. "Sorry. You had some flour on your cheek."

Her cheek moved in a way that told me she was gnawing on it from the inside. "Thank you."

I dipped my chin and moved to grab a stack of Tupperware. Sage did the same, leaving the trunk open as we headed back inside the library.

"Do you bake for events like this often?" I asked. Silence was deafening, and I was already feeling anxious being at this meeting. People would soon fill the space entirely.

Using a shoulder to push the door, I used my boot to keep it propped open while allowing her space to move past me.

"Sometimes. Working full-time at the cafe leaves me little free time to do things like this on the side, but if people ask, I'll always say yes."

I internally smiled at that. People pleasing was my best and worst trait, and it seemed to be hers, too.

Making our way through the library and back into the meeting room, we set our stacks beside each other on the table, then headed back out for the rest.

"Are you staying for the meeting?" I asked as I closed her trunk, balancing the Tupperware in one hand.

Her thumb idly rubbed at a spot on the bottom container as she walked beside me on the sidewalk toward the building. "I don't want to impose."

A burst of air blew through my nose as I kept my eyes trained ahead of me. "There's going to be fifty or so people here, Sage. You're not imposing."

Adjusting the containers in my hand, I opened the door for her again, but she paused, causing me to look at her. "Thank you for helping me with these."

My brows drew together slightly under the brim of my hat. She didn't need to thank me again. "No problem. You'd have taken twice the amount of trips back and forth alone."

She blinked, the corners of her mouth turning up the smallest bit. "You're right," she said, her voice quieter than before. She passed me and it took me a moment to follow. Was I doing the wrong thing by helping her? My mom had said she'd call when she arrived, and if she did, no one told me about it. Maybe she hadn't wanted help?

Either way, that didn't sit right with me.

After our short walk through the library into the back room, we sat our piles next to each other again.

"Did your mom have a certain way she wanted these set out?" Sage asked, keeping her gaze on the table.

"Any of the platters is fine."

She grabbed the ceramic beige oval one with green edges and set it next to the array of sliced sandwiches, getting to work laying the sweets out. Assuming she didn't need me watching her like a hawk, I went back to what I was doing before Sage walked in.

I wasn't sure if she planned to sit in on the meeting or wait outside until we were done, but a small part of me hoped she'd sit somewhere in here, if only so I could steal small glances at her throughout the hours-long meeting.

I shouldn't want that, but here I was, silently wishing for it.

9

SAGE

Romance novels held too much expectation for men in real life.

There was no way some guy would do all these sweet things like the man in this book was doing. I'd opted to stay in the main part of the building while the meeting took place in the back. I'd started the book while waiting, but was kicking myself for doing so because now I'd want to take it home and finish it.

It felt like I didn't belong in the room with everyone else, which was why I was now sitting on the floor in the romance section. I wasn't volunteering with the rescue, so I had no business sitting in on their discussion.

I wasn't sure how much time had passed, but I'd gotten seventy pages into this apparent fast-burn romance, and I secretly hoped it lasted a little longer so I could continue reading in peace. Obviously, I had to pick Avery up from her friend's house before nine, but having some much-needed quiet after the afternoon I'd spent getting everything ready was a blessing.

A throat cleared to my left and I pulled my face out of the book with a jump, then quickly wished I hadn't. The back of my head hit the shelf behind me and I winced.

"Shit, Sage. I'm sorry. I shouldn't have snuck up on you." Callan knelt beside me with a furrowed brow.

My fingers felt the back of my head as the pain eased, while my other hand still held the book open. "It's okay."

Warm fingers found mine and I froze. "Let me see if you're bleeding."

"I don't think—"

"Sage." My name was a rough command on his tongue, and I wanted to melt.

Moving my hand away, I angled my neck so he had a better view. His fingers gently prodded at my scalp, seemingly moving the hair away. After a few seconds, he pulled back.

"No blood." He stood and held a hand out to me. Closing the book, I reached up to grab it. He pulled me to my feet, though I was perfectly capable of getting up on my own, and it put us mere inches from each other.

"How was the meeting?" I asked.

"Long," he replied, glancing down at the book in my hand. "You like to read?"

I internally cringed at the thought of him seeing I was reading a romance and positioned the cover away from him so he couldn't see the title. "Whenever I can squeeze in the time."

"What genre?"

"What?"

"The book." He gestured to where I was very obviously trying to hide it.

"Uh." I moved to hold the book in front of me, looking down at the cover like it held the answers. "Romance."

He probably thought I was some hopeless romantic now.

"My mom likes romance, too. As a kid, after a long day on the ranch, I used to sit next to her as she read."

That was...unexpected. "Really?"

He gave a small nod. "There's nothing wrong with reading, if that's why you were hiding it."

My cheeks heated at his acknowledgement of what I was doing. "There's just a stigma around it. I guess I thought you'd think I was some hopeless romantic."

He looked confused, then said, "You shouldn't hide your hobbies just because others don't share them or understand why you have them."

Apperception shone in his eyes despite his words, like he, too, had hidden things before for the sake of not being judged.

"We're about to start cleaning up if you want to grab your Tupperware and the leftovers," he said, changing the subject.

"Yeah." I turned to slip the book back into its spot on the shelf. I wouldn't be able to check it out tonight even if I'd wanted to because the library was technically closed. They were only using the building for the back room.

Callan and I fell into step beside each other, heading past the computers toward the meeting area. A good majority of the people were still here socializing, so the area was pretty crowded, but I stayed close to the wall with Callan at my back as he followed me to the table full of mostly empty platters.

I eyed the one my pastries were on and bent to grab the empty container from where it was stashed under the table. Setting the remaining sweets in one of them, I popped the lid on it and slid it to the side before bending to grab the other Tupperware. Callan must have gotten caught up on the way over because when I glanced to my left, I found him standing about ten feet away, stuck in conversation with an elderly woman.

Instead of turning back to grab the containers, I stood there like an idiot, hoping he didn't see me watching him. His hair was just as it was that day on the ranch, curling at the nape of his neck up toward his tan cowboy hat. The button up he wore under his vest was fitted enough that I could see the definition of his biceps through the fabric. It was a light brown, close to the shade of his hat, and was tucked neatly into his jeans.

He was attractive. All of the Bronsons were, if I had to admit it. But Callan held a different level of charm with his awareness of those around him. Now that I thought about it, I realized none of his brothers were here, but I was sure they had other things to do. They had their lives and some, significant others, which made me wonder why Callan seemed to have the free time to help out. Did he have a girlfriend?

He seemed like the type of guy to drop everything on a dime if you needed him, and by the looks of it, he was always there for his mom.

"Sage." Lettie's voice caught my attention, pulling me away from Callan. "Everyone loved your white chocolate cranberry scones. You have to make them for every meeting!"

I smiled, pleased to hear that they enjoyed them. They were a favorite at the cafe. "I'm glad to hear it. You can take home the extras," I offered, sliding the container in her direction.

"You and Avery don't want them?" she asked.

"Trust me, we have way too many sweets at home. They're all yours." Avery and I indulged in my baked goods too often. It was nice to be able to pawn them off.

Lettie pulled me in for a quick hug as Charlotte walked up, sifting through the pocket in her dress. Lettie let me go, giving me a quick squeeze on the arm before disappearing to talk with a woman that was on her way out.

"Thank you for bringing all of these. They were wonderful." Charlotte held a folded paper out to me. "For the pastries and your time," she explained.

I hesitantly grabbed it, unfolding it to find that it was a check—a very large one at that.

"Oh, Charlotte, you don't have to—"

"No, I insist. It was very nice of you to squeeze this in at the last minute, and you blew it out of the park."

Taking money for my work was necessary, but it didn't stop me from feeling bad about it. Baking was my passion, and getting paid for it in return felt odd. At the cafe, it didn't feel the same because that was at an actual business. But as myself, I didn't feel good enough to be considered a business, let alone paid like one.

"Thank you."

Charlotte slipped the lid off the Tupperware to sneak another pastry as Callan came up from behind me. If it wasn't for her eyes lighting up at the sight of him, I would have known he was there by his sheer presence. My back thrummed with warmth like a heating blanket was draped over me and the man wasn't even touching me.

"Cal, sweetie, help Sage with her things," Charlotte got out after a quick swallow of her bite.

"Already on it," he said, moving around me to take a stack off the table. My shoulder brushed his chest as he did and, not knowing how to get out of his way with the table on my other side, I leaned to grab the other stack.

He angled his head and nodded in the direction of the door, signaling me to go first. He followed behind, only coming around to open the doors on our way out.

The sun had disappeared, the lamp posts and moon lighting up the street. Propping a knee up, I balanced the Tupperware on my leg while I felt around for the latch on the trunk. Callan was glancing both ways on the sidewalk when my trunk lifted.

We both set our stacks in, and he reached up above me to close the hatch.

Before he pulled it, he looked down at me, his face faintly illuminated now that night had fallen. Though the light was dim, I could see his eyes on me, and without blinking, he closed the trunk.

"Thank you for your help tonight," I said.

"My pleasure," he replied, then added, "The scones were amazing, by the way."

I gave a small smile. "They're definitely a favorite."

He rolled his lips together as he stuffed his hands in the pockets of his vest. "Get home safe, Sage."

I nodded once. "You, too."

Taking that as our goodbye, I turned, but before I could make it past my taillight, he said, "You look pretty tonight."

I stopped in my tracks, taking a step back to look at him. "Thank you. You do, too."

He smiled, and I was thankful it was dark out because I knew my cheeks were a deep shade of pink.

I just basically called the man pretty.

I got in my car and locked the doors before driving away, and through my rearview mirror, I saw that Callan still stood there, watching me go with his hands tucked in his vest.

He was just being nice. That's all the compliment was.

But some part of me couldn't help the pull of my lips on my drive to pick up Avery, a smile etched into my face the entire way.

SCRAPE THE BARREL

He called me pretty.

10

SAGE

The cafe had been slow all day, but that didn't ease the stress weighing on my shoulders like a cinder block. Gemma had come in for her shift early, which shocked me, but since our boss was here today, I figured that was the reason for it. Erica ran a few places scattered along the eastern side of Idaho, so she wasn't here very often. Despite that, she ran a tight ship, so when she did decide to pop in, it meant my day was always difficult.

Gemma barely lifted a finger around here. I was honestly surprised she was able to keep the cafe functioning when I wasn't around, but maybe she only worked hard when others weren't looking.

I highly doubted that, though.

"Are you heading home for the day?" Erica asked me as I came through the door to the back. Gemma was up at the register, taking over for the day.

"I am. I have to pick Avery up from her friend's house." Sometimes I was lucky and able to arrange a playdate for Avery, and I was thankful today was one of those days where it worked out. The last thing I needed was Avery running around here while my boss was in town.

"You have a minute before you leave?"

My hands fumbled with the tie on my apron. "Yeah, what's up?"

She was leaning back against the small counter that housed our microwave and sink, her hands braced on either side of her. Erica was a tall woman, with pin straight black hair and somehow even darker eyes. You honestly couldn't guess she was in her forties unless she told you.

"I just want to make sure you're able to handle this job."

My fingers froze on the tie. "What do you mean?" Penny and I were the two that practically kept this place afloat. If Erica had anyone to worry about, it was Gemma.

She moved to cross an ankle over the other. "I've heard you're having some troubles at home."

My brows shot up. "Excuse me?" I dropped my hands to my sides. To hell with this apron. "Who told you that?"

It had to be Gemma.

She ignored the question. "I want to be sure your performance won't suffer due to issues in your personal life."

"My personal life is no one's business." I shouldn't be getting defensive to my boss, but this was unbelievable.

She straightened, pushing off the lip of the counter. "I'm not asking about your personal life, Sage. As I'm not able to come into the cafe often, I want to be sure my business will stay afloat in the hands that I've trusted to run it."

My jaw clenched. "It won't interrupt my performance."

It was what she wanted to hear.

Nothing was even going on at home to make Gemma tell her this anyway, but sitting here defending myself wouldn't get me anywhere.

"Good." Erica grabbed her small black purse off the counter, looping the dainty chain over her shoulder. "I'll check in in a few weeks, see how things are going."

I gave a stiff nod as she passed me, disappearing through the swinging door.

My hand felt around in my purse, closing around my phone before I dialed Penny.

She answered on the third ring. "Another baking emergency?" she teased.

"Far from it. Can I come by your house before I pick up Avery?" I needed to cool down before I showed up at her friend's house.

"Uh oh." There was background noise as she moved on the other end. "Sure. I'll be here."

"Thanks." I hung up, stuffing my phone back in my purse before exiting the cafe, not bothering to even glance at Gemma on my way out. I didn't want to get into it with her today, or any day, really.

After pulling up to Penny's light blue home, I got out, heading up to her door. She swung it open before I could knock. "Porch or couch?" She held up two glasses of wine.

"This is why I love you." I took one of the glasses from her, heading over to the wooden chair she had outside. She closed the screen door behind her, sitting in the one beside me.

"What happened? Was it Gemma?" she asked. She disliked Gemma's attitude as much as I did.

Before answering, I took a large gulp of the wine. She hadn't filled it, knowing that I needed to pick Avery up after this. "When is it not Gemma?"

"What'd she do this time?" Penny crossed her legs in the chair.

"Apparently Erica is under the impression that I'm having problems at home and can't work to my best ability."

Her jaw dropped. "You're kidding."

"Who else would've said something like that if it wasn't her?"

She held her hands up, the glass gripped in one. "Definitely not me."

"Exactly. Do I say something to her?"

She mulled it over in her head, taking a sip while she thought about it. "She probably wants you to so she can create drama. You know how she is."

I slumped in the chair. "But why pick on me? And why now?"

Penny shrugged. "She's probably bored. But hey." She sat forward, setting a hand on my wrist where it rested on the arm of the chair. "Don't think too far into it. Erica will see that you're doing just fine. You won't lose your job over it."

"If I do, I don't know what I'd do."

"You won't. Don't let Gemma get under your skin like that. That's what she wants to happen. Just keep doing what you're doing and Erica will have no reason to fire you."

I blew out a breath. "Alright."

Besides, I hated confrontation. Even if I wanted to, I probably wouldn't approach Gemma on this. She could spin whatever lies she wanted, but I wouldn't let her ruin my life over it.

I was good at my job, I was a great mom, and a damn amazing baker.

Nothing could ruin any of that if I didn't let it.

***

Avery jumped out after I pulled into our driveway and turned the car off, still going on about her playdate with her best friend, Lucy. They'd been friends since we moved to Bell Buckle three years ago and thankfully, were in the same grade.

I beeped the locks on the car and headed up the path to the front door, unlocking it and stepping inside as Avery barreled in ahead of me. I couldn't comprehend how she still had this much energy after her playdate.

As she rounded the corner of the hallway, our cat, Pudding, let out a strangled noise like she'd been spooked and darted out of Avery's way. Instead of heading for the kitchen like she typically did when we got home so she could beg for food, she aimed right for the front door. I was just setting my purse on the entry table when I saw her blur of a body run by, and before I could reach the door to close it, she ran out.

I cursed, shoving the door open the rest of the way, and quickly followed her outside. I always warned Avery to be careful with Pudding because she could try to run out one day, but she must've thought it would never happen as she would still storm into the house like a tornado.

"Pudding!" I called as she darted under my car.

I dropped to my knees on the driveway and quickly wished I'd slowed my pace as pain ricocheted through my legs. But I couldn't pay attention to that right now. Losing Pudding would crush Avery.

"Mom?" Avery called from the doorway to the house.

"One second, Aves! Stay inside," I yelled back to her as I narrowed my eyes, checking for Pudding under the car. She was a gray tabby, which meant she practically blended into shadows.

"Why are you on the ground?" Avery asked from somewhere behind me. *So much for staying in the house.*

My hands slapped on my thighs as they dropped to my jeans. Pudding was gone.

I quickly stood, looking out at the street, then around our yard and the neighbor's lawn from where I was standing.

"What are you looking for?"

I could cry after everything that happened today. The knot in my throat formed and my eyes burned. No parent wanted to tell their child that their beloved pet was gone, but I couldn't see Pudding anywhere.

I turned to Avery, crossing the few feet to her and pulling her into my arms. "Mama, what's wrong?"

I sniffled, trying my best to hold back my tears. I had to be strong for her, because once I told her, she'd be a mess and I had to be there to pick her up.

"Let's go inside." I gabbed her hand and walked alongside her up the path to the door.

After I closed the door behind us, I knelt down to her level, my knees aching from the impact outside. There was no time for that now—no room for my feelings when I'd be holding hers in just a second.

"Do you remember how I asked you to come inside calmly after Pudding almost escaped that one time?" I asked. I really didn't know how to tell her. No one trained you to be a parent. You just figured it out as you went, and that made it even more scary.

Avery nodded, her brown hair falling in her face a bit. "I remember."

"I think the way we came inside today scared Pudding and she ran out the door." I braced myself, wishing there was an easier way to say that.

"She ran out the door?"

I ran my hands up and down her arms as I nodded. "That's what I was looking for, but I couldn't find her."

Avery's bottom lip swelled a bit as her eyes turned to glass. "Pudding's gone?"

I sniffled, my heart breaking at the crack in her voice. I pulled her to me, wrapping my arms around her as she broke on a sob. "We're going to find her, okay? I promise. I'll keep looking for her."

"But what if she doesn't come back?" she cried into my shirt, soaking the fabric.

Was I supposed to tell her she would? I couldn't make promises to her that I couldn't keep.

"We'll find her," I said, doing my best to keep the waver out of my voice.

We had to find her, for Avery's sake and mine. I hated seeing her upset. If only I had been faster and shut the door, this all could have been avoided.

If we didn't find her cat, it'd break me as much as it was breaking her right now.

11

CALLAN

Christopher, one of my students, hopped off the lesson horse while his mother and little sister stood from their bench and made their way to the gate of the arena to meet us.

"Do you think one day I can try cutting?" Christopher asked as we walked side by side through the sand, the horse following behind him.

I reached over to pat the top of his helmet. "Maybe once your balance is a little better."

Some kids just simply liked to ride, but others wanted to try various things like cutting, roping, and barrel racing. I was no rodeo teacher, and while I knew how to do those types of things, I wasn't a specialist in any of them. I helped take care of the rescues, the cattle, and taught my clients how to ride. My routine was simple, at least to me, and I liked it that way.

"How long do you think?" he questioned.

Unlatching the gate, I swung it wide for him and the horse to walk through. "I'll let you know once I'm confident."

"How was your lesson, sweetie?" Christopher's mom asked as he walked past her.

"Good like it is every week, Mom," he replied dryly with an eye roll, heading for the barn.

I closed the gate behind me as Christopher's little sister, Annie, made hearts with the tip of her finger in the dirt by her mom's feet.

I gave his mother a closed-lip smile and turned to follow Christopher when she laid a hand on my arm, stopping me. "How's he doing?"

I could reply the same way as Christopher, I supposed. But I was too polite for that. "He's doing great."

"Better than the others his age?" she pried with a flutter of her abnormally long eyelashes. They had to be fake.

I swallowed, biting the inside of my cheek. It was like a broken record with her. Every week, she tried to get me to say he was better than the rest. Each one of my students was unique and I enjoyed teaching them all for various reasons, but none of them were better than the others. They were all at different levels, and comparing them wasn't fair.

That was the problem with the "horse world." People thought too highly of themselves and compared themselves to every other equestrian out there. But it wasn't a comparison game. We should all lift each other up, give each other pointers;

not tear each other down because someone's seat wasn't as exact as the next person's.

That was the environment I was trying to create here on this ranch. No judgment, no expectations. Just ride because you want to ride, and do it safely.

"He's right where he needs to be," I answered.

She dropped her hand, shooting me a flirty smile. "I knew you were the best teacher around."

I gave her a tight nod. "Thank you. I have to go check on him and then I'll send him back out."

"Will you come say goodbye?"

My teeth worked on the skin in my mouth like they were about to tear it clean off. "I have another lesson in five minutes. I'll see Christopher next week, same time."

Her face fell a little, but she quickly covered it up with another flash of teeth. "Same time."

I turned, heading toward the barn where Christopher had disappeared. Bailey was stacking hay under the carport when he straightened, pulling his gloves off. His shirt was stained with sweat and dirt, his cowboy hat tossed to the side.

"You okay?" Bailey asked with a furrowed brow.

I heaved a sigh, oxygen filling my tight lungs. "Never better."

He tossed the gloves on the bale beside him and wiped the sweat off his forehead with a bandana. "It's no secret the moms drool all over you while you teach their kids, you know that, right?"

"I'm well aware."

"So why do you let it affect you?"

I crossed my arms. "Does this look like it's affecting me?"

He shoved the bandana in the back pocket of his jeans. "Sure as hell does. You've got your emotions written all over your face, Cal."

"Am I supposed to like them flirting with me while I instruct their kids how to ride a thousand-pound animal?"

"No. But maybe don't show them how flustered you get when they do it."

"I'm not flustered. I just don't like all the attention."

"Have you seen yourself? You can't look like that and not get attention. Trust me, if I wasn't with your sister, I'd be all over—"

"Okay! I'm going to go do my job." I pointed over my shoulder toward the barn. "And you can get back to yours. Nice talk, Bailey!" I turned on my heel, continuing on my way when something thumped against my ass.

I glanced over my shoulder to see Bailey's glove laying in the dirt.

"You should walk away more often!" Bailey shouted after me, following it up with a catcall.

"Jackass," I muttered under my breath as I flipped him the bird over my shoulder.

Most of the time, I tried not to give the moms the time of day when they came off like that to me. Not every mother was here to flirt with me, but the few who did made it very obvious, and if I was anything, it was afraid of conflict, so naturally I didn't put a stop to it like I should. I let it continue because I thought it was the nice thing to do to not make them feel bad, but in the end, I was the one left feeling like some spectacle on display in that arena while their kids rode. They should be watching their child make those memories and learn how to ride, not watching me.

My mind drifted back to Sage as she watched Avery ride for the first time and how all her attention was captivated by her daughter. She hadn't even glanced at me as Avery rode—her heart practically shone in her eyes.

For some reason, I hadn't minded the conversations with Sage. Usually, I was polite to parents and only spoke to them when I had to, but with Sage, I willingly started them. Opposite of everyone else, I didn't want to seem closed off to her.

My family knew I was overly empathetic, but I was only that way to the people I was close to. I was courteous when I had to be to others, but aside from that, I'd rather keep to my bubble.

But something about Sage made me want to care for her, too. Not in the aspect that I thought she wasn't capable of caring for herself, but more like when you look at someone and you just know they need a shoulder. Sage had that aura to her that screamed tired, like she'd been keeping the world afloat for so long that she just needed someone to throw her a life raft, even if just for an hour, and keep the world afloat for her, too.

There was only so long a person's meter could stay full for others without replenishing it for themselves.

SCRAPE THE BARREL

Before making my way over to Christopher at the cross ties, I glanced at my calendar to check for the twentieth time today that little slot of time blocked off for Avery's lesson.

A week between lessons was getting to be too long, and it was only her fourth one.

12

CALLAN

Sage's SUV came up the driveway right on time, and as soon as the car was stopped, Avery was jumping out of the back.

"I'm here!" Avery announced as she closed her door.

Sage turned off the car, getting out herself. Her movements were slow as she pushed the door shut, following a few feet behind Avery as she approached me.

My brows pulled together when I noticed she was catering to one leg, her steps off balance. I set my water bottle in the dirt and closed the distance between us, reaching for her elbow before I could think better of it.

"Are you hurt?" I asked, my voice foreign even to my ears.

Her forehead creased. "It's just my knee. The Tupperware is on the back seat with the pastries."

"What happened to your knee?" I ignored what she said about the baked goods and led her over to the bench by the arena, helping her sit down.

Avery had disappeared inside the barn, most likely to grab a halter and get ready for her lesson.

"I kind of...landed on them too hard? Concrete isn't especially cushiony."

I kneeled in front of her, eyeing her knee.

"What are you doing?" she asked, her eyes locked on me.

I gently ran my fingers over her knee and she winced.

"What do you mean you 'landed on them too hard?'"

"I wasn't thinking when I went to look under my car," she explained.

I looked up at her, bringing my hand back and dangling it over my thigh. "What's wrong with your car?"

Her brow furrowed like she wasn't sure why I was asking that. "Nothing's wrong with my car."

"Then why— I'm going to have my mom bring you some ice. I have to make sure Avery's not opening every stall in the barn. And no more pastries," I said, standing.

The look on her face made me instantly feel guilty. I didn't want her to think she was being a burden, but the way I said it, it definitely came off that way.

"It's okay, Sage. I'm fine with doing the lessons for free. Stay here and I'll keep an eye on Avery. I just want to make sure she's okay." *Now here I was, caring for the* both *of them.*

"You don't have to worry about the ice," she said. I wondered if she was going to ignore my comment about the pastries that easily.

Her knee was very clearly swollen under her leggings, and I wasn't going to do this lesson and ignore that.

"Let me help you," I practically pleaded. "Please."

Her eyes searched mine, like she thought I was going to strike at any moment and tell her to get off this ranch and never come back.

"Okay," she said softly. "And I suppose I can stop with the sweets as payment."

I gave a closed-lip smile. *Good*. She didn't need more on her plate. "Stay here. My mom will be out in just a minute." I pulled my phone out of my jeans and sent my mom a text, asking her to bring ice, water, and some pain meds as I headed inside the barn to find Avery.

I found her in the tack room looking at pictures on the bulletin board. Avery saw me come in and turned to face me. I couldn't help but notice she was already holding the pink halter in her hand.

"Am I riding Red today?" she asked.

I nodded. "Want to help me get him?"

"Yes!" She slipped past me, heading down the aisle in the direction of Red's stall like she'd been here a hundred times before. I followed, trying to clear my thoughts of Sage's injury and focus on Avery, but it was proving difficult to get Sage out of my head.

My concern for her was just that—concern. I only wanted to make sure she was okay and not in pain. That was it.

At least, I hoped so.

***

Avery was working on keeping Red up against the fence around the arena, learning to use her leg pressure gently as she rode at a walk. She had about ten minutes left of her lesson, and Sage had watched the entire hour, an ice pack resting over her knee that she had elevated on the bench, her leg outstretched in front of her.

It was hard to keep my eyes off of her. I was constantly battling my brain to keep my focus on Avery and Red, when all it wanted to do was check on Sage.

Avery's focus was on the horse underneath her, but while keeping Red to the wall, we were also working on keeping her eyes in front of her, not on the back of his head. It was the quietest I'd heard her since she'd begun her lessons here as she concentrated on all the moving parts.

"Is it alright if I use the restroom?" Sage asked, moving the ice pack off her knee.

I looked over to her as Avery rode on the other side of the arena. "There's one in the barn. Right by the tack room. Do you need help?"

Does she need help going to the bathroom? Really, Callan?

She waved me off, standing from the bench. Her knee seemed stiff, but she was putting more weight on it, most likely thanks to the pain meds. "I'm not completely disabled."

My hand moved out of habit to rub my arm. "Just shout my name if you need me."

She walked away, a slight lift to her lips, and disappeared into the barn. I turned back to Avery, but a ringtone sounded from behind me, bringing my attention back to where Sage was sitting moments ago.

Her phone was out on the bench, the ringer sounding until the call presumably went to voicemail. Avery rounded the arena, ignoring the phone.

Not ten seconds later, the ringtone started again.

Whoever was calling her must need to get a hold of her to be calling back to back like that.

The call came through another two times before Sage made it back. Coincidentally, the phone didn't ring again with her nearby, so I figured I should tell her.

"Someone was calling you," I said to her as Avery worked on her stop with Red.

Sage reached over to her phone, glancing at the screen. Her lips thinned and then she turned the phone off, setting it face down on the bench again.

I guess whoever it was wasn't important enough for her to call back at the moment.

"You ready to dismount, Avery?" I asked, looking at where she was stopped in the corner on Red.

"Can you help me down?"

I made my way over to her, my boots digging into the sand with each step. Reaching up, she dropped the reins and I hoisted her out of the saddle, helping her down.

Once both her feet were on the ground, I grabbed Red's reins, handing them to her. "Let's go take his saddle off and we can come back out."

"Okay!" she replied, leading Red toward the gate to the arena.

I swung it open, following her out.

About fifteen minutes later, Red was untacked, brushed, and back in his stall. Avery ran out of the barn to her mom as I trailed behind her. Sage was still sitting on the bench, her fingers picking at the edge of the ice pack, but as Avery approached, she looked up.

"Did you see me, Mama?" Avery asked, though it was clear Sage had. I hadn't missed Avery's glances at her mother to make sure she was watching all the little milestones.

"I did, Aves. You looked so good."

"Am I getting better?"

Sage looked up to me where I stood at the end of the bench with my arms crossed. "I think you should ask your instructor that. I don't know a thing about horses," Sage admitted.

"Maybe you can learn, too," Avery said to her.

Sage's eyes widened slightly. "I think all the learning should be for you right now. Maybe one day I will." But she didn't seem very convincing.

My attention caught on my mom striding over to us from the house. Sage followed my line of sight and stood, grabbing the ice pack off the bench.

"How's the knee feeling?" my mom asked her.

"A lot better, thank you." Sage held the now-melted ice pack out to my mom and she took it.

"Alternate between heat and ice and it should heal just fine. But to make today easier on you, I'm going to insist you stay for dinner."

Sage's brows pulled together. "Dinner? I can't do that, I don't want to impose—"

My mom waved her off. "Nonsense. It takes the stress of feeding this growing girl off your hands for the night. Please."

Sage glanced over her shoulder at me, then back at my mom. "Okay. Thank you."

My mom put a hand on Avery's shoulder. "Why don't you come get cleaned up in the house?"

Avery angled her head back to look at her. "Can I have a snack?"

"Of course. I have something I think you'll love." My mom bent down, whispering something in Avery's ear that made a smile light up her face.

They headed in the direction of the house and Sage turned to me, apology written all over her face. "Are you okay with us staying?"

I dropped my arms to my sides. "Why wouldn't I be?"

"I don't know. It's your family and we're just clients..."

I shook my head, not really sure what to say. I'd never had a student and their mother stay for dinner at my parents' house, but Sage didn't feel like all my other clients.

"You'll just have to excuse my siblings. They're a bit...unhinged, sometimes." Of all the nights for my mother to invite Sage and Avery to stay for dinner, it had to be the night that all my siblings would be here. Well, minus my younger brother, Beckham. He was competing in the circuit for bronc riding and didn't make it home very often in the summer, opting to stay with friends or at hotels for most of the season.

"I've handled your siblings just fine at the cafe," she pointed out.

"Not slightly buzzed and around family. Some of their comments—"

"Callan, it'll be okay."

She was reassuring *me* about dinner with *my* family.

I almost had to take a step back from the awe that slammed into me. The tightening of my chest had to be my imagination. For the first time, though, the tightness wasn't a bad thing.

Sage was making my heart swell.

My siblings weren't really people to apologize about, but a bit of a forewarning about them was helpful sometimes. *Especially* when it came to a few of them in particular.

I just had to hope that everyone was on their best behavior tonight.

13

SAGE

I was wearing leggings and an old t-shirt I got from a brewery in Portland—definitely not dinner apparel—but I got the feeling that the Bronsons didn't care what you wore as long as you showed up and had a smile on your face. They were so laid back and welcoming. It was a contrast to how I'd grown up.

My father left before I was born and my mother wasn't very present in the terms that she was always off with boyfriends and never home for me. I was an only child and took care of myself once I was able to. It was a miracle I survived with how careless she was, but I had my grandmother to thank for that. With her old age, there was only so much she could do with a young child, but she did her best with me, and I was thankful for every moment of it.

But you know the saying *the apple doesn't fall far from the tree*? I guess you could say that about my relationship with men compared to my mother's.

I'd always dated nice boys, but something about the edge in Avery's father made my heart rush, and that made me fall for him harder than the rest. But instead of falling into it, I should've run from it. From him.

I found out all too late.

He stuck around after Avery was born, but he was in no way loving after she came into our lives. Fatherhood was scary for any new dad, but Jason took it to the extreme. I'd expected him to help raise Avery, but he was rarely home, and if he was home, it was never pleasant.

I hid as much of it as I could from Avery, but thankfully, he was finally arrested when she was two and a half, so she remembered very little.

For a while after he was locked away, I still flinched at every sudden movement and triple checked the locks on the house every night. Because I was the reason he was put in prison, I could never be too sure that we were safe.

Safe was all I wanted for my little girl, and sometimes, I couldn't help but feel like I put her in a situation that was anything but.

We moved towns after he was arrested, landing in Bell Buckle and making a life here, but I feared that when he was released in two years, he'd somehow find us. No one in my past life knew where Avery and I were. It was for the best. But even so, those racing thoughts hit me all too often.

What if he came looking?

What if he took her?

Or worse, what if he was still mad?

I frequently had nightmares, my head conjuring up scenarios of all the what ifs. It wasn't enough that I lived my life in fear—he had to visit me in my sleep, too.

I snapped out of my thoughts, focusing on Callan chopping asparagus behind the counter. I was sitting at the kitchen island while Bailey and Lettie were outside with Avery. Charlotte was on the back porch, barbecuing the chicken breasts for dinner.

"Avery's loving the riding lessons," I started, not sure what else to talk about.

Callan laid the asparagus on a baking sheet beside the cutting board. "I'm glad."

I pursed my lips, poking at a crumb on the counter with my finger.

It was never this hard to strike up a conversation. I did it every day at my job, so why was this so difficult?

"Why have you never come to the cafe before?" I asked.

He set the knife down, rinsing his hands under the faucet. "I prefer to make coffee at home."

"We don't just sell coffee," I stated.

He dried his hands on a rag, eyeing me. "You don't say?"

I frowned. "If you don't like pastries, why'd you use that as part of our agreement?"

"I never said I don't like pastries." He draped the hand towel over the handle on the oven, then grabbed the olive oil from the pantry.

"So it's something against the cafe," I surmised.

"Didn't say that either." He drizzled the oil over the asparagus and shook the sheet to toss them lightly.

"You're not saying much of anything." I hated being the only one making conversation right now. It felt like the spotlight was on me, and I could feel my hands getting clammy.

He set the oil down and placed his palms against the counter, looking at me where I sat. When my eyes met his, I noticed his cheeks were slightly red. Was he blushing?

"When'd you start working at the cafe?"

"Three years ago," I answered.

"Your first job after you moved here?" he asked.

I nodded.

"Why not somewhere else?"

"I like baking," I reminded him.

"Where'd you grow up?"

"Oregon."

"Where in Oregon?"

"Portland."

"Ah." He finally dropped his eyes from mine, moving his attention to seasoning the asparagus.

"What?" I asked. Did he have something against Portland?

"Is that where you got your love for baking?"

My brow furrowed. "What?" I repeated. How did those two things go hand in hand?

He set the salt down, gesturing a hand at me. "Portland is known for their...coffee culture." He said the two words like they were foreign on his tongue. "So I assume there's a lot of cafes there."

"There is. But no. I got my love for baking from my grandmother." A swell of emotion hit me in the chest, but I pushed it away. It'd been years since she passed and I still missed her every day.

Callan moved to slide the baking sheet in the oven, then faced me after setting the timer. "Is she still..."

"Around?" I filled in.

His gaze met mine. His cheeks were still flushed, but his expression was soft, like he knew this might be a touchy subject. "Yeah."

"No." I cleared the rock in my throat that had suddenly risen with the subject of my grandmother. "No, uh, she passed before Avery was born." I wished she could have met her. She would've loved Avery.

"I'm sorry." His voice was so soft—so filled with sentiment that you would've thought he lost her, too. He moved around the island to take the seat next to me. "So tell me about yourself. Anything."

"You want to know more about your student's mother?" *Shit*. I was thankful for the subject change, but that didn't come out how I wanted it to. Obviously I wanted to talk to him, but how far was too far in the *get-to-know-you* department?

He shrugged, debating it in his head before facing me on the stool. "I guess I do."

"What do you want to know?" I asked.

I wish I knew how long it was until dinner. I didn't know how much longer I could sit here with all his attention on me like this.

His eyes were fixed at a spot on the counter for a moment before he asked, "Who was calling you earlier?"

My eyes widened. That was *not* the question I was expecting.

"You don't want to know my favorite color or something?" Avoiding the question altogether was my best option right now.

He glanced at the back door, his shaggy hair mussed up from pulling his hands through it after taking his cowboy hat off at the door. He opened his mouth to respond, but Avery came bursting through the door and I swiveled to face her. Rouge, Lettie and Bailey's Australian Shepherd, was on her heels, his tongue dangling as he panted.

"Mama!"

"Yes, Aves?"

"Bailey said Mrs. Bronson always keeps ice cream in the freezer," she said, trying to catch her breath from running.

"You can have some *after* dinner."

Her eyes lit up. "Do you promise?"

I nodded. "As long as it's okay with Mrs. Bronson."

As if on cue, Charlotte walked through the door with a plate of chicken in her hand. "Dessert is *always* okay with me."

Avery jumped up and down where she stood. "Yay! Okay, I'll be back in, like, five minutes." She turned and darted back out the door, leaving it open behind her.

I went to stand to close it, but Callan was already on his feet, heading in that direction. Rouge slipped out as he closed the back door and I averted my gaze before he could turn and catch me watching him.

It was unfair for him to be so attentive. Any other guy would have expected the mother to take care of their child's chaos, but he just stepped up and did it himself.

Ugh.

***

Callan's entire family was here—aside from Beckham. Oakley, Brandy, and Bailey were here as well, but I guessed they were considered a part of the Bronsons with how close everyone was. I longed for a family like that for Avery to grow up around. I always felt guilty for her not having cousins or aunts and uncles to shower her with love. She didn't even have her father to do that either.

So I made up for it. I made sure she always felt loved and never felt that hole like I did growing up.

The guys' plates were almost cleared as they devoured the food in front of them. Lettie and Oakley had been lost in conversation, barely touching their dinner, as Avery told Charlotte all about her lessons.

My attention was tuned in to the two of them, the rest of the table fading away. I watched with glassy eyes as Charlotte treated Avery like one of her own. I wished so badly in this moment that my grandmother was here to meet her.

"Is it good?" Callan's voice interrupted my trance.

I dropped my fork to the plate, the metal clattering on the porcelain. "What?"

Eyes glanced our way, but everyone continued their side conversations. I was seated next to Callan with Avery across from me. She'd wanted to sit in between Charlotte and Lettie, and I wasn't going to complain. Travis, Callan's father, was seated on the other side of Charlotte, and the others were at the opposite end of the table.

"The food. Do you like it?" he clarified.

I looked down at my plate, realizing I'd barely touched any of it as well. It was delicious, from what little I'd tasted, but my stomach was in knots over being here at a table full of people. I hadn't had a dinner like this in…well, ever. Not just the meal, but the people.

"It's amazing. The asparagus is lovely," I told him.

His brow furrowed as he set his own fork down. "Is something wrong?"

Nothing was wrong. Everything was just right. And that scared me. What if Avery wanted to do this more often? This wasn't our family to impose on. It was most likely just a one-time thing, and I didn't want to get her hopes up.

"My knee just kind of hurts," I lied. It was sore, but when I took my weight off of it, it didn't bother me as much. The bruise was an ugly shade of purple, covering my entire knee cap, but I didn't think anything was damaged.

"Here, I'll be right back," he said as he set his napkin on the table and got up.

No one at the table noticed, and when he returned, he held his palm out to me, two small pills sitting in the center as he refilled my water glass with the pitcher.

I gently grabbed them from his hand, my fingers brushing his rough calluses. "Thank you."

He sat as I swallowed each pill separately, followed by some water.

"Do you need me to drive you home later?" he asked.

I choked on the liquid, coughing to clear my throat. "No," I croaked.

His lips pursed as his cheeks stained a light shade of pink. He was *definitely* blushing. I took another sip of water to clear my throat, but it did little to ease the nerves coursing through me right now.

"And I told you, you're not fucking touching that horse," Reed bit out at the end of the table, pulling my attention away from Callan.

"Reed, language. There's small ears listening," Charlotte lectured.

Brandy scoffed. "You can't just tell me what to do."

Reed muttered something under his breath, shooting daggers at Brandy. "How many times do you want to go over this?"

Brandy lifted her glass of wine, a catty grin pulling at her lips as she said, "As many times as I want, because I'm breaking that horse."

"Maybe I shouldn't have brought it up," Lettie piped in softly as Brandy sipped her wine.

"No shit, Lettie," Reed grumbled. "If she gets hurt, it's on you."

Bailey sat forward. "Hey, now. Don't come at my girl."

Beside me, Callan let out a sigh.

Lettie rolled her eyes as if Reed wasn't her brother and she could handle him. "He's always got a stick up his ass, Bailey. This is nothing new with him."

"That's for damn sure," Brandy mumbled.

"What was that, Brandy Rose?" Reed asked calmly. It was almost more scary when he spoke in that tone. I'd seen a lot of sides to Reed when he occasionally stopped by Bell Buckle Brews, but never this.

"I don't know. Maybe if you pulled that stick out, you could hear me," she said sweetly.

Okay, the two of them speaking that way was much *more scary.*

Charlotte looked like she was about to pipe in again about the language when Avery blurted, "Does anyone know anything about cats?"

My lips parted slightly. I wasn't sure where she was going with this—though I was thankful for the attention shift—but I definitely didn't want her crying at this table over Pudding.

"I know Callan hates them," Lennon supplied with a smirk.

"You do?" I asked Callan.

His eyes narrowed on Lennon slightly before answering me. "I don't *hate* them."

Lennon let out a small chuckle. "The last barn cat we had, you wouldn't go anywhere near whatever barn it decided to stay in."

"That thing was mean, and you know it," Callan defended.

"It hissed at you one time," Lettie pointed out.

"Never thought a man could be scared of a ten-pound animal when he works with beasts a hundred times their size," Travis muttered, his gray mustache wiggling as he spoke.

Callan grimaced. "Listen, when you have giant fangs eye-level with you because you woke up a sleeping cat behind a bale of hay, you'd be scared, too."

"Oh, please." Lennon scoffed. "It was one time."

"Anyway," Avery interrupted, the sass clear in her tone, "my cat is missing."

Oh, fuck. Please help me.

"Avery—" I started.

"Missing?" Callan asked at the same time.

She nodded. "I need a team to help find her."

A team? This child was crazy.

"Avery—" I started again.

"I can help," Callan offered.

My jaw dropped and I turned to face him. "What?"

He seemed confused by my reaction. "I can help find her cat."

"This'll be good," Lennon remarked under his breath from across the table.

"So fucking good," Bailey agreed.

Charlotte let out a small gasp. "Bailey! Language."

Bailey bit back a smile, pressing his lips together.

"Do you know how?" I asked him. I didn't need him getting her hopes up just for Pudding to never come home.

I was so worried she'd never show up, but I had hope. I'd been out looking for her every evening after work, assuming that'd be when she was out and about. She was a night owl. Despite my search, luck was not on my side.

Pudding loved Avery. She had to come back home at some point for her little girl.

"I can do some research," Callan said.

Lennon barked out a laugh. "This'll *really* be good."

"Callan the Cat Wrangler," Bailey said through a laugh.

Lettie smacked him on the arm, but she had a smile on her face as well.

"Are you sure?" I asked him, doing my best to ignore the table so Avery didn't think that I thought this was a joke.

Callan shrugged. "How hard could it be?"

I wanted to slap a palm to my face. Finding a lost cat was not easy, yet Callan sat there like it would be as simple as spotting a horse in a freshly mowed one-acre pasture.

Avery piped in, considering Callan officially on her cat-catching team. "Okay, here's some things you need to know: Her name is Pudding, she's gray, she's a girl, and she likes when you rub your fingers together at her."

"Rub your fingers together?" Callan questioned.

Lennon and Bailey's fit of giggles only got worse as they watched Callan taking this seriously. I had to give it to him, he was acting like this was a job for hire and he was studying to pass the interview.

"Like this." Avery held her hand up, showing him what she meant as she rubbed her thumb across the tips of her other fingers. "Oh, and if you do this." She made a kissing noise with her lips.

I swear Lennon and Bailey were going to pee their pants as their faces grew red with laughter.

"Someone record this," Reed mumbled, having a hard time holding back his smile where he sat.

Travis's frown he wore all night was lifting at the edges, but Charlotte stayed silent next to Avery, most likely to make it known she didn't think her explanation was funny and what she was saying mattered.

Oakley had a hand over her mouth next to Lennon, but her eyes were watering, along with Lettie's and Brandy's. Apparently seeing Callan go into cat-loving mode was comical to everyone here.

"Alright, I've got this. You think of anything else, you tell your mom to call me," Callan said to Avery.

"How will I—" I started, but before I could finish my sentence, he set his phone on the table.

"Add your number," he said.

I tried to hide my shock as I picked up his phone and added myself as a contact, then texted myself on his phone so I had his number.

Lettie's mouth dropped open as she eyed the phone. "Did she just add her number?" she not-so-silently whispered to Brandy.

"I think she did," Brandy loudly whispered back.

Reed rolled his eyes as Bailey and Lennon's laughter ebbed.

"Text me your address and I'll come by tomorrow," Callan said quietly to me, most likely to keep his siblings' ears out of it to prevent them teasing him further.

Come by my house? The place was a mess, and it was already late in the evening, which meant I'd be up all night cleaning on my hurt knee.

"Can we do another day?" I asked hesitantly. I knew it meant we were less likely to find Pudding if we waited longer, but I didn't want him to see my disaster of a house. "Don't you have to research?"

"I can do it all tonight," he started, realizing the look on my face. "You don't have to clean the house top to bottom, Sage. Rest your knee tonight. I'm not going to judge you."

He could say that now, but one look at the current state of my home and he might be taking that back.

"I don't know, Callan..."

He set a hand on my thigh, most likely to reassure me, but all it did was center every ounce of my focus to where his warm palm rested over my leggings. A thin layer of clothing was all that separated me from feeling his rough skin on my bare leg.

"Don't worry about the house, Sage. It's okay. I promise."

I let out a sigh. He just wanted to help.

"Okay." I turned back to Avery across the table. "He'll come by tomorrow to help us find Pudding."

Avery smiled wider than I'd ever seen.

And Callan was the reason for it.

Well, and her cat possibly coming home.

But he wanted to help us find her, and that meant the world to Avery.

And to me.

14

CALLAN

Another yawn escaped me as I opened my truck door and grabbed the wicker basket off the passenger seat. Despite the three cups of coffee I'd had before leaving my house, I was still tired. I'd stayed up until two a.m. researching how to lure a lost cat back home. I'd written everything down on a piece of paper, which was currently folded in the back pocket of my jeans for safekeeping.

From what I could tell, Pudding meant a lot to Avery, and I wanted to do everything I could to get her cat back, but I hadn't a clue where to start with this. My specialty was horses, not felines. They hated me, I disliked them, so I never familiarized myself with them, but now I felt all too knowledgeable on the species.

I mentally recited what I'd memorized, on top of having written it down, as I knocked on Sage's front door, trying my best to calm my racing pulse. I'd made such a fool of myself in the kitchen yesterday with no clue on what to talk about with Sage. My thoughts were racing at the time, much like they were now, about how she was sitting in my parents' kitchen watching me cook, how she looked, how *I* looked. I'd been silently begging one of my brothers or even Bailey to walk in and spark a conversation, but I'd been left to my own devices. I shouldn't have asked who'd been calling her during Avery's lesson. I'd majorly overstepped with that, and I had to hope Sage had forgotten I'd even brought it up.

I didn't typically get anxious around people in particular—it was mostly just being out in town that did it for me. But something about Sage made my pulse skyrocket and my mind race as I worried I'd stumble over my words and embarrass myself.

Anxiety was a bitch like that. I could be having the most simple conversation and I'd still jumble words together and trip over my own tongue.

The door swung open and my gaze fell to where Avery stood before me. "You came!"

"Avery, I asked you not to open the door before I got there," Sage said from somewhere in the house.

"Of course, I came. I said I would," I told Avery.

Sage came up behind her daughter, her hair up in a messy bun atop her head, showing off her long neck. She was wearing an oversized t-shirt over biker shorts, her legs on display.

"Good morning," I greeted.

"Good morning." Her eyes dropped to the basket in my hands. "What's that?"

"A get-well basket." I felt bad that her knee was still hurting, so I wanted to bring her a few things to help her feel better.

Sage's lips parted, her attention stuck on the basket. I'd stuffed it full of tea bags, chapstick, hair clips—those were thanks to Lettie's input—two ice packs, a couple heating packs, a blanket, bath salts, and a lavender essential oil spray. To top it off, I'd gone back to the library to check out the book she was reading during the meeting. It was probably overkill, but caring for people was in my nature. Just because Sage and I didn't know each other very well didn't mean I couldn't get her a few things.

"You went back for the book?" she asked, her eyes shining up at me.

I nodded. "You weren't done reading it, and I figured with resting your knee, you might want to finish it." I hoped it wasn't too much. Now that I was looking at it, I almost wanted to shrink in on myself.

"Thank you. Really, that's so nice of you," she said, reaching for the basket. I passed it off to her and she disappeared inside. "Come in," she called over her shoulder.

Avery turned, following her mother as I stepped inside and closed the door behind me.

The house looked like a home—lived in and loved. Avery's toys were strewn about the living room, touches of pink set about, winter clothes still hanging on the coat rack.

"I'm sorry about the mess. I did my best to tidy up, but there's only so much I can do when Avery gets everything back out right after it's put away," Sage said as I entered the kitchen. She set the basket on the counter and bent to gently rub at the side of her knee.

"Does it still hurt?" I asked.

"Not as bad. The bruise is bright and shining, but I'm sure it will fade soon."

Avery stood by the kitchen table, her arms crossed. "So, Callan, how do you suppose you're going to find my Pudding?"

I cocked an eyebrow. The girl was smart for her age, I'd give her that. And sassy, too. I wondered if she got that from her mother—a side of Sage I had yet to see. "I wrote a list." I pulled the paper out of my back pocket, unfolding it.

"A list?" Sage repeated from behind the island.

I nodded, doing my best to read the scribbles I'd jotted down late last night. "Stayed up practically all night trying to find the best sources."

Avery came to my side, peeking at the slip of paper. "What's first?"

"Well, a lot of the websites said to set the food bowl and litter box outside, and that *should* attract her back here."

"I can go get those," Sage offered.

I looked up from the paper, eyeing Sage. "No. You rest. Avery and I have got this."

A look of shock passed by Sage's face before she blinked it away. "Are you sure?"

I nodded. "Positive. Rest that knee and use the heat packs. Take a bath if you'd like."

Sage opened her mouth like she was going to say something, then pressed her lips shut. "I think I'll watch some TV."

I turned back to the list where Avery was still studying it. "That's fine. We've got this handled."

Sage hesitated before heading for the living room while Avery and I stood there for a few minutes, going over where the best spot would be to set the litter box and food. Ultimately, we landed on placing it by the front door. Avery's winning point was that Pudding might smell her home with the front door cracked, and that would entice her more, so with the items on the porch, it'd be triple the smelling power.

I'd smiled at that.

We placed the litter box and food outside, and I waited while Avery filled the bowl with a heaping scoop of kibble.

"Do you think she'd come if we had wet food?" Avery asked from where she was crouched.

I scanned our surroundings, contemplating that. "What do you think?"

"Hmm, I think she would," she decided.

"Do you have any wet food for her?"

She stood, shaking her head. "No. Mom says it's too much money right now."

I glanced at the front door, then back at Avery. "I can buy you some."

Her eyes lit up. "Really?"

I nodded. "If you think it'll make Pudding come home."

"I do! Let me go tell my mom." She disappeared into the house but reappeared not even a minute later. "She's sleeping."

I slipped my cowboy hat off, running a hand through my hair as I looked out at the street. I couldn't take Avery to the feed store without Sage's permission, and I couldn't leave Avery here with her mother sleeping.

Setting the hat back in place, I looked down at Avery. "Let me call my brother."

I pulled my phone out, dialing Lennon. He answered on the third ring. "What's up?"

"Do you guys have any canned cat food?" I asked.

I could hear his snicker on the line. "I do. How's that going?"

"Currently setting up the trap." Avery let out a gasp and I quickly corrected myself. "The lure. We're luring the cat home. Do you think you can make a house call with that wet food?"

He was silent for a moment before speaking. "Oakley was about to go grab us some lunch. I can have her swing by with it. Just text her the address."

"Alright. Thanks, Len."

"Have fun wrangling cats," he said before we hung up.

"Wrangling cats," I muttered under my breath.

I was never going to hear the end of this from my siblings.

***

After Oakley dropped the can of wet food off, Avery had filled a separate bowl with it, then we headed inside. She showed me her favorite toys, gave me a little tour of her room, and then asked for something to eat. Without knowing what Sage had in her kitchen, I let Avery choose and made her a grilled cheese sandwich with tomato soup.

She'd devoured it, and shortly after, I'd suggested we clean up some of her toys in the living room. I'd pressed that we had to be quiet in order not to wake her mom, and I had to admit, it was pretty adorable watching Avery tiptoe through the living room to gather her toys. While she was gathering her toy ponies, I'd laid a blanket over Sage, careful not to wake her.

I cleaned up the kitchen, washing the dishes that I'd used for Avery's lunch, then got to work spraying down the counters. I wasn't sure if Sage would like me cleaning her house like this—not that it needed to be cleaned so thoroughly, it was a home, after all—so I didn't want to overstep by going through cabinets and doing laundry. I thought wiping down some counters would be okay.

"What are you doing?" Sage asked from the entry to the kitchen.

My eyes shot to her, my strokes with the paper towel pausing. "Cleaning?"

"I see that. But why?"

"To help out, I guess. I didn't want to wake you, and I didn't want to leave Avery alone while you were napping, so I figured I could do a few things."

Sage rubbed her eyes, blinking away the sleep and surveying the kitchen. "It looks...amazing."

A smile pulled at the corners of my lips. "Thank you."

"Mama! Did you see I cleaned up my toys?" Avery asked, running into the room from down the hall.

Sage crouched to her level, pulling her in for a hug. "I did, Aves. Thank you. I appreciate that."

After she stood, I asked, "Did you enjoy your nap?"

She nodded. "It was much-needed."

Avery headed back down the hall, presumably to continue playing with her toys she'd moved into her bedroom. I didn't say *every* room was spotless.

Sage glanced at the clock on the stove and cursed. "I have to get to work in thirty minutes. I didn't realize I'd slept so long." She turned toward the hallway and called out, "Aves, please get ready to go."

"I can watch her," I offered without thinking. *Yeah, right. Like she was going to trust me alone in her house with her daughter when she barely knew me.*

Sage faced me, her eyes wide. "What?"

"Avery. I can watch her so you don't have to bring her to work."

Her gaze darted around the room as she processed what I was saying. "You've already done so much, Callan. I don't want to use you like that."

I tossed the paper towel I was still holding in the trash, coming around the island. "It's not using me if it's something I want to do."

She studied me for a few moments before saying, "You want to watch a five-year-old while I go to work?"

I shrugged. "I like kids."

Sage shook her head, more in disbelief than as an answer. "I have a short shift. I'm just going in for a few hours until the cafe closes, so I should be home by five."

Four hours. That wouldn't be too bad.

"I can do that."

Her brows drew together. "You're sure?"

"Positive."

She eyed me like she was trying to tell if I was serious. "If something goes wrong, will you call me?"

I nodded. "I'll send you updates every thirty minutes."

Her brows raised an inch. "Okay."

There wasn't really a *good* way to reassure a mother that her child was in good hands because no matter what, they'd worry, so she'd just have to trust that Avery would be okay with me for four hours.

If watching Avery for the afternoon made Sage's day easier, I'd do it without hesitation any time she needed it.

15

SAGE

"No Avery today?" Penny asked as I walked in the door to Bell Buckle Brews, the cowbell above me letting out a clang.

"She's at home with…" Calling Callan a babysitter felt weird. He felt like more than that, like a friend doing a friend a favor. But was he my friend? "Callan."

Penny's eyes shot wide as I approached the counter. "Callan *Bronson*?"

"Why'd you say his name like that? Is he secretly a serial killer or something?" My luck, that'd end up being the truth.

The cafe was empty behind me, it's usual pace during this time of the day.

"No. I'm just surprised he'd be watching Avery. Are you guys friends or something?"

Or something sounded like the right answer.

"He's been giving her horseback riding lessons, and as of late, he's trying to help find Pudding."

Her eyes somehow widened further. "He definitely likes you."

I let out a nervous chuckle as I twisted my wallet in my hand. "No. Definitely *not*. He's just helping Avery."

She cocked a brow. "Helping Avery or trying to get close to you?"

I scoffed, shaking my head. I rounded the counter, heading into the back, but Penny just followed.

"He's not trying to get close to me."

"What would be the harm if he was?" she asked.

"Nothing." But everything.

I set my wallet in my tiny locker and grabbed my apron to tie around my waist.

"Come on, Sage. You haven't dated anyone since I've known you."

"Three years is not an abnormal amount of time to be single."

"Yes, it is."

I turned to her, my fingers finishing off the knot on the apron. "How long have you been single?"

She frowned as she shoved her own apron in her locker. "This isn't about me."

Pulling the strings taut, I brought my hands to the front pocket to be sure my pen and notepad were in there. "I'd much prefer it wasn't about me either."

"Come on, Sage, give a girl *something*."

"He's cute," I blurted.

I could've said anything *but* that. Literally *anything*.

A satisfied smile stretched Penny's lips. "Okay."

"Now get out of here so I can start my shift in peace. You're almost as bad as Gemma."

Penny gasped, slapping a hand over her heart. "That's the nicest thing you've ever said to me."

I rolled my eyes at the sarcasm lacing her tone.

"Let me know how Callan's night goes," she said as she turned to leave.

"Not my night?"

She looked over her shoulder at me, one hand on the swinging door. "Or your night with him. Whichever."

The corners of my lips turned down in a frown as she disappeared through the door.

Penny was such an instigator.

***

Three hours flew by and I surprisingly wasn't as anxious as I thought I'd be leaving Avery home with Callan, thanks to his promise of text updates every thirty minutes. A text came through every half hour on the dot and not a second later. Of course, I'd thanked him for each update, but it meant the world to me that he was doing this.

The problem with trusting any babysitter was that I'd want to know what was happening every second while I was away, and that was probably the last thing any of them would want to do—update the mother constantly. But Callan did it willingly. I hadn't even asked for them, he just *did* it. Everything he'd done today, between watching Avery for me and bringing me a get-well basket, showed just how thoughtful he was.

What guy did that? Because I was convinced men like that didn't exist.

But here Callan was, right in front of me, teaching my daughter how to ride horses and voluntarily stepping up to watch her for me so I didn't have to bring her to work.

Not to mention that he'd suggested I take a bath instead of sticking around to help out with the cat situation. And the fact that I got to nap? I hadn't had time for a nap since before Avery was born, but even then, they were few and far between because my ex didn't think they were productive.

I didn't want to confuse myself by getting caught up in the small things Callan did for me. He was just helping out for the time being, and then he'd be gone. I couldn't have him teach Avery for free forever, and I wouldn't be able to afford lessons once I had to start paying for them, so this kindness from Callan had to stop at some point.

I just feared I'd miss it too much when it did.

Callan was everything a woman could want: handsome, overly caring, thoughtful, and he worked on a ranch *teaching children to ride horses*. If your ovaries didn't explode over that, there was something wrong with you.

Sure, we got off on the wrong foot when I spilled coffee on him, but he hadn't held it against me. We'd both had a bad morning, and we started fresh after Avery's first lesson, but now I was starting to enjoy the little things he did, and that was dangerous.

I couldn't let myself get used to this. He was only temporary.

I stayed on top of the dishes and wiped the counters after each customer. I was not in the mood to stay late today, given I wanted to get home and make sure Callan and Avery hadn't burned the house down.

It was always slow in the afternoons, which was why Erica changed our closing time to five p.m. instead of seven about a year ago. It was costing us too much to stay open that late with not much foot traffic to justify it. I wasn't complaining though; it just meant the second shift was shorter if we split up the day. Most of the week, we'd work through from opening to close, but a few days a week, they were split, so one of us would have mornings and the other the afternoon. It was well balanced between Gemma, Penny, and myself, but the days that Gemma flaked, I'd have to cover if Penny couldn't come in, which sucked, but I appreciated the extra money. The schedule helped during the school year, but wasn't the most ideal in the summer when I'd have to drag Avery to the cafe midday.

My phone dinged with a text on the counter beside me and I picked it up, seeing Callan's name across the screen.

> **Callan:** Avery is telling me all the names of her My Little Pony's. Peanilla was an interesting one

I smiled down at the phone, typing out a reply.

> **Me:** Just wait till she gets to Chicken

Three little dots appeared and I stared at them, waiting for his response.

> **Callan:** I guess that goes hand in hand with the cat's name being Pudding

My cheeks ached as my smile widened, but before I could begin typing back, the cowbell above the door clanged. I locked my phone, slipping it into my apron.

"Good evening," I said to the man. He was wearing a black zip-up and blue jeans, and his dark hair was cropped close to his scalp.

"Hello, there," he greeted as he approached the counter. His eyes searched the small pink dining area before landing on me, glancing at my name tag.

"Midday coffee?" I asked.

"Black, please," he replied.

I typed it into the register and turned, pouring some beans into the machine and starting it up.

"You have a lovely cafe, Ms..." He trailed off, and I assumed he wanted me to fill in the blank.

"You can call me Sage," I said, leaning a hip against the counter as I waited for the coffee to brew. "But thank you."

He pursed his lips, giving a small nod.

"Would you like any food with your coffee?"

He shoved his hands in the pockets of his jacket, keeping his attention on me. "No, ma'am."

I turned back to the pot, my fingers finding the charm on my necklace. Unease crept through me with his presence. He filled the room, but given he was the only one here aside from me, there wasn't anyone else to focus on.

Once it was done brewing, I wiped my hands on my apron before pouring the coffee into a paper cup, then popped the lid on. Turning to place it on the counter in front of him, I read off his total. He handed me some cash, and I held his change out to him after counting it out.

"You live in town long?" he asked, pocketing the change.

"A couple years." It wasn't an odd question to ask around here, given people passing through always stopped for coffee and were looking for sights to see or things to do.

He tapped the counter twice with a finger, then grabbed his coffee. "Stay safe out there." The man turned, heading out of the store.

I watched his retreating back disappear through the floor to ceiling windows. It wasn't an odd farewell, but the way he said it sent chills down my spine.

I was probably just feeling off because I wasn't with Avery. That was it.

***

I pulled into the driveway and turned off the car, quickly unbuckling my seat belt. I inhaled deeply, telling myself that I had to calm down to not make it seem like I was so eager to get home that I broke the speed limit on the way here.

To be fair, it was only by five miles per hour.

I sat back in the seat, resting my head against the cloth headrest as I watched the house. The lights were on, giving my home a warm pull that made it feel somehow better to come home to. Callan was in there with Avery, most likely playing or eating a snack, and it made my heart swell with emotion.

It almost felt like what it would be if we had a little family, like I finally had that extra set of hands to help me when I needed it instead of taking the world's load onto my shoulders by myself.

But *this* wasn't a family. Callan watched her one time to do me a favor, and that was it.

Here I went looking too far into things again.

Maybe Penny was right to assume there was more going on.

After being alone for so long, I got used to not having someone to pass things off to, but my heart wanted this so bad that it was playing tricks on my brain. I had to approach this logically, not emotionally. Otherwise I'd get my heart broken and let Avery down.

Squeezing my eyes shut for a few seconds, I finally opened the driver's side door and got out. I beeped the locks on my car and headed for the house. The litter box and food brought a slight smile to my face. I just hoped it worked.

I tried the handle on the door, but it was locked.

Good.

Slipping the key into the knob, I unlocked it and stepped inside, relocking it behind me. Voices drifted down the hall, along with a giggle. I set my keys and wallet on the front entry table, then followed the sound to Avery's room.

I peeked around the doorway to where they wouldn't notice me watching with their backs to me as they sat on the ground next to each other. I raised up on my tiptoes to get a better view of what they were doing.

They were *painting*.

Callan, this big, teddy bear of a man, was on the floor with my daughter, *painting*.

And from the looks of it, he was painting a pink castle.

Avery moved to grab a different brush and must've seen me from the corner of her eye because her gaze shot to me, and I dropped from my toes. "Mama!" she shouted as she scurried to stand, racing my way.

"Hey, Aves. Did you have fun?" I asked her as she threw her arms around my waist.

Callan twisted where he sat, looking up at me.

"Thank you," I mouthed, and he dipped his chin in response with a smile.

"We had so much fun. We made pink slime, and then Callan helped me with my handstand, and then we played with my ponies and he met every one of them, and now we're painting. Do you want to see what I painted?" Avery's words tripped over each other as she couldn't speak fast enough to tell me all about their few hours together.

"Of course, I do," I replied.

She released me, hurrying over to her painting to pick it up and bring it to me. "It's not done yet, but Callan is helping me with the castle."

I stared at the piece of paper, the paint still wet, and swallowed back the lump in my throat. She'd painted herself standing on the grass next to a horse, with Callan and his cowboy hat to the left of her. Next to them was a field of flowers, and a big castle that was half filled in with pink.

"That's Boots," she told me, pointing to the horse, "and that's Callan and me."

Callan stood up with the wet paint brushes in hand. "I'm going to go rinse these."

I stepped to the side to allow him room to leave, his arm brushing against mine as he passed. His skin was so warm, like a walking heater, and I could imagine curling up next to him in the winter while snow fell outside, our Christmas tree twinkling in the living room as Pudding swatted at the ornaments.

I shook my head at myself. *Stop fantasizing, Sage. It's one time. This doesn't mean anything.*

"It's beautiful," I told Avery.

"He helped with a bunch of it, but the flowers are all mine."

I set the paper on her dresser, then bent to press a kiss to her forehead. "Why don't you clean up your paint while I make you some dinner?"

"Okay!" She bounced away, getting to work on tidying the paint supplies.

I headed out to the kitchen where Callan had his back to me at the sink as he ran the brushes under the faucet.

"I can clean those. You probably want to get going," I said to him as I opened the fridge.

"I don't mind. I had fun."

Grabbing some chicken breasts out of the fridge, I set them on the island behind me and closed the door. "I really appreciate you watching her for a few hours, and all that you're doing to get Pudding to come home."

He turned off the water, setting the brushes on a paper towel to dry. He dried his hands on the rag hanging from the oven door. "Anytime. I'll get out of your hair for dinner. I'll still be seeing you two in a few days for her next lesson, right?"

Anytime? Did he mean that? Surely he was just being nice.

"Avery wouldn't let me forget if I tried. We'll be there." I pulled a cutting board out of one of the cabinets, setting it on the counter. "And thank you for the texts. It helped ease my mind...a lot."

His brow furrowed. "Of course. I figured if she was my kid, I'd want updates, too."

God, why did we have to have that in common?

Shut up, Sage, every parent would.

"Is that why you don't have a babysitter for her?" he asked.

I opened the package of chicken, placing them on the cutting board to slice. "That, and the fact that not many people are up for watching a five-year-old, especially with my constantly changing schedule if I have to stay overtime."

"Your coworkers not very reliable?"

"Just one of them." I didn't want to get into it about Gemma right now.

He seemed deep in thought as he watched my knife slice through the raw meat, then said, "My mom or I can always help watch Avery."

My slices faltered, and I set the knife down on the board. The last thing I needed was to accidentally cut myself in front of him, *again*. "You don't have to—"

"Sage, it's okay to accept help if people are offering it. But I understand if you truly don't want us to."

My teeth gnawed on the inside of my cheek. I hated that he was right. I just felt bad asking people to help watch my daughter. Her father should be around doing that, but instead he was sitting in a prison cell because he was never taught how to respect women.

"Thank you." I had to be more open to people offering to make my life even a fraction easier.

As much as I wished I could, I couldn't carry the weight of the world on my shoulders and keep myself afloat, too.

16

CALLAN

I stomped up the steps to Reed's back porch, having come around the outside of the house instead of through. Lennon and Bailey were here, most likely a few beers deep already.

I hadn't planned on coming over tonight, but it beat being stuck in my house alone battling my thoughts, so I'd headed out the door and picked up a six-pack on my way.

A week had passed since I watched Avery while Sage was at work, and though I saw her at Avery's lesson a few days ago, I couldn't stop thinking of Sage every free moment I got.

Reaching the top step, I found Lennon and Bailey sitting on two sunbleached wooden chairs, their legs stretched out in front of them. The setting sun cast an amber glow over everything, the air still warm from the summer day.

"The life of the party is here!" Lennon announced when he saw me.

I lifted the beers up in display as Bailey sat forward in his chair and whined, "Hey! *I'm* the life of the party."

Taking the seat beside Lennon, I set the beers on the ground, grabbing one and popping the top off. "I agree with Bailey here. He knows how to leave a lasting impression. Me, on the other hand, I'm the polar opposite of that."

Bailey rested back against the hard wood. "Thank you. I like to think I'm pretty unforgettable."

The sliding door closed behind us as Reed said, "We could never forget Cooper."

Bailey took a swig, giving a short nod. "That's my intention."

"Didn't work on Lettie, though," I pointed out. "She seemed to forget you pretty easily."

Lennon's beer flew out of his mouth as he choked on the liquid while Reed's mouth ticked up at the corners. Bailey pressed his lips together, tipping his bottle at me. "That's fair. But now look at me. Happy as can be with her."

"Speaking of," Lennon started, "when's the wedding?"

"Probably next summer? She and Brandy keep going back and forth on different seasons for the wedding, but I told her the fall time would be best since we want to do it on the ranch. Not too hot, not too cold." He glanced at me and Lennon before continuing. "I was actually wondering if you two would be my groomsmen?" His focus moved to Reed. "And you'd be my best man?"

Reed had his beer halfway to his lips, his eyes glued to Bailey. "You want me to be your best man?"

Bailey's brows dropped. "Reed, you're my best friend. Obviously, I'd want you to be my best man."

"Ouch," Lennon hissed, but we all knew he wasn't actually hurt by that. It was no secret that Bailey and Reed were the closest out of any of us, despite their personalities being complete opposites of each other.

"I'll do it," I piped in, giving Reed a minute to process.

Bailey twisted to look at me. "Thanks, Cal."

I gave a nod, and Lennon lifted a shoulder in a half shrug. "I'm in."

We all three turned to look back at Reed, who was clearly not accustomed to the limelight being on him.

After a moment of us all simply staring, he raised his eyebrows. "Alright! I'll do it. Fuck. Don't any of you guys get a brain aneurysm, staring like that."

Bailey clapped him on the shoulder. "Thanks, man." Reed grumbled something before taking a long pull from his bottle, as Bailey went on, "So obviously, Lennon, you're with Oakley, and Lettie is already planning for Oakley to be one of her bridesmaids, so you don't really *need* a plus one." He looked at Reed. "Reed, you're with the maid of honor—"

"Hold on a fucking second—" Reed tried to interrupt, but Bailey continued, facing me.

"So that leaves us with Cal. Who are you planning to bring?"

"If you think for one fucking second I'm—" Reed kept talking from the other side of Bailey, but no one paid him any mind. Brandy was Lettie's best friend. There was no doubt in any of our minds that she'd be her maid of honor.

"I'm not sure," I replied. "I'll probably just go solo." I hadn't seen anyone since I'd been with my ex, and I wasn't in the best spot to date right now. I was so busy with lessons at the ranch, and it wasn't like I went to town enough to meet anyone.

"Fucking hell." Reed gave up on the battle, accepting his fate. There was nothing he could do about it. Whatever rivalry they had together could be set aside for one day.

Hell, it wouldn't even be one day. It'd be a few hours, and then they'd be free of each other.

"Bullshit," Lennon called out.

"Sorry?" I asked.

"Bailey's told me the way you look at Sage when Avery comes for lessons," Lennon said.

I turned a narrowed gaze on Bailey. "What is he talking about?"

Bailey rolled his eyes. "Don't act oblivious, Cal. It doesn't suit you."

I sat back, huffing a breath. "Someone please explain." There was no way in hell Bailey, or anyone for that matter, could tell I looked at Sage a different way than all the other women . She was gorgeous, but she also didn't flaunt it. She was the kind of girl who didn't see herself as beautiful, but the rest of the world did, and *that* made her more attractive.

But not just that. It was also the fact that she very clearly would hang the moon for Avery if she asked. She was selfless, maybe even a little too selfless, but so was I.

On the other hand, my ex was so beyond selfish that she'd given me an ultimatum. I'd chosen my happiness over following someone I knew wasn't my forever. From that day forward, I knew I'd made the right decision. After closing myself off for so long, something about Sage stuck out to me, and without me even realizing it, she became an everyday thought.

Maybe some people didn't believe in fate, or that things happened for a reason, but my choices led me right here, and I had to believe it was for the better.

Bailey kicked his feet up on the railing, his hands crossed behind his head. "All I'm saying is that you never give any of the other children's mothers the time of day, never ask *them* to go relax during the lesson. Never ask your mom to bring them a pack of ice for their knee."

"It was the nice thing to do," I defended.

"Oh, come on, Cal," Lennon piped in. "Don't act like that's the only reason you've done those things."

"I've seen it, too," Reed added quietly from the side.

Bailey tilted the tip of his bottle in Reed's direction. "See."

"You guys are looking too far into things." There was nothing going on between me and Sage. Nothing.

Bailey sprang forward, staying in his seat but pinning me with his stare. "Are you *seriously* dodging around this right now?"

"I'm not dodging around anything."

"If I've learned anything, it's that life is fucking short, Cal. Don't sit here wasting your time with this bullshit. Ask her out."

My eyes widened. "*Ask her out?*"

"Yes, you idiot! Ask her out." Bailey was passionate, I'd give him that. But just because he'd gotten together with Lettie after her disappearing for five years didn't mean he should start finding us girlfriends, too.

We had our mom to worry about with that.

"I barely know her," I pointed out.

"So?" Bailey exclaimed. "Asking someone on a date is an excuse to get to know them. A date isn't getting married. It's to talk, to learn more about each other."

"Since when are you such a fucking romantic?" Reed groused.

"Since I got with your sister, Bronson," Bailey quipped.

Reed shook his head. "Stop reminding me."

Lennon shifted in his seat. "There's no harm in asking her out, Cal."

My eyes scanned the horizon, wishing I could find the right answer there. It wasn't often I went out of my way to put myself into uncomfortable situations, and if Sage rejected me, it'd feel a whole hell of a lot worse than just uncomfortable. What if she never brought Avery back for another lesson? Then Avery would be upset, Sage would blame it on me, and I'd feel like shit.

"I'll think about it." Because if I said no, they'd just keep pestering me about it.

For the next couple hours, we alternated between water and beer, then we all headed home for the night. I hadn't decided what I'd do. I could take the risk and ask her out, and best case scenario, she'd say yes and we'd go on a date. But worst case scenario—I could ruin everything by doing it. Was I willing to risk that?

But the longer I thought about it, the more I was convincing myself that yes, I was willing to risk it if it meant I got to know Sage a little more.

There was so much I wanted to know about her, and not just her, but Avery, too.

I wouldn't tell the guys my decision because chances were, I'd chicken out, but for now, I settled on maybe.

Maybe I'd ask Sage McKinley on a date.

17

SAGE

"Are you sure you're okay with hanging out at Mrs. Bronson's house while I'm at work?" I asked Avery for what had to be the fifth time.

"Yes, Mama. I like hanging out with her," she said, like the two of them were best friends.

I pulled to a stop in front of the white farmhouse, turning the key in the ignition. I grabbed Avery's backpack off the passenger seat and got out, handing it to her where she stood.

I'd taken Callan up on his offer for his mother to watch Avery, but today was the first day, and possibly the last. I didn't want to inconvenience Charlotte in any way—she had to be busy with the rescue. I considered today a test run, though I was well aware she'd insist it was fine. She'd been more than eager when I called her a few days ago to set this up.

"I packed you snacks and your art supplies. There's also a few ponies in there you can play with," I told her.

She stepped forward for a quick hug, her voice muffled in my shirt when she said, "Thanks, Mama." She let me go, then smiled and waved at something—or *someone*—behind me. "Hi!"

"Hey, Avery." *That voice.* God, I hated how it made me buzz with awareness. Hated how just two words from him could make me want to fix my hair and double check that I didn't have any crusted bits stuck to my eyelashes.

Avery turned, bounding up the steps to the porch as I swiveled, finding Callan walking in my direction.

He came to a stop a few feet away from me, but I wished he'd step closer. It felt like forever since he was at our house, and while yesterday was my day off and I tried to be as present with Avery on those days as possible, it was extremely difficult when I kept remembering him standing in my kitchen, or playing in Avery's room, or cleaning the counter. This man had been to my house *one* time and I was daydreaming of him coming back.

What was wrong with me?

"Are you heading to work?" Callan asked. He was wearing a navy blue striped button up tucked into blue jeans. His boots looked so worn, I swore there had to be holes in the bottom.

"For a few hours. Charlotte's watching Avery until I'm off. I figured you'd be working, given the time." I wasn't sure how he expected to help watch Avery when he worked similar hours to myself, but since he was technically self-employed, I didn't really know what to expect out of his set schedule. That, and I also felt bad asking him.

"Yeah, no, I am. I'm in between lessons right now," he replied, reaching up to rub at the back of his neck, which was shaded by his cowboy hat.

"Do you typically work all day?"

"Sometimes. There's a couple days a week that I have a chunk of free time during the afternoon, and I give myself two days off. I'd work all seven, but my mom insists her kids take a break." He dropped his hand back to his side.

"It must be nice being able to make your own schedule."

"It is." His cheeks flushed as he shifted on his feet and reached up to take his cowboy hat off, running his opposite hand through his hair. "I had a question. And before I ask, let me preface by saying you can say no if you don't want to. I just, uh..." He glanced at the ground, kicking at a rock with his boot, then pinned those hazel eyes back on me. "I'll just outright ask. Sage, would you maybe want to go on a date with me?"

My eyes widened as I was unable to hold back my reaction. *Did he just... He just asked me on a date.*

Callan Bronson just asked me on a *date*.

"Me?" He couldn't have meant that.

His lips pursed together, concealing a smile as his cheeks turned a deeper shade of crimson. "There's not anyone else around, Sage."

"Right." A date didn't mean we were going to get any further than just one date. It was *one* date. There wasn't any harm in that. Yet here I was, overthinking it, and he'd just asked me not even a minute ago. "Are you sure?"

He let out a small chuckle, nodding. "I'm sure."

"It's just, I'm a mom and I have Avery—"

His brows furrowed. "What does that have to do with me asking you out on a date?"

My lips parted in slight awe that he didn't care that I was a mother before I replied, "I have a kid."

"I'm failing to see your point here," he said carefully.

"Why would you want to date a mom?" I blurted.

We weren't even on said date yet and I was already blowing it.

He shook his head. Any nerves there before were now gone from his gaze. "You're not *just* a mom, Sage. You're a beautiful woman who, despite whatever odds were thrown at you, made it through and are doing your best to take care of yourself and another human. That takes guts, and I admire that about you. I want to get to know *you*, outside of being a mom and a barista or whatever you call your position at the cafe. *You*. I would like to go on a date with you."

I stared at him as he stared right back, my mind reeling as my heart hung on to every word he spoke. I didn't know how long passed, but my mouth finally decided to work, despite every other part of me still trying to comprehend his words. "Yes."

"Oh, thank God." He let out a relieved breath, his rigid shoulders slumping slightly with the release. He gripped the top of his hat before setting it back on his head. "You had me scared there for a minute."

"Scared?" I asked, the corners of my mouth twitching.

Behind him, a car pulled up the driveway, slowing to a stop near the white barn. Callan glanced at it before turning back to me.

"Takes a lot of guts to ask a pretty woman like you on a date." He slowly started walking backwards. "I've gotta run, but I'll text you," he said. His cheeks were still red, and whether he knew it or not, he didn't seem to mind. The man wore his nerves on his cheeks, that much was for sure. Never in my life did I think I'd ever see a man blush, especially about me, but there Callan Bronson was, walking away from me after asking me on a date with his cheeks as red as roses.

I got the feeling mine were the same shade.

He was like a boy on Christmas, and my "yes" was on the top of his wishlist.

"You think I'm pretty?" I called before he turned around.

His teeth flashed with a smile. "I called you beautiful, didn't I?"

I guess he did.

I couldn't get this damn smile off my face, but neither could he.

He shot me a wink and turned, and I stood there watching him walk away before he disappeared. After a minute of attempting to process what just happened, I got in my car, heading toward town.

Callan Bronson just asked me on a date and I said *yes*.

Any moment now, I'd wake up and this would all be a dream.

After I had Avery and her father was arrested, dating never even crossed my mind because I didn't think any man would want me after having a baby.

Sure, Callan liked me now, but when it came down to it, I didn't feel beautiful enough to be loved the way other women were. I had a C-section scar, stretch marks—nothing about my body was the same from before I had her. And while I loved my body for growing and birthing my baby, it didn't stop my thoughts from spiraling.

From the fear of rejection from kicking in.

From my insecurities shining through, despite being told I was attractive or beautiful.

Because in the end, when I rarely looked in the mirror and saw my body for what it was now, all I had were my thoughts. And those thoughts weren't always on my side.

***

I'd been at Bell Buckle Brews for thirty minutes and was already told by Gemma twice that I needed to dial back on the "*cheeriness*."

Was it a crime for a girl to be happy?

I wasn't sure about Gemma's love life, but I thought she needed to be asked on a date. Maybe then she'd lighten up a bit.

Avery was in good hands, I was going on a date with Callan in the near future, and for once, my mind wasn't spiraling with my mental to-do list of grocery shopping, cleaning the house, or thinking about Pudding.

The cat still hadn't shown up, so I'd bought Avery a few more cans of wet food for her to replenish the bowl every night. She sat on the porch last night and read her book out loud in the hopes that Pudding would hear her voice and come home. It hadn't worked, but I wasn't giving up hope. Pudding was out there. We'd find her.

My grandmother always told me to keep the faith, so that's what I'd do.

"I'm heading out," Gemma said, her purse already slung over her shoulder.

I looked up from the cookie I was decorating. I'd been practicing a bit at work for Avery's birthday coming up soon. She wanted *My Little Pony* sugar cookies for her party, so I was doing my best to perfect them well before the event.

"Don't you have another thirty minutes?" I asked, setting the piping bag down.

She shrugged, chewing that ridiculous bubble gum she always smacked on. "I want to go home."

"Can I ask you something?"

She not-so-discreetly rolled her eyes. "What?"

"Did I ever do anything to you to make you hate me?"

Her chewing paused for the briefest moment, the only indication that what I said took her off guard. "No."

I pressed my lips together, doing my best to ignore the obnoxious noises that resumed coming from her mouth. "Is there a reason you don't like me, then?"

She shrugged. "No." Her tone suggested she was bored, wanting nothing more than to leave right this minute.

Talking to her was like pulling teeth.

"Alright." I picked the piping bag back up, turning back to my cookie.

"Finally," Gemma muttered under her breath, walking around the counter and out the door.

A pent-up breath escaped my lips as my phone buzzed on the counter. I glanced at it, keeping my hand hovering over the cookie.

> **Callan:** Forget I said I'd text you about the date

My heart sank. I knew it was too good to be true.

I went back to practicing with the pink icing when my phone buzzed again.

> **Callan:** Sorry Ace hit my elbow and I accidentally hit send too early. I meant to add - it'll be a surprise. Avery can come

I set the bag down next to the cookie, grabbing my phone to reply.

> **Me:** Ace?

Three dots appeared as he typed his response, my eyes glued to them the entire time.

> **Callan:** My horse. You'll love him

The corners of my lips inched up.

Why did meeting his horse feel like meeting someone's parents, or their child?

Like it was some kind of next step?

Stop it. I haven't even gone on one date with the guy and here I am trying to play house with him.

It wasn't only my feelings I had to think of, it was Avery's, too. Callan seemed like a nice guy, but I couldn't be too sure. I had to take this slow, for both our sakes.

I bit down on my bottom lip, sending my response.

> **Me:** I think I will.

But my brain feared it wouldn't only be the horse that I'd love.

18

SAGE

At Avery's next lesson, I leaned against the fence the entire hour, watching Avery become more comfortable on the horse. She'd been doing every lesson on Red, and it was clear they had a connection. He was a beautiful red roan, his head a darker shade than his body.

Watching Avery in the saddle made me wish I could give her more. The horse, the land, the ability to ride whenever she wanted. But right now, this would have to do, and Callan making this possible for her was everything to me.

After they wrapped up, I followed them inside the barn to untack, listening as Avery told Callan how she felt during her lesson. Her ability to open up so much to him about her fears was astonishing to me. She clearly liked him, and I had to say, I didn't mind at all. I was right there with her.

He was sweet and attentive, always paying attention to everything anyone said. A lot of people would blow off a five-year-old talking their ear off, but he replied to every single thing she said, listening with rapt attention.

"Has your cat come home?" Callan asked after putting the saddle away in the tack room.

Avery shook her head while simultaneously unclipping her helmet. She was still borrowing one from his rack, but I hoped I could get her one of her own soon. "Not yet. But I think she will."

"I think she will, too," he said with a kind of determination I admired.

It wasn't that I thought Pudding wouldn't come home. As a mom, my mind always went to the worst case scenario. What if she was run over by a car? What if another family took her in? Was she in the shelter and we just didn't know it?

"I think I'm gonna have my mom buy me a different flavor of cat food this time," Avery told him.

Callan rested a hand on Red's back as he looked down at Avery. "You think that will help?"

She nodded. "I do. Pudding likes different stuff sometimes."

His hand mindlessly rubbed on Red's back, and the horse was clearly enjoying it, with his head low and his eyes slowly shutting. "A variety, huh?"

"Yeah. Like maybe she wants chicken, or fish. Do they have others?"

"I think they have beef," he guessed. I was sure he knew more about pet food than I did, but I'd have to ask Lennon when I visited Tumbleweed Feed next. His brother owned the feed store, so he was a pro when it came to animal nutrition.

"I'll grab one of each kind," I told Avery from where I stood off to the side, my back against the wood-slat wall.

She turned to me. "Thanks, Mama."

I gave her a soft smile in response, hoping like hell a different protein was the trick to getting Pudding to come back home.

"Hey, Cal," Bailey interrupted, coming around the corner from the aisle. "Do you know where the rescue banner is?"

Callan looked over his shoulder at Bailey. "I think my mom has it folded away in the med room, but if it's not there, check the shed outside."

"You guys put shit in the weirdest spots," Bailey mumbled, turning around and disappearing down the aisle as he headed for what I assumed was the med room.

"Language, Cooper!" Callan called after him.

A door squeaked open, and the barn fell silent.

Callan ran a hand down his face, looking at me. "Sorry about everyone's cursing around here."

I waved him off, pushing off the wall. "It's fine. What's the banner for?"

"We have a parade we do every year to raise awareness for the horse rescue, so they're prepping for that."

"A parade?" Avery asked. "I wanna see."

He looked down at her again. "I can do you one better. You can be in it, but only if your mom says it's okay."

Avery's mouth fell open, then pinned her pleading look on me. "Pleeease?"

"I don't mind." A parade would be fun, and it'd give her something to look forward to.

She broke out in a huge, heart-stopping smile. "Yay! Thank you!"

Callan patted Red's back once, then dropped his arm and came around to his head, unhooking him from the crossties. "I'm going to put him away, then I have a surprise."

Avery gasped. "A surprise?"

He looked at me from under the brim of his cowboy hat. "If your mom has the time."

"She has the time! Right, Mama?" She turned to me, and the pressure of saying yes beat down on me. I didn't have work today, so I didn't have anywhere important to be, but did he mean for the date? I wasn't dressed for a date. I was wearing light washed jeans and an old gray t-shirt tied at the bottom with a hair tie. My hair was air-dried from my shower last night, and I wasn't wearing makeup. If he had any fancy plans, I'd have to take a rain check.

"I guess I do," I got out.

Callan headed over to Red's stall, leaving me alone with Avery.

"Can you stay here a moment, sweetie?" I asked.

"Yeah. I'll put away the brushes I used."

I couldn't help but smile. Doing these horse lessons was teaching her a level of responsibility I didn't think it could. She suddenly liked tidying the things she took out, making sure to put them away after she used them.

I followed after Callan, stopping by the door to the stall as he slid the halter off Red's large head. "Is this the date?"

He glanced at me and must've seen the alarmed look on my face because the corners of his lips turned up. "It is."

My hand grabbed the bars on the upper half of the stall door. "I'm not really ready for a date today." I looked down at my outfit, continuing to speak. "I didn't think you'd want to go right now, and I'm not dressed appropriately—"

I stopped talking when two fingers grabbed my chin, guiding my head up gently. My eyes met Callan's, his gaze soft. "It doesn't matter what you wear."

We were so close that the brim of his hat was mere inches from touching me. Though I was probably between five to seven inches shorter than him, with his head turned down to me, his hat was so close to touching my forehead.

I sucked in a breath as our eyes stayed glued to each other. "Where are you taking us?"

"Technically?"

I nodded.

"We're staying on the ranch."

My brow furrowed. "What are we doing on the ranch?"

"It wouldn't be a surprise if I told you, would it?" His thumb moved slightly against my chin, the touch like a caress. But I was imagining that. I had to be.

"No," I said, the word coming out like a whisper. "I guess it wouldn't."

He dropped his hand slowly, the movement seeming forced, like he didn't want to pull away. But that would be crazy, right?

He didn't step back. "Let me just go get some things from the house, and I'll be right back."

I nodded unconsciously, lost in his gaze. Hazel eyes had never been so hypnotizing, the swirl of various browns and golds stealing my breath just like before.

"I have to get by, Sage," he said, and fuck if his lips didn't wrap around my name like a goddamn purr.

"Right," I replied, but I couldn't get my feet to obey. From the looks of it, he didn't really mind. He looked just as lost as I was.

To my utter surprise, he lifted his hands and cupped my cheeks, but instead of closing the distance, he led me backwards into the aisle, removing one hand only to close the stall door behind him, not once taking his eyes off me.

Fuck. Why was that so hot?

"Mama?" Avery's voice filled the barn, and I jumped out of my stupor, inhaling a sharp breath as I pulled away from Callan.

"Yes, Aves?" I called back.

Her tiny form came out into the aisle. "Are we going?"

I worked to catch my breath, not realizing that I'd been holding it that whole time. "Yes, sweetie. We're going."

That was too close.

If Avery had seen Callan and I that close, it would only confuse her. Yet, I was going on a date with him, *with* Avery. She didn't know it was a date, though, which was for the better. Maybe it wasn't as serious to Callan as I thought it was. Maybe he was just being friendly, wanting to get to know me better without strings attached later on.

But if that was the case, we had to get on the same page.

Because wanting more with Callan Bronson wasn't what I needed to be focusing on right now. Wanting more with *anyone* only led to disappointment in the long run, and I didn't need any distractions from being the best mom I could be for Avery.

Callan and I would stay strictly friends, if we could even be considered that.

Acquaintances.

Yeah, that's what we were.

Just acquaintances.

19

CALLAN

Touching Sage was a bad idea.

My arms ached to reach out to her, my hand itching to feel her soft skin against my palms again. I shouldn't *want* her like this. I hadn't wanted anyone like this in…well, since my ex packed up and left.

So four years.

But even when I was with her, she didn't stop my heart like Sage did. She didn't steal the breath from my lungs, make my cheeks heat, just from being in the same room as her. Sage's presence could never fly under the radar. Her whole being demanded to be seen like the north star in an ink black sky.

You could look away, but you'd still *feel* her around you.

Sage McKinley was a fucking heart-stopper.

I didn't know the story behind Avery's father other than I knew he wasn't in the picture. For Sage to raise Avery all on her own while maintaining a full-time job absolutely blew my mind. She was so strong, and I had the feeling she didn't think of herself that way, but she should.

The tall grass brushed together as we walked through it, the field moving like ocean waves as a slight breeze ruffled the blades. Avery was skipping ahead of us as Sage and I followed, heading in the direction of the pond. Sage's pace was slow to cater to her still-healing knee, so I matched it, not wanting her to rush. She'd said the bruise was almost gone, but I should have driven them out here instead of walking. The pond wasn't too far out on my parents' property, maybe a fifteen minute walk, and the day was perfectly warm with the wind. Her knee still had to be somewhat sore, but she wasn't complaining, so I took that as a good sign that it was healing well.

"Are you going to tell me what all this is for?" Sage asked, glancing at the basket swinging from my hand, along with the fishing pole slung over my shoulder.

"Nope." She'd have to wait a few more minutes until we got there.

"If you think I know how to fish, you're out of your mind," she said.

Taking my eyes off of Avery in front of us, I faced Sage as we continued walking. "I'll teach you."

Sage snorted and I couldn't help the smile on my face at the sound.

She opened her mouth to reply, but stopped short when she saw my grin. "What's that look?"

"You snorted."

Her nose scrunched. "So?"

I turned my focus back to Avery to be sure she didn't get too far ahead. "It was cute."

From my peripheral, I saw Sage's mouth pop open, then snap shut again.

"Cat got your tongue?" I teased.

"In case you haven't noticed, I'm currently cat-less."

A soft chuckle escaped me. "Touché."

Minutes later, we emerged from a row of trees, coming out right on the shore of the pond. Beside me, Sage stopped in her tracks, but ahead of me, Avery was already close to the water, picking up stones.

The two of them were already pulling me in separate directions.

I set the picnic basket down, pulling out a blanket and laying it on the grass. Setting the fishing pole beside the blanket, I reached back into the basket, grabbing what had me most nervous about this date.

Before I could stand up, Sage spoke up from behind me, where she was still frozen in place. "Is that..."

"Sage," I finished for her.

"You brought me a bouquet of sage?"

My cheeks instantly lit up like a fire was burning in my skin, and I wanted to shrink into myself. Did she hate them? I knew this was too much.

"Callan."

I looked up at her, the sun shining behind her, casting her silhouette in a bright glow. Her eyes searched mine for a moment before she took the two steps to the blanket and lowered herself to my level, taking the bouquet from me. I'd picked them myself, the bundle smaller than one from a floral shop, tied with an ivory ribbon at the stems.

"I love them. Thank you."

The vibrant purple of the flowers looked pale in comparison to the light that Sage held in just her physical appearance alone.

"You're welcome." I turned back to the wicker basket to hide my face, knowing my cheeks were as red as cherries, but also to dig out the snacks I'd brought along.

I set the water bottles on the blanket, then laid out the wrapped sandwiches, chips, and fruit. I'd brought Avery her own Tupperware of string cheese, applesauce pouches, gummy bears, and graham crackers. I wasn't really sure what she liked or if she was picky, so I'd packed what I'd seen other parents bring their children as a snack after lessons in the past.

"This is for Avery," I said, setting the container down on the blanket.

Sage stared at it like it was going to sprout teeth and bite her.

"What's wrong?"

"You packed Avery a lunch?"

I nodded hesitantly. "Yes... Is that okay? Is she allergic to anything?" I should've asked before I packed it.

Her gaze snapped to mine. "No." She shook her head. "I mean, no, she's not allergic to anything. Thank you for thinking of her."

I studied her for a second, wondering why this was a shock to her. "Well, I did include her."

"I know. It's just...I thought you had her come along because there was no one else to watch her."

My brows pulled together. "No. I wanted her to come." Besides, if that was the case, I was sure my mom would have been more than eager to hang out with her for an hour or two.

Sage shook her head in disbelief.

"Is there something wrong with that?" If there was, I wanted to know.

"Not many guys would invite someone's child along on a date willingly... Let alone pack them their own separate lunch."

"If it's overstepping—"

"It's not," she interrupted. "I'm sorry. I really appreciate all of this. I'm just not used to...dates."

I nodded in understanding as she adjusted herself on the blanket, setting the bouquet beside her.

"Do people swim here?" Avery asked from the shore, staring down at the small ripples in the water.

"Sometimes," I told her. "It depends on the season. In the winter, it ices over, but in the summer, it's the perfect temperature."

Avery looked over at us. "Does that mean we can swim?"

"Maybe another day, Aves," Sage answered. "You don't have your swimsuit."

"We'll make time soon," I added once I saw the deflated look on her face.

From my side, Sage turned to me. If shock and confusion were a picture, that would be it. I wasn't sure why she was so surprised I was willing to include Avery. Sage was a mother, and I had no problem accommodating that. Plus, from what I'd seen, Avery was far from a handful compared to the other kids that have come through this ranch for lessons.

Sage reached for Avery's Tupperware as she said, "Why don't you come over here and have something to eat? You can get all messy in the dirt after."

Avery strode through the grass, which was shorter around the pond, and sat next to her mom on the plaid blanket.

"I wasn't sure what to pack, but there's those applesauce pouches with the fancy tops," I started.

"Those are my favorite!" Avery squealed, reaching her hand into the container once Sage had the lid off.

Sage let out a small laugh. "Have at it."

Avery took the container from her, digging through the contents. You would have thought I'd gotten her a pony or something by the look on her face.

"I brought her a sandwich, too, just in case," I told Sage.

"Thank you. She might not eat it, given her current infatuation with the other things you brought her, but she appreciates it. *We* appreciate it."

I nodded, unwrapping my sandwich. Sage picked one up, doing the same.

We sat in silence, listening to the birds chirp in the pine trees as we ate. Even Avery was quiet, looking out at the pond. An occasional dragonfly would swoop down for water, then flutter away.

Nature calmed a wild mind, its presence drawing even the most stressed person to a point of relaxation. You couldn't help but feel content out here, which was why I frequently visited. Sometimes, when life was too much, sitting outside with only the sounds of the countryside was the one thing I needed.

My fears, my nerves, they all disappeared when I was out here. Whether it was on horseback or foot, *this* was the only medicine I needed. And here I sat, sharing it with the two girls who came into my life unexpectedly.

While it was different, sharing this peace with them, I wouldn't change a thing.

That should scare me, make me run to the hills and not look back, but it didn't. Ever since my ex instilled such a huge self-doubt in me, I hadn't wanted to share any parts of my life with someone else. But yet, here I sat on a date that I'd put together with the two of them.

I just hoped I was making the right decision.

***

"This is too hard," Avery complained from my left.

"Maybe you just need a smaller pole," I told her. I should have brought a kids' pole, but I hadn't been thinking.

I was already fucking this up.

"I don't have one of those," she said while reeling in the line. The hook had already caught on a rock, a tree limb, and now grass under the water.

I watched the line come in, sending ripples through the pond. "I'll get you one."

"You don't have to do that," Sage said from the rock she was sitting on a few feet behind us.

I cast a glance over my shoulder at her. "Fishing takes practice, and—" I turned back to Avery just as the hook reached the tip of her pole. "—you need practice."

"What if I'm just never going to be good at fishing?" Avery asked, a slight quiver to her voice.

I knelt beside her so we were eye level, setting a gentle hand on her elbow so she'd face me. "You don't have to be good at everything, but don't expect it right away." I looked at a tree behind her, trying to think up an example, then brought my eyes back to hers. "Remember your first day of lessons? When we went over the small details, like leg pressure and how to hold the reins?"

Avery nodded.

"Well, think of fishing like that. Right now, you're just getting used to the pole, the same way you got used to the horse. Once you're comfortable with the pole, then you focus on the small details. Like aiming where you want your hook to land or how long you want your bait in the water." I dropped my hand from her elbow, then wrapped it around hers on the pole, giving a reassuring squeeze. "You don't have to be a pro at everything the second you start, right?"

She shook her head. "But I want to be good at it."

I dropped my hand to my knee. "You will. I'll help you." Rising, I kept my eyes down on her. "But that starts with a fishing pole meant for your size. Next time we come out here, I'll make sure you have one."

"Next time?" Avery and Sage questioned in unison.

I gave a stern nod. "Next time. Now why doesn't your mom give it a shot?" I turned to Sage.

Her eyes widened. "No way."

"I promised I'd teach you."

Sage crossed her arms. "I think Avery wants to keep trying."

Avery held the pole in her mom's direction. "You can have a turn."

Sage gave a tight-lip smile, clearly wishing Avery hadn't said that. "Are you sure?"

Avery nodded. "Super sure."

Sage stood, coming forward to reluctantly grab it from her. "Alright."

Avery ambled over to the blanket where she had a pile of rocks she was collecting and sat, sifting through them.

Sage held the pole toward my chest. "Teach me, ol' wise one."

I cocked a brow. "Wise one, huh?"

She shrugged, pink tinging the apples of her cheeks as a small smile played on her lips. "You seem to be very knowledgeable in a lot of areas."

I wrapped my hand around hers on the pole, pulling her toward me and then spinning her so her back was to my front. My other hand grabbed the one she didn't have on the pole and led it to the reel so she could get a feel for it before casting out. But instead of telling her what each part did and how to use it, I did the most ludicrous thing I possibly could have done.

I held my chin just above the shell of her ear, the both of us looking out at the water. "I can teach you a lot of things, Sage," I murmured.

Her chest rose and fell as her breathing deepened. "Can you?" she asked breathlessly.

Her hair brushed the stubble on my cheek. "Like you said, I'm knowledgeable in a lot of areas."

What the fuck was I doing?

Playing a dangerous game of *how far can I go* was not how I had planned this to turn out. But here I was, standing behind Sage, hoping like hell that my boner wasn't touching her ass, all because there were a lot of *other* things that popped into my mind the moment she said that.

I should definitely *not* be thinking of her this way. *Especially* on our first date.

Blinking the thoughts away, I adjusted her hand on the pole. "You hold the bail as you cast, then release it when it's out. It'll stop your line when you're ready. Then wind here—" I moved her hand to the handle on the reel. "—to bring the line back in."

She studied the reel for a moment. "This seems too easy."

I took a step back, gesturing to her. "Have at it, then."

She tested her hands, trying a few different positions to get comfortable with the feel of it, then slung it over her shoulder carefully, eyeing the hook. "It won't bounce back and stab me, will it?"

The question was cuter than it should've been. "No, Sage, it shouldn't."

She nodded, looking back out at the water. I could tell she was hesitant to cast, so I came back behind her, wrapping my arms around her to fold my hands over hers on the pole. "Like this." I slowly swung it behind us, setting a finger on the bail, then cast it out, her arms easily moving with mine. When the hook hit the water, I released the bail, letting the end of the line sink a bit. I tugged on it gently, mimicking the movements of a fish with the bait, and slowly reeled it in with my hand still placed over hers.

She let me have complete control, watching each movement like if she didn't memorize it, she'd fail the test. She didn't have to know how to fish or ride a horse for me to be entranced by her. Opposites attract, right? And though Sage wasn't my opposite in every way, she didn't have to know everything I did for us to have fun or get along.

I got the feeling she'd been through a lot more than I had in life, and that was fine. I'd take Sage for who she was, and if she wanted to learn things, I'd show her. But I wouldn't mold her into someone she wasn't.

I stepped back, letting Sage try her hand at it on her own. Taking a seat at the rock she was sitting on previously, I watched her get a feel for the weight of the pole and how to get the hook to land where she wanted it to.

I glanced over at Avery, who was making some kind of tower out of her rocks, but it kept falling over when it got too high. Scanning the ground, I found a few flat rocks and made my way over to her, taking a seat next to her on the blanket.

"Maybe these will be easier to stack," I told her, placing the rocks next to her pile.

She picked one up, studying it like the shape of the rock was the difference between life and death. "This might work."

She began her stack again as Sage's phone buzzed on the blanket next to the basket. I shouldn't have done it, but I glanced at the screen. Whoever had texted her, the number wasn't in her contacts.

"Do you think we can come back here after my next lesson?" Avery asked, keeping her focus on the rocks as she balanced another on top.

"You'll have to ask your mom. But if she's okay with it, I'd love to." Maybe I could teach Avery how to skip rocks next.

Stop it.

Avery was a student, and Sage was her mother. Thinking of future plans with them was not what I needed to be doing. It was one date, and chances were, Sage wouldn't want to continue whatever this was.

This could very well be nothing, though.

One date didn't mean jack shit, yet here I sat, my unforgiving brain growing attached to something that didn't even exist.

Lost deep in my thoughts, I didn't hear when Sage walked up to us in the grass.

"We should probably head back," she said.

My eyes shot up to hers, then I quickly pushed to a stand. "Right. I'll pack all this up." The way Sage said it made me sure she wouldn't want a second date. What the fuck was I thinking? I was stupid for even asking. Stupid for letting my brothers talk me into this. All that talk about Lettie and Bailey's wedding had messed with my head, and now here I was, envisioning a future with someone I'd just met weeks ago.

I got to work putting everything back in the basket as Avery put her rocks back on the shore.

"Thank you for today," Sage said quietly.

My hands slowed as I was rolling up the blanket. "Of course. I hope I wasn't overstepping in any way."

Her brows pulled together. "What? No. This was so thoughtful, Callan. Avery and I had a lot of fun."

I nodded.

Fun.

SCRAPE THE BARREL

That's all this was.

But why was it so hard to get that through my fucking head?

20

SAGE

"Don't forget this!" I grabbed Avery's pink lunchbox off the passenger seat, holding it out the window to her.

"Thanks, Mama," Avery said, wrapping a tiny hand around the handle.

"Have a good first day, sweetie. I'll be back to pick you up later."

She gave a small nod and a quick smile, then turned to run up to the fence where her friends were already waiting at the playground. First grade was a big step from kindergarten, but she hadn't been scared. My little girl was fearless and so beyond excited that she'd barely slept at all last night.

I liked to think that she got it from me, but I couldn't say I was exactly brave all the time. There were too many moments in my life that I'd stayed quiet and let the worst happen.

Heading out of the U-shaped parking lot after drop-off, I headed toward Bell Buckle Brews for my shift. I'd be off by the time Avery got out of school, so I didn't need to worry about her pickup situation today. Most days during the school year, I could get off around the same time she was released, but on the occasional day that wasn't possible, I'd either have her go to a friend's house after or I'd use my lunch to pick her up and bring her to the cafe. At least, that worked for kindergarten. First grade was a whole different ball game.

A few minutes later, I pulled into my usual parking space out front of the cafe and headed inside. As the cowbell above the door sounded, my phone dinged in my back pocket, but I ignored it until I passed through the back doors to clock in.

With school drop-off, I got in a little later than I usually liked to, but I didn't want to drop Avery off at the crack of dawn just to get a head start on some pastries. I already dropped her off about forty-five minutes before the first bell. Thankfully, her teachers didn't mind, seeing as a lot of parents dropped their kids off early so they could head to work as well.

The beauty of working in a cafe meant I could bake and cook things all day—it didn't all have to be done before opening. Sure, we might run out of things, but it wouldn't be the end of the world if a customer had to wait ten minutes for a specific baked good to be done in the oven. We had a variety of items to choose from anyway.

That was the nice thing about places like Bell Buckle—life didn't move too fast to where people couldn't wait a few minutes for their food. In the city, though? That would cause havoc and a bad Yelp review.

Thank goodness for small towns.

I slid the baking sheets full of assorted items into the ovens in the back, my wrist slightly twinging with the weight, but I ignored it and headed to the front to deal with the register and other opening duties.

My fingers worked to tie a knot with the strings on my apron as my phone buzzed again from my jeans. Remembering I had ignored the text from earlier, I pulled it out to check who it was.

An unknown number sat in the message field of both text messages, and I clicked it to read them. This time, it was a different number than the one that texted me during my date with Callan.

> **Unknown:** You've been ignoring me.

> **Unknown:** You know who this is. I know what game you're playing.

My fingers froze, clutching my phone like my grip might keep the fear away and erase what was on the screen. If this was him, how was he texting me? Did he get someone to smuggle a burner phone into the prison? There was no way he could be out. He still had just under two years left of his sentence at the Oregon State Penitentiary.

I didn't know if a minute passed or ten, but a knock on the glass caused me to jump out of my spiraling thoughts. My hands retracted from my phone like it might bite me, the device landing on the counter with a clang. My eyes shot to the window, my heart beating out of my chest. My whole world had frozen with the terror that crept into my mind at the thought of him being free. That he might be able to find me and Avery.

Oakley stood outside the window, her hand lifted in an eager wave as a smile creased her cheeks. She pointed to the handle on the door and I realized it was locked.

Shit. How long was I standing there for?

Leaving my phone where it landed on the counter, I rushed to the door to let her in.

"Good morning," Oakley said as I held the door open for her.

"Morning," I replied, checking both ways on the sidewalk and across the street before closing the door again. The damn cowbell dinged with the movement, making me flinch. I never hated the thing as much as I did right now.

"You okay?" she asked as I turned to her, wiping my palms on my apron.

"Better than ever." I pasted on a grin.

Her eyes narrowed slightly like she knew I was lying through my teeth. I was a baker—not an actress. "You're never late to opening Triple B."

"Late?" It was just seven-thirty when I last checked the clock.

"It's fifteen past opening," she stated hesitantly.

Swallowing the tremor that was building with my inability to lie, I said, "Must've lost track getting the food ready."

Oakley nodded slowly as I passed her, heading back behind the counter. She followed, eyeing my phone where it laid face down on the counter. I swiped it away, stuffing it in my apron.

"Typical order?" I asked while maintaining eye contact. Avoiding looking at someone was the telltale of a lie, right? Or was it the opposite? I should've glanced away, made it seem natural. How the fuck would I make something look natural when I was so obviously lying that I was okay? I was freaking the fuck out.

"Yep," she answered in her typical cheery voice, but it sounded skeptical.

Fuck. I should've blinked.

I turned around to prepare her and Lennon's coffee order.

"Is something burning?" she asked from behind me.

"Burning? No. I never burn anything," I said, my voice coming off a little too airy.

"Sage? Do you have something in the oven?"

My eyes bulged out of my damn head.

Fuck.

Leaving the coffee to do its thing, I rushed through the door to the back, finding the room clouded with smoke.

This was not good.

I ran over to the oven, switching it off before opening the door. I yanked a mitt off the counter, slipped it on, and pulled the tray out.

Even through all the smoke, I could see every pastry was blackened to a crisp. It was all ruined.

Coughing filled the room from behind me and I turned to see Oakley waving a hand in the air as if it could do anything against this amount of smoke. "Are you okay?" she asked, doing her best to cover her mouth and nose.

"Fine," I croaked as the air stung my eyes.

"Is there a window?"

"The door," I said as I put my foot on the lever of the trash for the top to pop open. I angled the tray, all of the wasted food sliding into the bin with a thud.

The back door to the cafe creaked open as Oakley propped a chair against it to keep it open.

I surveyed the room, thankful that the only damage was smoke and a few burnt pastries. I didn't burn the place down, but I still felt guilty. It could have been way worse. He wasn't even in front of me and he was affecting me this badly.

I squeezed my eyes shut as if that could keep the overthinking at bay.

"Come outside with me," Oakley said from her spot by the door. "Your eyes are probably on fire with all this smoke."

I followed her command, heading after her out the back. I leaned against the brick building, needing the support.

"Can Penny come in to cover your shift?" Oakley asked, standing a few feet from me.

"I'm not leaving work because of some burnt pastries."

Oakley tilted her head in a disbelieving manner. "This isn't just some burnt croissants or whatever the hell was in that oven. Something's on your mind, and I think you need a day off."

I shifted my attention on the asphalt to her. "I can't afford a day off."

"PTO?"

I sighed. I did have PTO, but what if I needed it for a sick day for Avery?

"Come on, Sage. Take some time for you."

I scoffed, adjusting my stance against the wall to lean my butt against the back of my hands where they sat folded behind me. "And what? Sit at home instead? Pass."

"Come to the bar with us."

"Us?" But who would watch Avery?

"Lettie, Brandy, and me. We weren't planning on it, but they'd never pass up an excuse to day drink."

I could, though. "I don't know, Oakley. It was Avery's first day of school today. I want to be there for her."

"And you will be. But you can't be the best mom you can be if you don't take care of yourself first. You don't even have to drink if you don't want to. Just come have some girl time. We'll find someone to watch Avery. I'm sure Charlotte would love to."

I gnawed on my bottom lip, hating the idea of not being there for Avery. Now with these texts, I couldn't be sure if we were even safe, and leaving her felt like the worst decision right now. But if Charlotte was watching her at the ranch, she might be safer than if she was at our house.

What if he knew where we lived?

I shoved the thoughts away. I couldn't let him have power over me, not anymore. I wouldn't put our lives on hold any longer for him.

"Okay."

Oakley's answering smile could've blinded me if it wasn't for the sting of smoke still burning them.

21

CALLAN

"Same shit, different visit," Beckham mumbled from his horse to the left of me. He was in town visiting for a few days, so the lot of us were spending as much time together as we could.

"You complaining about ranch chores now?" I teased, keeping my eyes on the land to look out for any down cows. It was rare that it happened, but I liked to be aware in case we stumbled across any.

"He's a rodeo star. This shit is boring to him now, don't you know?" Bailey said from where he was riding Nova, his black quarter horse, a few feet off to the side of Beckham.

Lennon scoffed. "I wouldn't say star."

Beck hinted at a grin. "I agree with Len on that."

"Then quit," I said, my tone flat.

Beck let out a sigh, shaking his head. "Maybe you should quit with that shit, Callan."

"Not gonna happen." I hated how he rode broncs like it wasn't one of the most dangerous things you could do. To get on a horse primarily for the animal to try to buck you off was reckless to me. What if he broke his spine? His neck? Hell, just any part of his body? There were much more useful things he could be doing that weren't so dangerous.

From the corner of my eye, I caught Beck adjusting the reins in this hand. "I should've said same broken record, different visit, then."

"How's it feel to be on a horse that doesn't want you dead?" Bailey asked, trying to lighten the mood in his typical way. It was a miracle he put up with us Bronson brothers.

"Boring," Beck replied. "Wanna race?" he asked Bailey.

"We're supposed to be—" But before I could finish my sentence, they were off. "Checking the cows," I finished, my tone quieter.

"Not your fault they never grew up, Cal," Lennon said. He had the day off work while Oakley held down the fort at Tumbleweed Feed with their coworker, Jacey, so he decided to spend it with us. I wondered if he was rethinking his decision yet. Lennon was the most mature out of all of us, but that also probably stemmed from him being the oldest.

I liked seeing the carefree side of Beckham, but I wished he'd put his adrenaline junkie personality to use elsewhere rather than in rodeo. Every time he rode, I flipped the footage on, whether it was on TV or a live stream from a smaller event, but I'd only watch till he jumped. Then I'd turn it off. I didn't care to hear the stats. I just wanted to see that he was okay. Each ride was just as ruthless as the last, and to see my brother thrown around like a rag doll never sat right with me, but he wouldn't quit. I'd tried everything, and all it did was annoy him.

Up ahead, Bailey and Beck circled around, trotting back to us.

"So, Cal, how're things with Sage?" Bailey asked, a huge smile lighting up his face.

"Fine," I clipped. I didn't feel like being teased to the end of days at the moment.

"Bullshit. We want the tea," Beck said.

Lennon barked out a laugh. "You're spending way too much time around those buckle bunnies."

Beck shot him a glare. We all knew he wasn't one to sleep around, but his use of the word was a bit funny. If he wasn't at events, he was staying with friends or visiting home. If I was being honest, Beckham only had eyes for one girl his whole life, and if I had to guess, that most likely hadn't changed to this day.

"I took her on a date. That was all," I said.

"Don't forget the part where you brought her daughter," Bailey added.

"You what?" Beck asked. "Might as well walk down the aisle now."

"There's no harm in including Avery," I defended.

Beck's eyebrows rose. "A woman letting her child around the guy she's going on a date with? She definitely thinks it's serious."

"It was one date," I reminded him. "Plus, I'm Avery's instructor. So she already knows me by default."

"A lesson isn't the same as a date," Bailey piped in.

"Come on, Cal. You can't keep yourself hidden away forever," Beckham said, his tone a bit softer now.

My thumb picked at the leather rein in my hand. "I'm far from hidden."

"Is that so?" Lennon asked.

I nodded in response. "Yep."

"Then how come you only just met Sage a little over a month ago for the first time because you'd never been to Bell Buckle Brews before?"

"Lots of people don't go to cafes," I told him.

"False," Beck said. "Everyone in this town goes to Triple B."

I frowned. "I doubt that."

"Proof's in the pudding, angel baby," Bailey teased.

"What fucking pudding?" Now I was just getting irritated, and that didn't happen often. What were they trying to say? That I should hop out of my comfort zone to just make myself uncomfortable for fun? Pass. "This is why Reed stays away from all of you and your lady talk."

Beck smiled, his chin held high. "I'm single, so no lady talk for me."

"Don't even get me started on your woman problems," I said to him. "Woman as in singular."

Beck's smile fell, knowing exactly who I was talking about. He wanted to give me shit about Sage? I could throw it right back in his smug face.

"Brothers," Bailey murmured, like he wasn't already one of us.

"Zip it, Cooper," Beckham warned, as if he read my thoughts.

"Anyway," Lennon started. "Oakley texted me that Sage and the girls are going to the bar tonight, if you all wanted to join."

I turned to look at him as my horse, Ace, continued on his way. "Sage is going to the bar?"

"Yeah?" he replied, like that wasn't abnormal. Was it? I didn't know Sage enough to know if she went to the bar often or not. I figured she didn't because she didn't typically have anyone to watch Avery, but what did I know?

"I'll go," I said quickly.

Beck let out a snort and I sent a glare his way. "What?"

"Don't act too eager," Beck teased.

Smart ass.

I wasn't too eager. I would've gone either way. Sage hadn't joined us on any of our bar nights before and I'd gone to almost all of them. It wasn't *just* because of her.

Okay, a *little* bit was because she would be there. But we'd gone on a date and I hadn't seen her since, so of course I wanted an excuse to see her. Plus, I liked Outlaw's Watering Hole. The place gave that nostalgic feel and somehow, my nerves never shot up in the neon lit bar.

"Oakley said something about Mom watching Avery," Lennon added.

"Is Sage bringing her by the ranch before they go?" I asked.

"Hoping to get back in time to see her?" Beck questioned jokingly from the side, but I continued to ignore him.

Lennon shook his head. "Mom's in town picking up some supplies, so I believe she's picking Avery up on her way back here."

That made sense. It wouldn't be logical for Sage to drive all the way out here to drop her off just to go back into town to the Watering Hole.

"When you say 'the girls,' you mean Brandy will be there, too, right?" Beck asked. Brandy had been Lettie's best friend since kindergarten, so I saw her as a little sister. We were pretty close, but that's all she was to me. Another little sister to love and care for.

I turned my attention to Beck. "What other girls do you think would be coming?"

"His buckle bunnies," Bailey teased with a grin.

Beck gave him a mocking grin with a shake of his head and then said, "No, dipshit. But you've got to invite Reed."

"Oh, God, Beck. Please. For once, I just want one fucking peaceful night at the bar," Lennon complained.

Beck pouted. "I'm only here for a few days. I miss them sometimes."

"So miss them separately," Bailey said. "Even *I* can't handle them in the same room together."

"That's saying a lot, seeing as you're with our sister," Beck joked.

It was Bailey's turn to smack him on the shoulder now. They'd go back and forth like that all day if they could.

They continued poking fun at each other until we made it back to the barn about an hour later. The silence that met me in my truck was bliss as I headed home to shower off the smell of the ranch.

Something about the familiarity of Outlaw's Watering Hole made me feel at home, how strangers rarely hung out there and you could always expect the same thing when you visited.

Seeing Sage in that bar made me anxious with excitement, like if she fit in there, somehow she could fit into my life, too.

I'd made the mistake long ago jumping into a relationship too quickly, and I was all too aware that I could be repeating history. But something about Sage McKinley drew me in like a moth to flame, and damn, if I got burned in the process, would it really be all that bad if I got to be near her for even a fraction of my life?

22

SAGE

Maybe mixing alcohol with the thoughts swimming through my head wasn't the best idea.

My eyes trailed the condensation rolling down the side of the glass as the ice melted, turning the already-weak margarita to water. I didn't know if they served wine at bars, so I'd opted for a margarita, really only because I didn't know what else to order.

I got pregnant shortly after I was legal to drink, so I didn't spend much time at bars. This was the first time I'd been to one since…well, before Jason went to prison. He didn't like me going out to bars all that often anyway. He thought I'd cheat on him. I guess what they say is true—the ones who are paranoid are more than likely the ones doing it themselves.

Unfortunately for me, I didn't figure it out until after he went to prison. But even if I had found out before, I wouldn't have been able to get away from him. He may be locked up in a concrete building manned with guards at all hours, but the real prison was my mind, and I wished I could say my sentence ended the day he was taken away.

Thoughts of him still haunted me, and while I thought it was getting better, today just made them come back around tenfold. I tried to keep my glances at the entrance to the bar minimal, but all I kept expecting was him walking through that door and dragging me out of here.

Avery was safe with Travis and Charlotte. We had no connection to that ranch for Jason to find us there, which meant she was okay for tonight. It was after she left there that I had to worry about.

From where Oakley, Brandy, Lettie, and I were seated, we had a clear view of the door as it swung open.

"Look who finally decided to show up," Brandy remarked over the beat of the country music filling the dimly lit bar.

Bailey, Lennon, Reed, Beckham, and Callan strode in. Their almost matching attire would have made me laugh if it wasn't for the look on Callan's face, how it settled with relief once he saw me. I offered him a small smile and they made their way over to us. The bar wasn't packed, but there were enough people that they had to maneuver around a few groups.

Lettie set her drink on the high top table, meeting Bailey halfway to wrap her arms around his neck and slam a kiss to his mouth. The others left them standing there and closed the distance to where we were still seated. Lennon bent to kiss the side of Oakley's head and she leaned into him, a blush lighting up her cheeks.

"You guys weren't having too much fun without us, were you?" Beckham asked, surveying the drinks on the table.

Brandy slid off the stool, holding her arms wide. "Can't have fun without the life of the party, can we?"

He grinned down at her and pulled her in for a tight hug, rocking her back and forth before letting her go.

"We missed you," Brandy told him.

"I missed you guys, too. Pool?" Beckham asked, looking at each of us with the question.

Callan ignored him, keeping his eyes locked on me with a slight furrow to his brow. I offered him another smile, but it didn't ease the look on his face.

"I'll play," Bailey offered. "Teams?"

"Len and me, you and Cal?" Beckham said to him.

Callan tore his attention from me and I heaved a deep breath. "I'm good," he said.

"Reed?" Beckham asked, facing Reed where he was leaning against the half wall that surrounded the area with the pool tables.

Reed adjusted his arms from where they were crossed. "You buying drinks?"

"Loser buys," Beckham said, like he was reminding him of a rule they had.

"I'm not playing if I'm not drinking," Reed stated.

Beckham clapped his hands, rubbing them together. "Always the picky asshole. Brandy?" He faced her.

"I'll get them," I offered before she could respond.

"Great," Beckham said.

Callan gave him a stern look, then reached into his back pocket to pull out his wallet. "I'll go with."

"It's okay," I told him.

"We'll go with her," Lettie cut in, coming up beside Brandy.

Callan hesitated a moment, then pulled a wad of cash from his wallet and handed it to me. I took it because I knew damn well I couldn't afford drinks for everyone. "Thanks."

He gave me a short nod. "Let me know if you need help carrying the drinks back."

"That's what she's got us for," Brandy said, looping her arms through mine and Lettie's.

Lettie did the same to Oakley on her other side. "You're coming, too."

Oakley laid her hand on Lettie's arm. "If you insist."

"Beers?" Lettie clarified with the guys.

"Whiskey, please," Beck said while the others nodded.

"Four beers and a whiskey. Got it."

With one last look at the guys, the four of us headed toward the bar on the other side, keeping our arms locked together.

"So," Lettie started as we approached the worn wooden bar, "what's the look on your face for?"

"What look?" I asked as we all dropped our arms. Each barstool was taken aside from the two at the end that we grouped behind.

"What can I get you?" the bartender asked, his tattooed arms flexing as he threw a rag over his shoulder and leaned against the counter.

Lettie listed the guys' beverages, then ordered herself some mixed drink, along with Brandy's and Oakley's.

"You?" the bartender asked.

"I have a drink back at the table," I said, gesturing behind me.

"She'll take a lemon drop," Oakley told the guy.

He nodded once and got to work on all of the drinks as I faced Oakley.

"What?" she asked innocently.

"I have a margarita," I reminded her.

Oakley leaned an elbow on the bar. "It's been sitting there for almost an hour. It's probably watered down and gross. Plus, lemon drops are delicious. You'll love it. And if you don't, I'll drink it."

"Do you guys wanna dance?" Lettie asked.

"Dance?" People still did that?

"Yes, dance!" she exclaimed, grabbing my hand. "Come on."

"What about the drinks?" I'm sure the bartender would hate to get them all ready and then look up to find us gone.

"We'll come back for them," Brandy said.

I looked back at the guy as he filled beer glasses, then turned to the others. "You guys go. I'll wait for them and come get you when they're all done." I couldn't imagine he'd be long making them anyway. But I'd wait with the drinks while they had their fun to whatever country song was on the jukebox.

"Are you sure?" Oakley asked, her red hair draped over her shoulders like silk.

"It's only a few feet away," I pointed out.

The three of them glanced at the makeshift dance floor and then back to me like they were mentally measuring the distance.

They looked at me like they didn't want to leave me, which was nice of them, but I'd be fine. "I don't know how to dance. I really don't mind."

"One song," Brandy promised.

I gestured to the group of people already doing some cohesive dance as I sat on the second stool from the end. "Get going, then!"

They headed off toward the group of people stomping and twirling as I swiveled on the seat to face the bar. There were already two beers in front of me, and I was sure the rest weren't far behind. Even if they wanted to dance for a few more songs, I could take Callan up on his offer to help bring the drinks back to the table. It'd give me an excuse to talk to him and right now, I needed the distraction.

The bartender set what I presumed to be the lemon drop on the bar in front of me and I eyed it for a moment before picking it up and taking a long sip. It was sour, but it covered up the taste of vodka well. It was almost like drinking an extra tart lemonade.

I'd have to pace myself with these if I wanted to stay aware of my surroundings.

The chance of something happening tonight was slim, but I didn't want to be too comfortable and caught off guard. Jason was good at showing up when I least expected it.

To my left, the barstool scraped against the ground and someone sat in it. I avoided making eye contact only because I didn't want to give anyone the wrong impression. I was here to have fun, according to Oakley, but that didn't mean I had to give every stranger the time of day.

"Sage, is it?" the man asked.

My heart jumped in my chest at the use of my name and I turned. My spine was stiff, my breath caught in my throat. "Uhm—"

"You work at the cafe," he explained, and my chest eased a fraction. He was just a customer.

"I do."

He held out a hand and I looked down at it before hesitantly setting my palm in his. He shook it, his grip hard. "Can I buy you a drink?"

I pulled my arm back, folding my hands together in my lap as I glanced at my drink. "Already have one, but thanks."

His brows pulled down as he ignored the drink on the bar. "I can buy you something better than that girly drink."

My chest tightened like a brick was placed on it as I recognized him from the other day when he tried to get my last name. He'd made me feel a little off then, but right now was solidifying the fact that he was a creep. "I'm okay. Thank you, though."

"Please, I insist," he said, his voice laced with demand. He held a hand up for the bartender to see and gave him a nod.

"Really, I'm okay—"

"You're not one for pleasantries, are you?" he asked, cutting me off.

"I—"

"I think she said no," Brandy's voice interrupted before I could get a word out.

The man paid her no mind. "Little busy here, princess."

The nickname he spit out so casually took me by surprise, and I looked at Brandy to find her fuming.

"What did you just call me?" she gritted out.

Lettie and Oakley strode up behind Brandy, smiles on their faces as they clearly didn't know what was currently going on.

"He get our drinks?" Oakley asked, referencing the bartender, who was stuck in a conversation at the end of the bar, holding two of our drinks hostage.

This time, the man looked at the three of them. "Only buying for one tonight."

"Not you, you fucking pig," Brandy seethed, and before I could blink, she was shoving his chest.

23

CALLAN

Beckham must have glanced over at the bar for the hundredth time when he dropped his pool cue and stood ramrod straight. "Uhm, guys."

"What now?" Reed complained right as a loud bang sounded from my right.

My head twisted toward the bar so fast that I had whiplash, but I didn't give it a second thought when I beelined for the girls. The others weren't far behind as we pushed through the few groups of people that were now staring at the commotion.

Brandy was yelling in some guy's face as Sage tried to scoot off her seat behind the man. His barstool had tipped over when he stood up, blocking her exit. She looked cornered and scared and it ignited a rage inside of me that I'd never felt before.

Lettie and Oakley stood behind Brandy like her backup, but they were so focused on the man that they didn't see Sage trying to get away. It was like slow motion as I rushed over. She tried to balance a foot on one of the metal rods on the stool, but her sneaker slipped and she careened forward. Breaking into a run to close the ten feet still separating us, I caught her around her waist as she braced her hands on my chest.

"I've got you," I murmured into her hair as she shook against me.

Making sure her foot wasn't caught in the stool, I kicked it away and pulled her to me. Her entire body trembled as my hands tightened on her waist.

Seconds later, Beckham was in the man's face, sending a punch straight into his jaw. He was a swing first, ask questions later kind of guy. Brandy tried to get a punch in, but before her fist could land true, Reed was picking her up by the waist and slinging her over his shoulder.

"Let me go!" she screamed, but Reed didn't pay her demands any mind as he hauled her away.

"Are you okay?" I asked Sage. Her eyes were frantically searching the bar, so lost in her head that she didn't hear me. "Sage."

Lettie and Oakley were already backed away from the fight, Bailey and Lennon now pulling Beckham off the man. Beck had him on the ground, sending punches to his jaw.

Sage's chest was rising and falling like she'd run a mile. I needed to get her out of here. The signs of a panic attack were clear to me, and she was on the verge.

I reached for her hand and she ripped it away, eyes flaring up to mine. "It's okay, Sage. I'm going to get you out of here, okay?"

She blinked, clearing whatever fog she was stuck in, and nodded quickly. I gently grabbed her hand, her trembling fingers folding around mine. Leading her toward the door with the trust that Bailey and Lennon would take care of the rest, we exited the bar.

As soon as the music was muffled by the door closing, I could hear her rapid breaths. Stopping in my tracks, I turned, quickly scanning her for injuries, and then cupped her cheeks.

"Breathe with me, baby. Okay? In and out."

She nodded, the movement frantic. I inhaled deeply through my nose, then out through my mouth, watching her the entire time. Her chest was still heaving, pressing against mine with each rise. Tucking her hair behind her ears, I tilted her head up toward me.

"Sage, look at me."

Her eyes found mine, the green in them glossed over from tears threatening to fall.

I spoke slowly to be sure she heard every word. "You're okay. You're safe. Slow breaths, in and out. Can you do that for me?"

She nodded again, her body still wracked with tremors. I inhaled deeply, then exhaled slowly, repeating the action until she was doing the same.

My hands smoothed over her hair, resting back on her cheeks. "Good. That's good. How was work today?"

"Bad."

My thumb brushed a tear that fell down her cheek. "Why's that?"

"I burnt the pastries."

"That's okay. Things like that happen. How was Avery's first day of school?" She'd texted me last night that Avery was jumping all over her bed, excited to see her friends.

"Good. I called her after your mom picked her up."

"I'm sure she had a lot of fun seeing her friends. Probably told them all about the horses, too."

Sage nodded, the movement slow. Her eyes were too damn far away, lost in whatever spiral the fight sent her into.

"Did he touch you?"

"No," she said quietly. Her throat worked on a swallow, and I knew her mouth was dry from the panic.

The urge to storm back in there and beat the shit out of the guy with Beckham eased the slightest bit.

"Come with me." I grabbed her hand again and led her over to the passenger side of my truck. I opened the door and reached in, all while keeping her hand in mine.

After blindly feeling around, I turned to her, letting go of her hand to twist the cap off the water bottle. "Here."

She grabbed it gently, taking a few deep gulps.

"Thank you," she said, handing the water back to me.

I set it in the cupholder, then faced her again. I had a million questions about what the fuck happened in there, but mostly, I was kicking myself for not keeping a closer eye on them. On her. I should've been watching. Hell, I should have gone with.

"Are you okay?" she asked.

My focus on the door to the bar snapped back to her. "I don't matter right now. You do."

"You always matter."

My teeth ground together, the urge to kiss her too fucking strong with all the adrenaline coursing through me. Now was not the time.

"I'm okay."

I couldn't tell if she was only worked up about the incident inside or if it was a combination of things. Something was off when I walked in earlier, but it wasn't my place to pry.

She stepped forward and wrapped her arms around my torso, laying her head on my chest. Without hesitation, I folded myself around her. What if we hadn't been here tonight and the girls went out alone? We wouldn't have been here to protect them, and the thought ate away at me. Anyone I loved— No. Anyone I simply *knew* being in danger made my gut twist.

"What did he do?"

Sage kept her head against my chest as my thumbs began to stroke circles on her back. "He wanted to buy me a drink."

That couldn't be all. "What else?"

She hesitated, then said, "He wouldn't take no for an answer. Then he called Brandy a princess, and she blew up."

My veins felt like they were on fire with the knowledge that he wanted to force a drink on her. But not just a drink. If he had...

Sage pulled back slightly to look up at me. "I'm okay."

The look on her face assured me of that, but feeling her shaking just minutes ago, how scared she was, I wanted to fucking kill him for making her feel that uncomfortable.

Lost in the rage that still coursed through me, I didn't realize it when she raised herself up on her toes slightly. Only when Sage pressed her lips to mine did I snap out of my fog and breathe again. I breathed *her* in. Her sweet, lemony taste danced on my lips as she slipped her tongue past mine. My hands fisted in the back of her shirt, tugging her closer to me.

I was kissing Sage McKinley in a bar parking lot, and it felt a lot like what I imagined heaven to be.

My hands slid up her back, coming around her neck to rest on her cheeks. Tilting her head, I deepened the kiss, our mouths molding together like they were meant to. She arched into me and let out a soft moan, and all I could think about was her. Her soft skin, her lips, her voice, just *her*. She took over every sense that my body and mind had, and I quickly realized I didn't want this feeling to ever end.

Her hands wrapped around the back of my neck, and I reached up to take my cowboy hat off, setting it on top of the truck. Her fingers slid up, tangling in my hair and pulling me closer to her, if that was even possible.

Across the small parking lot, the door to the bar opened, letting music filter out into the night.

"Hey, you fucks!" Beckham shouted, and I reluctantly pulled back.

We both turned to find everyone filing out of the door, letting it slam shut behind Bailey.

"You guys okay?" I asked, not having to raise my voice too high with the small lot we were in.

"I'm fucking amazing," Beck said, striding up to us with the others tailing behind.

"Your hand says otherwise," Lennon remarked.

Beckham whirled, his feet a little unsteady. "I can shove it where the sun don't shine if you want to feel it."

"That's disgusting, Beck," Lettie said, a hint of revulsion on her face. Other than her frown, she was fine. They all were.

"He asked!" Beck exclaimed.

Lennon draped his arm over Oakley's shoulders. "I didn't ask shit."

"How many shots did you have after we left?" I asked Beck. He was slurring and not very stable.

Beck's grin grew. "Bartender gave me free drinks for slugging the guy. Can't not take advantage of that, can I? Speaking of," he started, his expression sobering up the slightest bit, "you okay, Sage?"

She nodded next to me. "Thank you for…punching him?"

Beck saluted her. "My pleasure."

Behind them, Brandy came storming out of the bar, Reed close on her heels. His black cowboy hat was pulled low, but he looked frustrated as shit. I could practically see the veins bulging out of his tattooed arms.

"Leave me alone," Brandy spit out at him, not bothering to glance back as she headed for her Bronco in the parking lot.

Reed grabbed her arm, stopping her in her tracks. We all watched them, knowing what was coming next.

"Get your fucking hand off of me," Brandy seethed, her tone lethally calm.

"No. You're not getting in that fucking car drunk," Reed gritted out, his voice gravelly.

She ripped her arm from his, though it took little effort. "Callan will drive me."

I swallowed as Reed turned his glare on me. Brandy was practically my little sister, and though I'd come to her rescue from Reed countless times to avoid further drama between the two of them, tonight was not one of those nights.

"Reed will have to take tonight, B," I said to her.

Brandy turned to me, a look of betrayal passing over her. I couldn't keep getting in the middle of them. Sooner or later, they'd have to figure this shit out and get over whatever the fuck was going on between the two of them.

Brandy crossed her arms. "Then I'll walk."

"Like fucking hell you will," Reed grumbled. "There's two other vehicles here. Take your choice."

Brandy was doing this to get a rise out of him. She always did. She practically reveled in him getting worked up.

I turned to Sage, blocking the two of them out as they all situated who was driving with who. "Ready to go?"

She sucked in a deep breath, nodding. Though she'd come with the girls, there didn't seem to be any question that I'd be driving her home. I braced one hand on the already opened passenger door while the other hovered at her back as she got in. I wanted to give her space rather than assume she'd be okay with me touching her again.

Once she was buckled, I closed the door and rounded the truck, giving everyone a short wave before sliding behind the wheel.

"My parents' place to pick up Avery?" I asked as I turned the key.

She shook her head, leaning back in the seat. "No. Your place."

24

CALLAN

My parents were fine with Avery spending the night once I called them, but I wasn't sure what Sage wanted out of tonight. Was it too soon to take her to bed? Did she just want to chat? I'd talk with her all night if she wanted, but I didn't want to ruin whatever this was between us. If there even was anything between us.

She could have only kissed me because of the rush, but a part of me knew it wasn't just that.

It'd been so long since I'd been with anyone that I didn't really know what classified as dating. We'd gone on one date and shared one kiss, but did she want more?

I turned onto my driveway, heading toward the house. It wasn't too far from the street, but the dirt road was bumpy as we approached the white two-story.

"This is your house?" Sage asked from beside me, finally speaking after keeping quiet the entire ride.

"It is." Shifting into park, I killed the engine and hopped out. I took steady breaths on my way around the hood to open her door for her. The nerves were settling in, but I did my best to keep them away. I didn't need to be nervous around Sage. She was like sunshine after a blizzard, warming every cold inch that she shined on. Any fear I may have felt about having her in my home couldn't touch me.

After sliding off the seat, she looked up at the house while I closed the door. "You live here alone?" she asked as she turned to me.

"Aside from the crickets and coyotes?" I joked. "Yeah, I do. My brothers give me shit for having a house like this until they're the ones crashing in my guest rooms."

"*Rooms?*" she repeated, emphasizing the *S*.

"Just two." Guilt slammed into me like a train. She and Avery were living over in town in a small two-bedroom cottage-like house, and I was out here living alone in a structure four times that size.

Shifting on my feet, I set a hand on her lower back, leading her toward the front door. After I unlocked it and headed inside behind her, I bolted the door again. It didn't matter that I lived in the middle of nowhere, safety was always a priority. Plus, after tonight, the last thing I needed was that guy coming around for revenge. Speaking of...

"Did you know that guy?" I asked as she studied my kitchen.

She took a moment to respond, like the setup of my appliances and cabinets was all that interesting, then said, "No."

I cocked a brow. "That doesn't sound like a very confident 'no.'"

She looked over her shoulder at me as I set my keys in the dish on the counter and my hat on the hook on the wall. "He was in the cafe a few days ago."

"Ah, so you know *of* him."

"Not really."

"You didn't speak to him, then?"

She tensed for a split second, but even though it was brief, I didn't miss it.

"I did."

I closed the distance so that I was standing directly behind her, her back now lightly pressed to my chest. Reaching a hand up, I brushed the hair away from her neck, then leaned closer to her ear. "Do I have to keep prying things out of you? Because I can."

"So demanding," she teased, her voice full of satiny lust that wrapped around my senses, heading south.

"This? This is nothing, Sage." I brought my lips to her ear, faintly brushing a kiss to the lobe. Goosebumps freckled her neck and I smirked. "What'd you talk about?"

She inhaled deeply, her chest rising with the action, accentuating her breasts in the fitted white tank top she wore. I wanted to clamp down on them, suck on her peaked nipples for hours. I wanted to do a fuck ton of things to her in this moment, but

I had no idea what she wanted out of being here. She was the one to ask to come to my house, but that wasn't an invitation to have sex with her.

"He asked for my last name and if I'd been in town long," she stated, her voice harder than before.

I stopped, pulling my lips away from her ear. "He did what?"

She turned, our chests now touching. "It wasn't anything, but then he wanted to buy me a drink at the bar and…" She trailed off.

"And now you don't think it's nothing," I filled in.

She nodded slowly, her eyes shining with worry, though she did her best to mask it. She didn't have to hide it around me. Whatever her battles were, whatever her insecurities or problems consisted of, I wanted them all. I wouldn't let her be alone in that beautiful mind of hers.

She went to take a step back, but my arms quickly came around her, holding her to me. "Tell me what's on your mind."

She let out a slight scoff. "That's a lot to ask."

"Well, I'm asking."

She pulled her bottom lip in between her teeth, and all I wanted to do was suck it right back out.

Where the fuck was this sudden hunger for her coming from?

"He just gave me the creeps and kept pressing to buy the drink. That's all."

If she thought I'd believe that was all, then she must think of me as a fool. But I wouldn't press. Tonight, Sage was fragile, and I'd handle her with the delicacy she needed.

"If he comes near you again, you call me, okay?" It wasn't a question, more so a demand.

"Okay."

"Men like that deserve the worst of what's coming to them. Don't feel bad sticking up for yourself, and don't feel guilty calling me." Because I knew she would. Sage and I, we were alike in more ways than one. Like calls to like, and my entire being called to Sage like a lighthouse to a ship lost at sea.

I reached down, grabbing her hand in mine. "Come on."

Leading her down the hall and around the corner, I opened the door to my bedroom and led her in.

My king-sized bed sat in the middle, dark brown sheets folded over a cream comforter with more pillows than a typical bed for one held. Women weren't the only ones who liked pillows.

A floor to ceiling mirror sat against the wall across from the bed, gold rimming the edges with intricate detail at the top. To the left was the door to my bathroom, and behind the bed was a wall of windows that looked out over the land, but the curtains were drawn, blocking us in and the world out.

"You're very neat," she stated from where we stood just a few feet inside the door.

"Ranch work and lessons are messy by definition. I need some kind of cleanliness in my life." People always talk about the gruff, messy cowboys, but never about the ones that still took their immaculacy at home into account. We weren't all unhinged in that department.

Her hand slid from mine as she made her way over to the antique mirror. I'd found it at an auction and couldn't pass up the price, and with such an empty house, I figured it would add some character. By the looks of it, Sage approved.

"It's beautiful."

I slowly stepped behind her as she looked up at the top of it, admiring the weaving of gold around the frame. It was the most expensive thing in this house. I didn't indulge in pricey items often, but I was learning to treat myself every now and then. Life was short.

My hand reached up to her shoulder, gently trailing down her arm. My fingertips passed over the strap on her tank top, then slid down her bare skin. Like before, goosebumps rose in the wake of my finger, and I wondered how long it'd been since she'd been touched.

"Just like you."

She met my gaze in the mirror as I pressed a kiss to the crook between her neck and her shoulder.

"Tell me if this isn't something you want to do," I murmured against her skin.

"It is," she whispered, keeping her eyes on mine in the reflection.

Her arms slid up to fold around her stomach, like she wanted to hide.

That wouldn't do.

I reached around her, clasping her hands and bringing them to her sides. "Keep them here."

Releasing her, I watched as her chest rose with a big inhale while her fingers on her right hand rubbed together.

"Don't get in your head, baby," I told her as I slid my hands along her belly.

"I have a scar—"

"Sage."

Our eyes met again in the mirror. Our silent communication was clear. She didn't have to explain her body or worry that I wouldn't love it. She was still standing here fully clothed, and I was harder than I'd ever been my entire life.

My fingers wrapped around the hem of her top and she worried her bottom lip again. Keeping one hand on the fabric, I reached up with the other, using my thumb to free the pink flesh. "I'm not judging you, Sage. I'm going to visually *devour* you, so that when I physically do the same, it's that much sweeter."

Just because she had a baby years ago didn't make her body any less beautiful, any less breathtaking. She was the definition of perfection, and I hated that she didn't see that. If anything, I wanted to worship this body harder than I thought possible with that thought in mind.

She was astonishing.

Moving my hand from her mouth, I cupped her chin, making sure her gaze stayed locked on the mirror. I slowly inched her top up, only enough to give me easier access to her pants. I didn't want to scare her, but I wanted her to know that I wasn't shying away because she didn't think of herself as worthy of this. Of being admired openly.

My fingers undid the button on her jeans with ease, moving to the zipper to pull it down. Sliding her jeans down her legs, I bent to take her shoes and socks off. She stepped out of her jeans with my help, all while keeping her hands to her sides.

So obedient.

I rose, leaving her black lace panties on. Reaching back around her, I bunched the material up in the front so the center was a thin strip, revealing her pussy. "Did you wear these on purpose?" I asked her, my voice low and smooth.

"Maybe."

Pulling up, the fabric went taut against her clit as I whispered in her ear, "Only clear answers, Sage."

She swallowed, keeping her eyes on my hand in the mirror as her thighs inched apart ever so slightly. "Yes."

"Did you hope it would be me who saw you in them?"

She nodded and I tugged the fabric down, only to let go so it shot back to her center.

"Use your words like a good girl, baby."

Her legs were practically shaking. "Yes, I hoped you'd see me in them."

A smirk pulled at the side of my mouth as I ran a hand over the smooth skin of her thigh. My fingers lightly ran a path up the inside of her leg, the sensitive skin prickling under me. She was so hyper aware of everywhere I touched her and I fucking loved it. I could play with her for hours.

Gliding my hand up her center, dragging it over her clit through her underwear with slight pressure, I grabbed onto the hem of her tank top and began to lift it.

Her fingers twitched at her sides like she wanted to pull her shirt back down. "You deserve to be worshiped, baby," I murmured in her ear.

"What if you don't like what you see?" she asked, a slight tremor to her voice.

I immediately let go of the fabric, twisting her around to face me. Clasping her chin in my fingers, I stared into her eyes, my words hard as I said, "There's no fucking way I won't love what I see. Just because you think your body looks different than what people think the norm is does *not* mean you're not worthy. Do you hear me? You. Are. Worthy. You deserve the same sex as the rest, the same love, the same admiration, and I'm going to give it to you."

Her eyes shone. I didn't want her to cry, but she needed to hear it. I fucking hated whoever instilled in her mind that she wasn't beautiful.

"Now let me show you."

Turning her back around, I stood between her and the mirror as I gently pulled off her top, tossing it to the ground.

"You keep your eyes on that mirror the entire time, and don't focus on anything other than how good this feels."

"How good what—" But before she could finish her sentence, I dropped to my knees in front of her, practically ripping her panties as I yanked them down her legs.

I peppered kisses over her thighs, my movements now slow again, but once I got to the main course, I wouldn't be holding the same restraint. The slight stubble on my jawline scratched against her thighs, but instead of moving her legs away, she pressed them closer together.

"Rule number one," I started, using my hands to pry them back apart. "No hiding."

Sage let out a small whimper, and it was now my ultimate goal to make her louder. Make her scream. I wanted the neighbor a mile down the road to hear my name on her lips.

"Rule number two," I said as I lifted each of her feet to pull her underwear off the rest of the way. Once they were off, I looked up at her, but like the obedient girl she was, she had her gaze on the mirror. "No holding back."

"No holding back?" she questioned.

I dragged my eyes down her body from where I was kneeling in front of her, my gaze snagging on the way her breasts seemed to want to spill out of her lacy bra.

"Meaning, no keeping quiet when I do something like this." In a flash, my mouth was on her clit, sucking it into my mouth. There was no slow preparation this time, no working up to it. Her pussy was mine to conquer tonight, and I'd own it.

A moan slipped out of her, causing my dick to twitch against my jeans. Tonight wasn't about me, so I did my best to ignore the urge to stroke myself.

Sucking her clit, I let it go with a *pop*, then moved to drag my tongue up her center. "You taste so sweet," I mumbled.

I speared my tongue inside of her, not able to get enough of her. My new favorite meal was Sage, and I was fucking starving.

I fucked her with my tongue for a moment, then moved my mouth back to her clit. Flicking my tongue over the sensitive bud, I felt her belly jump with the sensation.

Removing my mouth from her, I ran my hands up her thighs, then used my thumb to rub circles over her clit.

"Rule number three," I began again. "We're honest with each other."

She let out a small, breathy laugh as the sensation of my thumb clouded her head. "You want to talk honesty right now?"

"I'm not talking about just outside of the bedroom. I mean right now. You want me to do something else to make you come, you tell me. The way I'm touching you isn't good enough? You tell me. I always want your words, and never false pleasure."

She audibly gulped, nodding.

"Now sit on the edge of the bed."

I dropped my hand from her and she took three slow steps backwards until the backs of her thighs hit the mattress. She lowered her ass to the comforter, her eyes moving to me. Standing, I stalked over to her.

"You want to watch, Sage?"

With her eyes aimed up at me, my dick twitched again, and an image of her lips wrapped around me flashed in my mind. It wouldn't be happening tonight, but soon. So long as she wanted to continue this.

Whatever *this* was.

"Yes," she said, her voice slightly higher and full of need.

Kneeling again, I opened her legs wider.

"Eyes on the mirror, baby."

Her gaze moved to the mirror right as I slid a finger inside of her, and her mouth parted on a moan as I crooked my finger right against her sensitive spot.

Lowering my head, I lapped at her clit, matching the pace of my finger as I kept it deep inside her, only moving the tip of it.

Adding a second finger, I reveled in the way her opening stretched around me. She'd feel fucking phenomenal around my dick.

She braced her hands behind her, not once straying her gaze from the mirror. I sucked, licked, and fucked her all at the same time, feeling her pussy slowly start to clench around my hand.

"Just like that, baby. Feel my fingers so fucking deep inside you. How wet you are on my hand. How all I can taste right now is you."

She whimpered, her elbows bending a bit as she fought the urge to lie back.

"You want to lie down, do it. Do whatever you need to get there."

Her head tossed back as her back hit the comforter and I fingered her deeper, pulling her clit back into my mouth to flick my tongue against the bud.

She arched her spine, her fists clenching in the sheets, and then she exploded.

A scream filled the air as her hands quickly moved to my hair, gripping it so hard that I had no choice but to keep my mouth firmly against her. Not that I'd want it to be anywhere else. Pleasuring Sage was my new favorite hobby. Just seeing her unravel like this made me feral.

Her whole body quaked with her orgasm, her pussy clenched so tight around my fingers that I was sure the blood had stopped circulating to them. But fuck, she could keep them. I was weak for her.

As she came back down, I gently slid my fingers out of her, then wiped my tongue over her center one last time, like I was so hungry that I had to lick her clean. Her body twitched slightly as I passed over her clit, the bud even more sensitive than before.

Gliding my mouth up a few inches, my lips ghosted over her scar, pressing a gentle kiss to the skin. I peered up at her. "Don't ever feel ashamed of the body that brought life into this world. Every inch of your skin is flawless."

She stared at me for a moment, blinking as she let my words weave through the dark crevices of her mind. Standing up, I laid on the bed beside her, pulling her to me so that her head lay on my chest.

We lay there in silence for a while, my hand idly running over her hair. For a second, I thought she may have fallen asleep, until she spoke up. "I haven't done that in a long time."

"Been fingered?" I asked, staring up at the ceiling. Her body was a welcome weight on me, and I never wanted to move again.

"No," she said, adjusting her leg over mine. "Orgasmed."

My hand froze on her hair. "How long?"

I felt her cheek move against my chest as she must've been chewing on it, deciding how to answer. "Since before I had Avery."

Crinkling my brow, I lifted up on my elbows slightly, the changed position causing her to have to sit up with me. "I don't understand. How?"

She inhaled deeply, like she was preparing herself to voice it. "Well, I was too pregnant for… When I was that big, I guess he didn't want to…" She stuttered over the words before taking another steadying breath, then continued. "He didn't want to unless he got something out of it, and I was too pregnant for sex to be enjoyable, so after about five months, we stopped. And then I had a C-section, and he didn't…" She looked down at my shirt as her words trailed off.

"Hey," I muttered, crooking a finger under her chin to bring her eyes back to mine. I loved when she looked at me. "I'm sure you already know this, but he's an asshole, okay? Real men don't treat women like that, and I promise, as long as you'll let me, I'll make sure you know every day how important you are."

Her expression changed from sad to piqued interest. "As long as I'll let you?"

"I like you, Sage. I don't know if that's clear after what we just did, but I want more. Not just of that, though I'd gladly take that every day," I admitted with a smile, "but I want more of you. As much as you're willing to give, I'll take it all."

"Are you saying you want to date? Officially?" she asked.

I nodded. "Do you?"

She blinked a few times and I dropped my finger from below her chin. "I mean, yes. But—"

"Baby, don't think of the buts." I lay back, pulling her on top of me so that she was straddling my hips. I brought my hands up to her cheeks, brushing her hair behind her ears. "We've got a million years to think of the reasons we shouldn't, but what if instead, we spent those thinking of the reasons we should?"

A smile reached her lips, and all I wanted to do was kiss her again and again and again.

"I think that sounds like a good plan," she said, inching her face closer to mine.

"A million years, then, yeah?"

Her smile widened, and right before she pressed her lips to mine, she murmured, "A million years."

25

CALLAN

All I could smell and feel was Sage wrapped around me in the early morning light that peeked through the crack in the curtain. I'd stripped down to my boxers after we talked for a bit, crawling under the covers with her. She'd worn my shirt to bed, but from the waist down, she was bare. We cuddled all night, and even now, her leg was in between mine, pulling my thigh closer to her as the rest of her was draped over my chest. Her breathing was still deep with sleep, so I took the time while I waited for her to wake up to recite last night's memory in my head.

Her moans were my new favorite sound, along with her laugh. Her smile, how fucking bright it was, was the only image I wanted to see from this point forward. I was falling too damn quickly for Sage, but I guess life didn't have a timeline, so why would I pump the brakes?

I could waste precious time by holding back with her, but where would that get us other than delaying right where we both wanted to be?

An inkling of doubt crept in, reminding me of how I'd had the same thoughts before, and it left me heartbroken and alone for years. Trust wasn't easy to hand out, but something about Sage made me want to open my walls again, tear down the fortress that I'd built in my mind to protect myself, and let her in.

She was already in.

I didn't consciously realize it, but every lesson she came to with Avery, every interaction we shared from the moment we met at the coffee shop, it all piled together and I was tumbling down in an avalanche of feelings that I couldn't hide any longer.

I liked her.

And she liked me, too.

Sage shifted, letting out a small sigh as she buried her head deeper against my bare chest. Her hand moved, dragging across my stomach to awaken the butterflies that hid inside.

"Good morning," I said, stroking a hand down her hair.

"Good morning," she mumbled, her voice laden with sleep.

"Sleep well?" I asked.

She lifted her head, and I instantly missed the weight of her on my chest.

"I slept better than I have in a long time," she admitted, blinking the haze out of her vision as she looked at me.

Brushing a lock of hair behind her ear, I admired her like this. Just woken up and beautiful. Raw, untouched, and wholly herself.

"I'm glad. Coffee?"

"Yes, please." I wished I had everything she needed to make her special coffees she liked at Triple B, but black would have to do today.

With her off of me, I sat up, swinging a leg over the edge of the bed.

"Did you sleep well?" she asked as she sat with the blanket still up to her hips.

"Amazing," I replied, not bothering to put on pants or a shirt. I wanted some time with her in bed before we had to go pick up Avery. "I'll be right back. Stay here."

Heading to the kitchen, I brewed two cups of coffee. I grabbed two bagels from the pantry and put them in the toaster to warm up while I whipped up a couple eggs and a few slices of bacon. With the coffees at the perfect drinking temperature now that they'd had a moment to cool down, I assembled the breakfast sandwiches and headed back to the room, balancing the two mugs and a plate with both bagels.

She'd opened the curtains while I was gone and was staring out the window at the open field, the morning sun shining a pinkish haze over the yellow grass. She was still wearing my shirt, which fell to about mid thigh. If I had to guess, she wasn't wearing her underwear still either.

"I wish I had a view like this at my place. Avery would love it," she said.

I set the mugs and plate on the dresser, then came up behind her. Wrapping my arms around her waist, I rested my chin on her shoulder and gazed out the window. I wasn't really seeing anything, though, because Sage didn't just cloud my thoughts. She was my only vision.

"Are you hungry?" After last night, she had to be.

"Starving." She turned her head to look at me and I took the opportunity to press a light kiss to her mouth.

She returned it, kissing me slow and soft. When she pulled back, she made an emphasis on sniffing the air. "Did you make food?" She turned, eyes landing on the bagels. "Oh my God."

"What?" Did she hate bagels? Maybe she ate them too much at the cafe.

"You made me breakfast."

Was that too far? I mean, I had her for dinner last night, so I assumed breakfast was the least I could do. "Is there something wrong?"

Her eyes found mine again. "It's just— It feels nice to have food made for me."

It dawned on me then, with her being a mom and working at Bell Buckle Brews, how food would become a chore to her. Someone had to take care of Sage, and if it wasn't her, it'd be me. I'd gladly take on the task.

I folded my hand in hers and led her to the bed. "Sit. I'll bring it to you."

She did, getting under the covers and leaning her back against the headboard. I smiled at how cute she looked in that moment, like being served in bed was the biggest turn on for her.

Grabbing the plate and her coffee, I walked back over to her and handed her the mug as I set the plate on her lap. I grabbed my bagel off the top, then rounded the bed, grabbing my mug on the way, to sit beside her.

I'd never felt the importance of breakfast in bed, but this felt so damn nice.

Sitting beside Sage on a weekday morning with our first meal of the day felt more intimate than what we did last night.

We were quiet while we ate and sipped our coffee. The morning rays of light streaked across the room, and when I glanced at Sage after I'd finished my bagel, I noticed a rainbow reflected on her cheekbone.

Unable to help myself, I reached over to brush my thumb along the array of colors. She looked at me, leaning slightly into my touch.

She was the beauty after the storm I'd been through the past few years. My sign of hope.

Leaning forward, I captured her mouth with mine, kissing her deeply and with meaning. I hope she felt the capacity of my feelings flowing through my lips, because I sure felt hers.

She shifted, and then a thump sounded on the ground. Pulling apart, she looked over the edge of the bed to find the plate on the floor.

"Oops," she said with a smile.

I returned it, then stood to grab the plate off the ground.

"We should go get Avery," I said, grabbing her now empty mug off the nightstand. "It's almost seven, and I think she has school today, right?"

Sage looked at the clock, then shot out of bed. "Shit."

She grabbed her pants, yanking them on while I picked her shirt up off the ground. She tore my shirt off of her, and I swear my entire being froze at the sight. My brain, my heart, most of all my dick.

She reached for the shirt in my hands and I released it, though part of me wished she had stayed in my clothing. Another part of me wished she'd keep the shirt off altogether.

Pulling it over her head, she moved to her shoes and socks while I worked on getting myself dressed. In less than a minute, we were heading for the door. I grabbed my cowboy hat and keys, locked the door behind us, then followed Sage to my truck. Opening the passenger door for her, I waited until she was all the way in before shutting it and coming around the front.

Double checking that she was buckled, I started the truck and headed for my parents' house.

Within a few minutes, we were pulling up to the ranch. As I approached the house, I could see Avery on the swing out front with my mom. With the sight of her daughter, a smile lit up

Sage's face, and if I wasn't driving, I would've photographed it. A mother should see those raw moments with her kid.

"She looks...happy," Sage stated.

"She does," I replied, shifting the truck into park. "Is that surprising?"

She unbuckled. "It's her first sleepover like this, so I wasn't sure how she'd be."

"Like this?" I questioned.

Sage reached for the door, setting her hand on it. "She usually only has sleepovers with kids her age."

She didn't see her grandparents?

Now wasn't the time to ask, but before I could even think of forming the question, Sage was out of the truck and meeting Avery halfway. Avery wrapped her arms around her mom as Sage peppered kisses to the top of her head.

I could watch them all day.

Getting out, I approached the two of them. "How was your night, Aves?" I asked.

Avery let go of her mom, the biggest grin on her face. "It was so much fun. And Mama, look!" Avery fished around in the pocket of her jeans, then pulled out something white and tiny in a clear plastic bag. "I lost a tooth!"

Sage kneeled to get a better look at it. "Wow, that's very cool. Was it wiggly?"

Avery nodded. "All night. I kept playing with it, and then it just fell out. It didn't hurt at all."

I wondered if Sage felt bad for missing a moment like that, but from the looks of it, she was more happy for her than anything. Regardless, she shouldn't feel guilty for it. She needed a night out to herself, and this was good for her.

"Did Pudding come home last night?" Avery asked, looking up at her mother with hope shining bright in her eyes.

Guilt visibly slammed into Sage like a train, so I stepped in, ruffling Avery's hair. "She will soon. Don't worry."

Avery nodded, quickly moving onto explaining the other activities she did with my mother last night.

Leaving the two of them to talk about the tooth, I headed up the porch steps to my mom. "Good morning."

"Have a good night?" she asked, a mischievous hint to her tone.

"It was fine, Mom," I replied. "Where's her booster seat?"

"Right inside the door," she said, moving to grab it.

"I'll get it," I told her, motioning for her to sit back down on the swing.

Opening the front door, I found the seat propped right next to it. I grabbed it, coming back out.

"She's a sweet girl," my mom said, pausing me in my tracks.

"She is," I agreed, watching them talk in the driveway.

"I was talking about Avery."

"So was I."

She made a humming noise and I rolled my eyes, continuing down the porch steps to the truck.

I looked up a quick video on my phone on how to install the booster and got to work. After I finished securing the seat, I walked back over to Sage and Avery. Avery was still talking her ear off, going on about the painting she made last night.

"Ready when you two are," I said.

"Ready!" Avery exclaimed, then skipped over to the truck. I helped her in, then watched as she buckled herself to be sure she was set. Closing her door, I waved goodbye to my mom before hopping in the driver's seat. Sage was already buckled in on the passenger side with a small smile on her lips.

"What?" I asked as I started the truck.

"Nothing," she said with a shake of her head.

I shifted into reverse, putting a hand on the back of Sage's headrest to look behind me. These newer trucks had reverse cameras, but I liked it better this way. After making it down the drive, I looked both ways, then continued onto the road. I shot Avery a wink, and she returned it with a smile and a small kick of her feet.

Facing forward, I put the truck in drive and headed down the main road, but I didn't miss the way Sage watched me.

"Okay, really, what?"

"You're really cute, Callan," she said.

I glanced over at her to find a slight blush staining her cheeks. Reaching over, I set a hand on her thigh, keeping my other gripped firmly on the wheel. "Right back at you."

We drove like that the rest of the way, with Avery in the back humming to the country song on the radio and my hand on Sage's leg.

And after years of feeling like my mind was stuck in an isolated black hole, life was good.

26

SAGE

After Callan dropped me and Avery at home, I drove Avery to school just in time for the first bell to ring. Since it was my day off, I didn't have to rush to work afterwards, so I went home and deep cleaned the entire house.

It took all I had in me not to go back to the ranch to see Callan while Avery was at school, but she had a lesson today, so I'd see him then anyway. I feared I was getting too attached to the idea of us too soon, like this was too good to be true. But nothing about Callan gave me the impression that he'd be anything like Jason, so I had to stop comparing.

As I sat in the school pickup line with my car idling, all I could think about were those two texts. I hadn't received any more since, but that made me even more nervous than if he'd kept trying. If he wasn't texting, that meant he was finding another way.

Though the car wasn't moving, my hands were still gripped tight to the wheel, like my hold on the leather could keep everything from falling apart.

The back door popped open and I jumped, the fog in my head clearing with Avery's voice. "Hi, Mama."

"How was school?" I asked, turning around in my seat to make sure she buckled herself in.

"Good. Lucy and I wanna have a playdate," she said as she situated her backpack on the middle seat, then worked on her seatbelt.

"Today?"

Her little fingers clicked the buckle in. "She had to go to the dentist, but probably soon."

Turning back around, I shifted into drive and pulled out of the pickup line, going around the other cars. "Just let me know what day and we'll figure something out."

"Okay. Are we going to the horses?"

Flicking on my blinker, I headed onto the main road. "Yep. Why don't you put your boots on while we're on the way?"

She was silent for a moment, then said, "Did you bring them?"

"They're not in here? I thought we left them in here from the last lesson."

I glanced at her in the rearview mirror as she shook her head. "No. I put them inside, remember?"

I didn't. "It's okay. We'll stop by the house on the way, then."

It wasn't too far out of the way, but we'd be late to the lesson regardless.

A few minutes later, I pulled up our driveway and got out at the same time as Avery. I was getting the key ready when she let out a little shriek. I followed her line of sight to the front porch, where Pudding was sitting like she'd been waiting this whole time.

"Pudding!" Avery squealed, running up the steps. The cat unfolded her tail, standing with the anticipation of being pet. She scooped her up, hugging her tight. "Mama, do you see her?"

"I do. She looks so happy." Really, the cat's face was squished against Avery's cheek and she squirmed slightly. "Let's get her inside before she takes off again."

I unlocked the door, letting Avery in first, and made sure to shut it fully before Avery set her down. Pudding instantly rolled to her back with her tail swishing.

"I didn't think she would come back!" Avery exclaimed, bending to pet her belly.

I could hear the cat's purring from here. "Do you still want to go to your lesson?" She looked too excited to leave the cat so soon.

"Yeah, I wanna go! Pudding will be here when we get back, won't you?" She looked down at the cat for an answer, giving her a rub on her cheek.

"Alright, then. Get your boots or we're going to be late." Even though we already were with our little detour.

Avery bent to kiss Pudding on the top of her head, then jumped up and ran to her bedroom. Seconds later, she reappeared, pink boots in hand.

"Anything else you need to grab?" I asked.

She shook her head. "All good."

I ushered her out the door, making sure that Pudding stayed put. Locking the door, we hurried back to the car, and I waited to pull out until Avery was buckled in.

She swapped her shoes for the boots on our way there, humming along to the song on the radio. The sky was slightly overcast, but as far as I was aware, the forecast hadn't called for rain. If it did, I just hoped it held off until Avery's lesson was over.

As we pulled up, Callan was coming out of the barn with a black box in his hands. He wore a casual smile under his dirt-stained cowboy hat, and in that moment, I wanted to forget about everything else and soak him in. He looked like the sunshine peeking through the clouds that had hovered over me for far too long.

"Sage, Avery," he greeted as we got out.

"Guess what!" Avery squealed as she approached him.

"What?" he questioned with a small chuckle at her excitement.

"Pudding came home today!"

He seemed a bit shocked at first, but quickly wiped it away with a bigger grin. "I told you our little trick would work. Which flavor food drew her in?"

Avery scrunched her face. "Salmon."

"Ah. Typical fish to lure in a cat."

Avery's eyes fell to the box, like she hadn't seen it at first. "What's that?"

"It's for you." He knelt down so she had a better angle to open the lid on the box.

"For me?"

"Yep. It's a gift."

Avery swiveled her head to look at me. "Can I open it?"

"Of course."

She turned back around and gently slid off the lid, then peeled away a piece of plastic wrapping. I peered over her shoulder, seeing something pink in the middle.

Avery reached in and pulled out a helmet, all pink with black straps. I didn't have to look to know she had the biggest smile on her face.

"A pink helmet!" she exclaimed with a little jump.

"Now you don't have to borrow any of the ones here," Callan said, setting the lid back on the box.

"It's all mine?" she asked.

Callan nodded. "All yours, Aves."

I was already smiling, but it grew with the use of the nickname. Something about it felt more personal. I called her that all the time, along with a few other people, but Callan saying it felt different. It felt like another step into whatever this was between us.

"Can you help me move the strap thingies?" she asked.

He nodded. "Put it on."

She did, then he reached up under her chin and adjusted the straps so it fit her nice and snug. "How's that?"

She tossed her head back and forth to be sure. "It's perfect," she replied, and then threw herself at him, wrapping her arms around his neck with such force that he almost fell back on his ass.

He looked at me, a few pieces of her hair clinging to the stubble on his jaw. He was...beaming.

"Thank you," she murmured into his shoulder.

"You deserved to have one of your own," he said.

She let him go and stepped back as he rose. "Can we ride now?"

He nodded, and fuck, I could truly watch the two of them interact all damn day.

"We can ride."

***

Rain didn't come for the entirety of Avery's lesson, the looming storm having mercy on us before it decided to strike. I'd watched the entire time, only taking my eyes off of Avery to check the driveway behind me. Though no cars drove up it, my mind was playing tricks on me, making me imagine the sound of tires on gravel when there was none.

He hasn't found me. We're okay.

And even if he had somehow managed to figure out where Avery and I were, I had to believe that Callan wouldn't let anything happen to us. I needed to tell him what was going on, but I was scared that it would make him run the other way.

The last thing I wanted to do was put all my baggage on his shoulders when we'd just started getting to know each other.

"Want to go for a ride?" Callan asked, pulling me out of my thoughts.

I turned to him. "What?"

"Just out in the field. Not far or anything," he explained.

"I can't ride," I said. I'd never been on a horse before.

He and Avery must have decided on this plan before she untacked, because behind Callan, she came walking out of the barn with Red strolling behind her.

"I've got the perfect horse for you." He took a step to the side as Avery came up beside him and gestured to Red.

My eyes widened slightly. "Him?"

Callan shrugged. "Avery is pretty confident that you'll be a pro right off the bat."

I eyed Avery. "Is that so?"

She nodded with way too much enthusiasm, the thought of throwing her mother on a horse way too appealing. "You're good at everything you do, Mama."

Emotion hit me like a tidal wave. It was such a light comment, but it held so much weight.

Not at keeping her hidden.

The thought came out of nowhere, and I wanted to shove it away, but that little voice was telling the truth.

I couldn't even keep her away from him, and now that she was older, she'd know what was happening if he came near her. She asked about her dad sometimes, but she knew he wasn't a good person. I just didn't want her to know how cruel he could really be.

"Mama?"

I blinked, coming back to the present. "I can try."

Sometimes, like right now, I had to remind my fear that I was the one who held the reins. It wouldn't get a hold of me today.

She smiled, offering the leather reins to me. My eyes moved to Callan, who was staring at me with...concern. He had to have seen my emotions displayed on my face. But he didn't know what they were about.

I had to tell him soon. Otherwise, he'd find out some other way, and I wanted him to hear it from me.

Stepping forward, I grabbed them from Avery, then came around the side of the horse.

"Why don't you go get your horse tacked up while I help your mom?" Callan said to Avery, and she took off back into the barn with a nod.

Callan came up behind me and I inhaled, measuring the height of the horse compared to my size. I could barely see over the saddle.

"Want to tell me what that was about?" Callan asked as my gaze moved to the stirrup.

I could lie and tell him everything was fine, but the idea felt sour on my tongue.

"There are some things that I need to tell you about, but now probably isn't the time."

He set a hand on my waist, then reached around me with the other to position the stirrup at an easier angle for me to slip my foot in. "Later, then."

I lifted my leg, the height slightly awkward, but slipped the toe of my shoe in, then hoisted myself up. With Callan's hands both on my waist now, he helped balance me as I swung my leg over and situated my opposite foot in the other stirrup.

He repositioned the stirrups to better suit me, then set a hand on my thigh as he looked up at me. "But we will be talking about it."

I nodded. "I promise. I just— I don't want to in front of Avery."

His eyes softened, understanding written on his face. Before the shift of his features, I hadn't realized just how worried he was. It was all over him, his concern out in the open for me like the pages of a flipped open book.

I wasn't very good at hiding things, but I was learning it was especially difficult to keep things from him.

I didn't even have to say anything for him to know something was wrong.

All of a sudden, it hit me that it was a trait I wished everyone held—the ability to tell if something was wrong just by looking at someone. So many people were blind to others suffering, but Callan spotted it like a shooting star in a midnight sky.

Maybe Callan could be my shooting star, making my wishes of safety come true.

27

CALLAN

After teaching Sage some of the basics of riding, we rode through the empty pasture. The cows were in a different field this time of year, and in a few months, we'd move them over here.

Avery was on one of the ponies I used in lessons, and though it was her first time on a horse other than Red, her confidence was still glowing. She wasn't nervous like some people were when they got on a new horse. She just got on and did the damn thing.

Avery pulled Butterscotch to a stop and twisted to look at me and Sage behind her. "Can I pick flowers?"

I lifted a finger to my chest. "For me?"

Avery scrunched her nose. "Boys don't like flowers."

"I do," I said. "A certain flower in particular."

Out of the corner of my eye, Sage looked down at her leg with a slight pink tinge on her cheeks.

"I'll find some pretty ones!" Avery said, hopping off the horse.

Sage was riding beside me, her legs and arms stiff with Red's every step. Despite the tightness of her body, she seemed to be enjoying herself. With time, she'd feel more natural in the saddle. I'd take her out as often as she wanted.

I reached over to set a reassuring hand on her thigh, then pulled it away so I didn't piss Ace off with being too close to Red. He liked his space.

She looked over to me. "You can relax," I said.

"What if I fall?"

A small chuckle escaped me. "I won't let you fall, baby."

Her eyes clung to my mouth like the endearment was unexpected. "I don't think you'd have time to catch me."

"Oh, really? Are you doubting my speed to get off this horse?"

A smile teased at the corners of her mouth. "Maybe."

"I can prove it to you. I'll even show you just how fast I can get you off *your* horse."

She adjusted her hands on the reins, glancing at the horn of the saddle. "I'd really like to stay—" But before she could finish her sentence, I had pulled my reins, stopping Ace in his tracks, jumped to the ground, and was reaching for her.

"*On*," she said through a laugh as I grabbed her by the waist and lifted her off. "Callan!"

I hoisted her up and over, slinging her over my shoulder as she laughed. "What's up?"

"Tickle her!" Avery shouted from up ahead.

I shot her a wink and moved my hands to Sage's sides. In an attempt to get down, she moved her hands to my shoulders to push away. As soon as I felt the pressure against me, she hissed in a breath as she winced, like she was in pain. Immediately setting her feet to the ground, I looked over her body.

"What happened? Did I hurt you?" I asked hurriedly, worried I'd injured her.

She held her wrist in her opposite hand, her brows pulled together. "No. No, you didn't hurt me." Her voice was slightly strained with each word.

I grabbed her hand from her, flipping it over. My eyes landed on a long, thin scar that stretched a few inches in diameter. She pulled her hand back, dropping her arm to her side.

I couldn't take my eyes away from her dainty wrist. The only sound I could hear was the blood rushing through my veins. "What happened?"

"I broke it a long time ago," she said, her voice small.

"You did, or someone else?"

Her eyes bored up at me, but all I saw was that scar. How had I missed it before now?

"Don't try to tell me someone didn't do that to you," I warned.

"I slipped—"

"You don't slip and get a scar like that, Sage." She very well could have slipped and broken her wrist, but I got the feeling that was far from the truth. She'd begun to recite her response on impulse, like she'd trained herself to answer with that when people asked. I knew when people were being genuine, and right now, Sage was covering something up.

I slowly raised my gaze to hers, and the fear I saw in her eyes was a sight I never wanted to see again. I could have gone my entire life without seeing that look.

I gently grabbed her hand again, but instead of examining the scar, I cradled it in both of mine, like it could break any moment. "Who did this to you?"

"My ex."

My jaw locked, my teeth threatening to break with the pressure.

"How?"

"He grabbed it," she whispered, a strain in her voice. The term was putting what he did to her lightly.

I pulled one of my hands back, clenching it into a fist. The muscles were pulled taut with how hard my grip was. We had to talk about these things, and while it wasn't the most ideal time, we couldn't avoid hard topics. I wanted to know everything about her, the good and the bad.

"I got flowers!" Avery announced.

Sage's head whipped in her direction and she inhaled deeply, pasting a smile on her face. "What kind?"

"Purple and yellow," she replied.

"Good job, honey. Why don't you make me a bouquet?"

"Do you want more purple or yellow?"

"Purple, please," Sage said.

"Okay!" Avery turned back around, the pony's reins in her hand as she walked over to a patch of purple wildflowers.

"Sage," I murmured, shifting her attention back to me now that Avery was occupied.

Her eyes shot up to me. "Yes?"

"Do you want to talk about it back at the barn?" I didn't want to put her on the spot, but something as extreme as her ex breaking her wrist was not going to be brushed under the rug.

Her eyes shone up at me, unshed tears brimming in them. "Please."

"Okay." I leaned forward and brushed a kiss to her forehead, running my thumb across the back of her hand. "Later."

Standing in the middle of the field with our horses waiting quietly and Avery a dozen feet away probably wasn't the best time to discuss it. I wasn't sure how much Avery knew, but if I knew anything about Sage, she'd want to protect her at all costs. Mentally and physically.

The tip of my nose brushed hers. "Why don't we head back?"

Sage nodded right as a rain drop fell on her forehead. "Yeah."

Reaching up, my thumb wiped the drop away.

"Rain!" Avery yelled out along with a high pitched giggle.

Taking my hat off, I leaned forward, lightly pressing my forehead to hers. "You're okay," I murmured.

She closed her eyes, giving a small nod. The rain started coming down faster, droplets sticking to her hair.

After a moment, I straightened, setting my hat on her head. "Come on, Aves," I called out.

"Coming!" Avery replied. She hurried back over to us, the bundle of flowers gripped tight in her tiny hand.

"Need some help?" I asked, turning to Avery as she came around the side of her pony.

"No, thank you." She hiked her foot up and tried a few times, but eventually got the momentum she needed to hoist herself up.

Once we were all back on our horses, we headed for the barn. We hadn't made it too far out in the field, but we still got drenched in the sudden downpour.

Instead of dismounting outside the barn, we stayed on until we were in the aisle and out of the rain, then got off. I grabbed Butterscotch's reins from Avery and nodded toward my parents' house.

"Why don't you go see Charlotte and give her your flowers?" I asked her.

"Do you think she'll like them?" Avery questioned.

I nodded. "She loves flowers. Especially purple and yellow."

Avery grinned. "She's gonna love mine, then."

She skipped off through the rain and I watched her until she made it to the house and slipped inside the front door. Turning, I found Sage staring at the reins in her hand where she was picking at the leather.

"Here, let me take care of Red for you." I gently took the reins from her, leading all three horses over to the cross ties. One by one, I hooked them in, then turned to Sage again. She was still standing in the aisle, staring down at her hands.

"Sage."

She slowly brought her gaze to mine, my hat shifting on her head, its size too big.

Instead of asking her to come to me, I crossed the distance to her and pulled her into my arms. She leaned against me, my hat teetering on the edge of sliding off her head.

"You can talk to me," I reminded her. I thought back to the bar when she'd had a panic attack over that guy. He couldn't have been her ex, but for her to react like that meant the asshole did some lasting damage on her, and that fucking wrecked me. In an instant, I wanted to find him and kill him. Murder had never been as appealing as it seemed right now.

She sniffled, shifting in my arms, then looked up at me. "I had surgery to put pins in my wrist because the bones were so badly broken," she said quietly.

I could feel my heart threatening to beat out of my chest.

"That's where the scar is from?"

She nodded. "He mutilated it. It still hurts if I use it wrong, but I try to ignore it. I was already barely eating at the time because I was so depressed, so I was weak. I was so *weak*." Her voice broke slightly on that last word, and my hands instantly moved to cup her cheeks.

"Hey, look at me. You are *not* weak."

She sniffled again, and I could tell she was trying to hold back tears. "But I was."

I shook my head. "But you're not anymore. You're strong, Sage. Raising Avery on your own, working at the cafe, balancing all of that on top of everything life has thrown at you. Not many people can do that, and look at you. I bet even fucking angels are jealous of you."

She let out a sad laugh, and while her laugh was one of my new favorite sounds, hearing it like this destroyed me.

I wiped an escaped tear off her cheek, moving my hands to her neck. "You can cry, baby, but cry because you're free. Never because of him."

She pressed her lips together and nodded.

"Is there a possibility he may come around?"

One of her hands came up to play with her necklace. "He was in prison."

"*Was?*"

"He was sentenced for four years, but I think he got out early."

Everything in me froze. "Why do you *think* he got out early?"

She inhaled a shaky breath, her hand tightening into a fist on my shirt. "I've been getting these texts and some phone calls, but I block the numbers. He just keeps getting new ones."

"Why was he in prison, Sage?" I asked, enunciating each word carefully.

"Domestic abuse," she stated, her voice barely audible.

A muscle in my jaw pulsed. "Were the charges from you or another woman?"

"Me," she admitted quietly.

Fuck.

"Does he know where you are?"

"I don't know. Maybe? I don't think he could have figured it out, but there's a chance."

"What do you mean?"

She let go of her necklace to run a finger under her eye. "The guy from the bar. He was in the cafe before and wanted to know my last name."

I nodded, remembering her telling me that. "You think your ex had something to do with that?"

"It's possible. I don't want to jump to any conclusions, but he could be Jason's friend or someone he hired to find me."

One of the horses whinied behind us, but I barely heard it over the blood rushing through my ears. I was tempted to tell her I'd be glued to her side for the foreseeable future until we knew for sure what was going on with her ex, but I didn't want to suffocate her, and I definitely didn't want Avery to wonder what was going on.

"Does Avery know?"

She shook her head. "No. And please don't tell her. She doesn't really know anything other than he's not nice. She's just... She's too young, Cal." Her voice broke again.

I pulled her against my chest, letting my hat slip off her head and fall to the ground. My fingers stroked through her hair, the pieces frizzy from the rain. "I know, baby. We'll keep her safe."

I fucking meant it. These two girls were quickly becoming everything to me, and I wouldn't let anything happen to them, regardless of what it took.

28

SAGE

The last seven days went by slow, each day dragging on. I hadn't spoken to Callan more than a couple times since our conversation in the barn because we were both swamped with work.

I'd taken on a few extra morning shifts at Bell Buckle Brews, working until Avery got out of school. She had a science project that was due in a few days, so we spent every day after we got home working on the assignment. Callan was booked with lessons anyway, so even if we had time to go see him, he was busy, too.

It'd been a few hours since I opened the cafe, the customers few and far between this morning, so when the cowbell above the door dinged, I perked up immediately. Much to my surprise,

Erica came strolling in wearing her black pencil skirt and vibrant purple blazer.

"Good morning," I greeted, straightening my posture. The last thing I wanted to look in her eyes was bored. I didn't forget that she was under the assumption that my efforts at work were lacking recently.

She surveyed the tables before looking at the counter I'd scrubbed endlessly all morning. Without many customers coming in, all I could do to fill my time was clean, organize, and bake.

"Morning. Not a lot of foot traffic today?" she asked.

I shrugged. "It's been steady."

She came around the counter, eyeing the pastries in the bakery case, presumably trying to see if they were fresh or days old. "The place looks good," she said before disappearing into the back.

I stayed up front, assuming she wouldn't want me to leave the register, before she called, "Sage, a moment, please."

Wiping my hands on my apron, I reached for the bell below the counter, setting it in the center of the counter in case anyone came in while I was in the back. I took a steadying breath before heading through the swinging door. Erica was by the oven, peeking inside at the pastries I had going.

"Is there something wrong?" I asked, doing my best to keep the slight waver out of my voice.

"Nope," she replied, closing the oven door and then moving on to look in the mini fridge below the counter.

She looked in every drawer, wiped a finger along every surface, likely checking to make sure everything was in order. That was what every good manager did. I didn't need to worry.

And yet...

"If it was something Gemma said—"

"Gemma?" Erica interrupted, rubbing her two fingers together after having checked for dust atop the spare coffee machine on the counter.

"You said you were going to check in."

She turned on the faucet for a brief moment, running her fingers under the water, then grabbed a paper towel to wipe her hands dry. "Right. Well, everything looks in order here."

My hand reached for my necklace on impulse, but I forced it back down. "Was it her?"

She tossed the paper towel in the trash bin, then faced me. "I'm not sure what you're talking about."

My brows pulled together. Surely she had to remember. "You said someone made a complaint about my work performance."

The slightest bit of recognition shone when her chin tilted slightly higher in the air. "Ah, that." She was quiet a moment, crossing her arms as she leaned a shoulder against the cabinet beside her. "I can assure you it wasn't Gemma who made the complaint, as to keep the peace here in the cafe."

My forehead creased further as her words didn't make anything any clearer. "I'm confused. Who filed the complaint, then?"

Her finger tapped her arm a few times as she contemplated telling me. "All I can say is that it was a male who spoke to me on the phone."

My eyes widened slightly before the worst case scenario started flying through my mind. Was it the guy from the bar, the same man who came in asking my last name? Was that why he'd come in, so his complaint was more viable if he had my full name?

Or could it be Jason?

With that thought alone, the blood drained from my entire body.

"A Food Safety Inspection guy is supposed to come in next week, if you and the girls can keep up the cleanliness around here," Erica said, though her voice barely penetrated my thoughts.

I forced a nod.

"Right, well, I need to get going. I have a long week of meetings in Boise, but if you have any questions, don't hesitate to call."

I nodded again, and I barely noticed when she walked by to leave.

If Jason was trying to sabotage my job, he knew where I worked.

And if he found my place of work, he could find where I lived.

Where Avery and I lived.

SCRAPE THE BARREL

I blinked a few times before crossing to the sink to fill a paper cup with water, taking a long gulp. Once it was empty, I filled it again, chugging the water like it could somehow clear my head.

None of it was confirmed.

I had no idea who had made the complaint to Erica, and for all I knew, it was an angry customer that got one sugar instead of two.

I dug around in the top drawer for the bottle of Advil we kept back here, taking two pills to keep the impending headache at bay. I tossed the cup in the trash, giving myself a minute to breathe in through my nose and out through my mouth, just like Callan told me to.

I attempted to distract myself with questions, but it didn't work as well as when he did it.

Grabbing my phone from my locker, I shot Callan a text.

> **Me**: What's your current view?

In less than a minute, he was typing back.

> **Callan**: Ace attempting to bite a soccer ball. What's yours?

> **Me**: Unfortunately not the same

> **Callan**: Is everything okay?

> **Me**: Other than my boss stressing me out?

The three dots appeared and disappeared three times before he replied.

> **Callan**: I'll come by once I'm done with my lessons. Call me if you need me, okay?

> **Me**: Okay. Thank you

> **Callan**: Always, baby. I'll see you soon

I shouldn't want to rely on him in this moment, but I wished his arms were around me and his voice was speaking soothing words in my ear. It'd been so long since I had someone I felt like I could turn to in a time like this, and now Callan was the only one I wanted to take my mind off of everything.

I needed him, but I wouldn't put that burden on his shoulders. I could get through this until he was able to come by.

I was strong.

***

My shift was ticking by at a snail's pace, every minute feeling like an eternity. Tomorrow was my day off, so naturally the entire day was dragging on.

I lost count of how many times I'd scrubbed the counter, but I was wiping at the same spot I'd just been working on twenty minutes ago. I was even more eager to see Callan than I was to be off. We'd texted and called since our talk in the barn—we even fell asleep on the phone together the other night—but neither of us had brought up my wrist or my ex. It was hard to figure out if he didn't want to hear about it, or if he was simply not bringing up the topic for my sake.

The cowbell above the door announced a customer coming in, so I tossed the rag on the counter and turned to greet them.

But rather than words flowing out of my mouth, my heart stopped instead, my breath getting stuck in my lungs.

"Hello, Sage," Jason said, and the greeting was anything but warm.

I swallowed, trying my damned hardest to compose myself. I did *not* want him to see that I was scared.

Fear only fueled him.

"What are you doing here?" I asked, but even I didn't miss the tremor in my voice.

He prowled up to the counter, his movements slow and predatory. Each step echoed through the small eating area, pounding in my ears with the panic I tried to keep at bay.

"You weren't replying to my texts." He took another step, but instead of stopping in front of the counter, he turned to come around the side. "Or answering my calls."

"You're supposed to be in prison," I said, not allowing myself to take my eyes off of him.

He came around the corner, facing me. I inched backward a step, holding onto the edge of the counter for support.

"Good behavior gets you a long, *long* way on such a bullshit charge."

But we both knew it wasn't bullshit.

Or at least, I did. Maybe he still believed that what he did was fine. To take charge. To control.

But that wasn't how you treated a woman, and I knew that now.

All those years spent thinking, *maybe this is the last time. He loves me, he wouldn't possibly do it again.*

"What do you want, Jason?"

He held his hands out, palms up. "I'll make it easy on you. I don't care about seeing Avery. Just pay off my debt and give me money every few weeks to make up for the hell you've caused me, and we're good."

The hell *I* caused him? As if he never treated me poorly? Never raised a hand to me? He thought he did nothing wrong, as if he had been falsely convicted of domestic abuse.

I hadn't realized I was shaking until I slid my hand on the edge of the counter as I took another step back from him. He was still slowly coming closer, cornering me.

I have to move. I can't let him corner me,

"I can't afford that. I'm barely getting by as it is," I said. My words were hurried, my voice more high-pitched than normal.

He was a foot away from me now, staring me down like a lion would his kill.

I took another step, and my back hit the wall. I flinched when my shoulder blades connected with the wall, every nerve ending inside of me standing at attention.

One more step, and he was in my face, lowering his gaze slightly so that we were eye to eye. His hand came up to roughly grip my jaw and it took all I had in me not to make a sound. "Then figure it out."

The cowbell rang out with the door opening, but before either of us could look that way, a voice said, "Step the fuck away from her or I'll cut your fucking hand off."

Callan.

Fuck, fuck fuck.

If he got involved, if Jason hurt him, I'd never forgive myself.

Jason moved his hand from my jaw, patting my cheek twice before he removed his hand. I closed my eyes tightly against the touch, wishing I could just fucking disappear. His hands on me made my skin crawl, fear pounding in my ears. This was nothing compared to what he'd done in the past.

In front of me, I could tell Jason had straightened, and I opened my eyes. Callan was standing in the middle of the cafe. All I wanted was to go to him and sink into his arms and let him hold me.

Jason scoffed. "You run off to some cowboy, Sage?"

Callan approached, coming around the back of the counter. "Step away from her."

Jason faced him. "Or what, big boy?"

Callan kept his calm, but I could see the rage building inside him with the slight flare of his nostrils.

"You need to leave," Callan demanded.

Jason chuckled. "Am I really being threatened by a hick right now?" He reached behind him, grabbing my arm.

"Jason, let go," I begged, trying to pry his grip off of me with my other hand.

His grip slid down my arm to my wrist and he tugged. Pain shot up my arm, my hand going numb as I hissed in a breath.

"My girl and I were just leaving actually," Jason said.

As if he had the fucking right to claim me.

"You're hurting me, Jason, please." Tears stung my eyes as my arm laid limp in his hold. When the pain got too bad, my nerves would burn and my hand wouldn't want to function. That's how it felt as Callan took two steps forward and swung.

Jason dropped my wrist as Callan's fist connected with his jaw. He staggered a few steps to the side with the impact, and before Jason had the chance to react, Callan was reaching around him to urge me toward him. His hand at my lower back, I quickly moved out from behind Jason, only to be moved behind Callan's back now.

His hand slid into mine behind him as he warned, "You swing back, and you'll end up right back in that prison."

My hand was still numb, doing its best to hold onto Callan's.

Jason wiped the blood from the corner of his lip, looking at the red drop of liquid glistening on his finger. "You picked a fight with the wrong guy, hick boy."

Callan's thumb gently rubbed along my wrist. "I don't pick fights I won't win, and I'd suggest you do the same. Bell Buckle doesn't take kindly to guys like you, so unless you want this whole town on your ass, I suggest you leave."

I didn't doubt for a second that the Bronson brothers would put Jason in his place. I was sure the entire town would, too, but I didn't want that on my conscience. I already felt guilty for involving Callan.

Jason dropped his hand from where he was admiring the blood, staring daggers at me. "Remember what I said."

Then he shoulder checked Callan on his way past him, and I couldn't take a breath until the cowbell chimed.

Callan turned, carefully lifting my hand to examine my wrist. "Are you okay?"

My breaths were too short, but I nodded, then shook my head. "It's not bad. It's okay."

Callan's cheek pulsed as his jaw clenched.

"Your hand. Is it okay?" I looked at his knuckles as he cradled my hand. The skin was red.

He let out a disbelieving breath. "You're asking if I'm okay."

"I'm not the only one who matters here, Cal."

He eased my hand back down to my side as his gaze darted between my eyes, searching for answers I wasn't sure he wanted to find.

"What did he mean?"

"He wants money." And apparently me.

Another tick in his jaw.

"How much?" he asked, though I knew he wasn't asking with the intent to actually pay him.

"I don't know. He wants me to pay his debt, then give him an allowance." But I couldn't do that even if I wanted to. I didn't have the money to support us and him. If he was the one who made the complaint about me, how did he expect me to pay him if I was jobless? Unless he expected me to go back to Portland with him.

Callan reached up, running a hand over his mouth, then gently wrapped his arms around me. I folded into him, finally able to take a full, deep breath. My lungs expanded in relief.

Some people sprayed lavender on their pillow to calm themselves, but all I needed was Callan and I could breathe.

"We'll report him to the police and he'll go back to prison," Callan said, his chin resting on top of my head.

"What if he hides? It could make him more mad." More angry at me.

Callan leaned back, cupping my face in his hands so I was looking up at him. "Baby, I can't live with myself knowing you or Avery could be in danger because he's here. I would love to stick by your side twenty-four-seven, but we both know it's not possible."

I blinked, nodding. "Okay. I'll report him."

"*We*," he corrected. "We'll both report him."

"You don't have to—" I started.

"Sage," he interrupted. "It's you and me, together. You're not in this alone anymore."

After all these years, I didn't know I needed to hear that to truly feel safe.

Even with Jason out there, walking the streets, Callan made me feel protected. Like I didn't have to worry about every what-if on my own.

I had him to lean on when I needed it.

And that was freeing in itself.

29

SAGE

After reporting the incident at the station, I had gone home to spend some time alone. The sheriff had one of his officers doing a drive-by every couple hours to make sure Jason didn't show up here, which eased a bit of my worry. I hoped he wouldn't and that this was all just an extra precaution. If he did, I at least hoped it wouldn't be when Avery was here.

Charlotte had picked Avery up from school, and when I called to let her know I was on the way to the ranch, she'd offered to let her spend the night. I guess Callan had told her some of the details through text when he'd asked her to get Avery from school. She understood immediately and dropped everything to help in any way she could.

I ached for a mother figure like that.

My grandmother had filled that void while my mom was out with a new boyfriend every week, and Charlotte only made me miss her presence more.

Oh, what my grandmother would say if she saw me now.

Don't get hung up on boys that aren't hung up on you.

But that was the problem.

Jason was hung up on me for all the wrong reasons; he wanted control, and he saw me as an easy target.

Callan was hung up on me for all the right reasons, but I felt guilty for it.

And the sad part was that I fucking shouldn't.

I should let him be there for me, but every instinct in my body told me to shut down and leave. To take Avery as far away from here as possible so Jason could never find us again.

But I'd already tried that once, and it didn't work.

Ruining the life I'd built here wouldn't create a better one. It'd just restart the cycle.

So I had to hope that the police found Jason and he was sent back to prison for violating his parole by crossing state lines. I'd filed for a restraining order yesterday as well, which made Callan feel at least a little better.

We all knew a piece of paper wouldn't keep Jason away, though, which was why I'd been too scared to do it years ago.

I'd barely slept last night, staring at the ceiling with Pudding laying on my stomach and wondering when this would all be over. Every noise made me jump, and I was thankful Avery wasn't at the house. After hours of laying in bed, I'd gotten up sometime around four a.m. to make coffee. With only a few hours of sleep and my spiraling thoughts, the caffeine didn't help all that much, and now I was just an anxious mess.

All I wanted was to call Callan, but he had a life. A job. A family. I couldn't just disrupt it because I needed him.

I didn't want to become a burden. The problems I had with Jason were already laid bare for Callan, and though he hadn't moved a single muscle yesterday when I told him everything Jason had done to me in the past, I didn't want to interrupt his life because of mine.

Scooting the dining room chair back and setting Pudding on the ground from where she'd been laying on my lap, I got up and went into the kitchen. I wished for nothing other than the smell of cookies to fill the house, but I couldn't find the energy to make them.

Baking was my therapy, but even now, thinking about getting the ingredients out made me want to curl up in a ball on the floor and waste the day away.

I ran a finger along the knobs on the front of the oven, staring at the numbers and dashes that indicated certain heat levels. It wasn't anything fancy, but I didn't need fancy appliances or kitchenware. The comfort they provided was enough for me.

A knock at the door made me pull my hand back as I looked over my shoulder toward the front entry. My heart seemed to skip a beat, a bass drum thumping in my chest like the soundtrack to my own doom.

It wasn't Jason.

He wouldn't just show up here.

But he'd shown up at the cafe, hadn't he?

I grabbed the closest thing to me, gripping the wooden stirring spoon in my hand as my feet dragged themselves to the front entry. Twisting the lock, I wrapped a fist around the knob and turned, opening the door an inch to see who it was.

My shoulders relaxed, my grip on the spoon loosening. "Callan?"

He eyed the crack in the door, probably wondering why I wasn't opening it further, then in less than a second, realization struck. Taking a step back, I pulled the door open wider.

"What are you doing here?" I asked.

He held a grocery bag up in his hand. "Figured you might want company."

A crease formed between my brows. "What's that?"

His eyes fell to the spoon in my hand. "Why do you have a spoon?"

Dropping my gaze to the utensil, I twisted it in my fingers, momentarily having forgotten that I was even holding it. "I, uh, I thought you were someone else."

His face fell, his hand that was holding the plastic bag falling to his side. "Sage..."

"I know, silly me. A spoon wouldn't save me." *Nothing will.*

He stepped over the threshold, closing the door behind him, then folded himself around me. "Baby, you should've called me."

But calling him would've let on to how scared I was, and in my experience, men either loved scared women or they hated them.

"I'm okay," I lied. I wouldn't be okay until he was behind bars, but even before, it took me years to stop looking over my shoulder.

"You know you don't have to lie to me," Callan murmured, running his free hand down my back.

"I promise, it's much better than the truth," I told him.

The rough timbre of his voice vibrated through his chest, giving me the comfort I so desperately needed. "I only want the truth with you. No matter how bad it may be. Remember my rules?"

I inhaled deeply, a sense of calm washing over me now that Callan was here. How could I forget the rules he instilled in me that night in front of his mirror? Yet even then, he hadn't demanded anything. He laid a path for me to follow if I chose to.

Pulling back slightly, I looked at him. "Only truths, then."

He pressed a kiss to my forehead. "Only truths."

After he removed his lips from my skin, I looked down at the bag. "Did you buy me groceries?"

He grinned, removing his hand from around my waist to grab the handle of the bag, holding it open. "I brought ingredients to make cinnamon rolls."

Arching an eyebrow, I said, "Middle of the day craving?"

A blush heated his cheeks. "I wouldn't say I was craving cinnamon rolls."

The unspoken words clung in the air, tension radiating between us.

"Hmm. I wonder why you'd bring the makings for them, then," I wondered out loud.

The corner of his mouth ticked up. "I want you to teach me."

I wanted to learn a lot of things from him, but Callan taking an interest in what I did and wanting to learn how to do it himself? My mouth would've dropped open if it wasn't for me asking, "To bake?"

"Yeah. What else would you be teaching me with all of this?"

A warmth spread through my chest, crawling up my neck as I smirked. "How to have fun with it, too."

***

"You want me to just wear this?" Callan asked, holding the fabric up in his hands.

I nodded.

"No boxers?"

"That's up to you."

I'd immediately dragged him down the hall to my bedroom and rifled through the dresser to find my spare apron. If this was supposed to be all about having fun and getting my mind off everything else, I was going to take advantage of it. I'd much rather have my attention on his body instead.

"Alright. Out," he instructed.

"I don't get to watch?"

He smiled, waving his hand at me to shoo. "You'll get to see the final result."

Watching Callan strip in front of me seemed a lot more enticing than the cinnamon rolls now.

"Go on. Close the door behind you."

I let out a *hmph* and turned around, pulling the door shut and heading back to the kitchen. I'd debated changing into an apron myself, but kept my pajamas on instead. The shorts were a bit too short, the top a bit too flimsy, but I doubted Callan minded.

I got to work setting out all the ingredients we'd need for the recipe, aside from what he'd brought, as I waited for him to come out. Minutes later, the door down the hall opened.

I grabbed the cinnamon from the cabinet and turned to find Callan standing in the opening to the hallway with one arm propped up on the wall.

My jaw fucking dropped.

My cheeks had to be a million shades of red as I took him in.

"You actually did it," I said, disbelief ringing in my tone.

"I did it for you, and if you tell anyone—"

"Oh, don't worry. This is all for me." All six-foot-whatever of him was mine tonight.

I eyed the apron slung around his neck, his broad shoulders exposed. His arms were fucking mouthwatering. Muscles like that should *not* be allowed. He was all toned, tanned, and delicious, and I wanted a taste.

He shoved off the wall, coming over to the kitchen to join me. When he turned, I saw he had kept his boxers on. "No commando?" I pouted.

He looked over his shoulder at me with a lift to the corner of his mouth. "I figured you might want to remove those later yourself."

I was glad he turned back around to grab the bowls out of the cabinet because I was on fucking fire.

The way his words affected me could make this whole place go up in flames and I'd still stand here relishing in the fact that this man was in my kitchen in nothing but boxers and an apron.

He set the bowls on the counter next to me, leaning a hand on the edge as he homed in on me.

"Ready to get started?" he asked.

My eyes trailed over his arm, up his shoulders to his collarbones, then slid up his neck to meet his gaze.

"Yes." On more than just the cinnamon rolls.

He reached around me to turn the knob on the oven to start the preheat, his hand dangerously close to me. As he pulled his arm away, his fingers gripped my ass softly, all while keeping his eyes on me. "Then let's get to it, baby."

We got to work on prepping the dough, bringing all the ingredients together to make a ball. As we waited for it to rest, I moved on to the icing as he wiped the counter where we'd made the dough.

"Taste this," I said, dipping my finger into the bowl. I held it out to him and he faced me, wrapping his lips around the digit and sucking the icing into his mouth.

He made a low humming sound in the back of his throat, his tongue thoroughly licking my finger clean before he released it. "It's delicious. Cream cheese frosting was the way to go. Have you tried it?"

I nodded. "I just wanted to make sure you liked it."

He inched closer. "Here, have another taste."

Callan dipped his finger into the bowl, gingerly coating his skin. He held it out to me and I opened my mouth, letting him slide his finger in.

Fuck, this was hot.

This man had me sucking icing off his finger, and all I could think about were the many other places I could be licking it off of his body.

"Good?" he asked as I twirled my tongue around it with another suck. He pulled his finger out, watching me intently.

"Amazing."

He dipped his finger into the bowl again. "Get on your knees and try it again."

Oh, fuck.

Though he was the one standing there in only an apron and boxers, I quickly became the one at his mercy. He hadn't needed to wear the apron, but he'd done it for me. Now all I wanted to do was return the favor in any way he wanted it, and if being on my knees was what he desired, then I'd do it.

I lowered myself, keeping my eyes glued to his as my knees met the ground. I opened my mouth and he brought his finger to my tongue, letting me close my lips around the digit.

Was it wrong that I wished I was sucking something else of his instead?

"That taste good, baby?"

I hummed, nodding as I took his finger the slightest bit deeper.

After it was licked clean, he removed his finger again. He eyed me, then dipped back into the bowl, but instead of staying where he was, he casually crossed the kitchen, leaning back against the wall. He watched me from where he stood, hunger shining in his eyes.

But it wasn't hunger for the icing or the cinnamon rolls or any of that.

It was for me.

"Crawl to me."

My palms lowered to the ground, and slowly, I prowled toward him, never once removing my eyes from his.

He watched every movement, his stance nonchalant, like he had all the time in the world to visually devour me.

Like nothing else mattered but me.

I stopped once I was right in front of him, removing my palms from the ground to perch up on my knees.

"Now be a good girl and suck my finger like you wish it was my cock."

My lips parted, wrapping around his finger again, but instead of stopping at the knuckle, I took his finger all the way in, letting the tip of it hit the back of my tongue.

I liked to think men had big hands for a reason, and this was one of them.

My cheeks hollowed as I sucked, my tongue twisting and twirling around him, and my mouth ached to be full. Sucking his finger was fine, but I wanted more.

My mouth slid off of him. "I want more."

"Oh, yeah?" he questioned. "How much more?"

"You. All of you. Inside me."

He reached down, hooking his hands under my armpits, and hauled me up so that I was standing before him.

"Inside you here?" he asked, running a finger over my lips. He trailed down my jaw, over my chest, and past the hem of my shorts. His touch sent goosebumps down my thighs as he shoved the leg of my shorts aside and slid his hand up to my pussy.

I *knew* he felt how utterly soaked I was.

"Or here?"

"Both." The word came out like a plea.

"My finger not enough for you, baby?"

I wanted to whimper at the thought of him filling me with his dick instead. "I want more." It wasn't just the sex I wanted more of with him, it was everything else, too. I wanted this to be more than what it was, and with us crossing this line, it solidified us. "As long as you do, too."

He brought his hand to my cheek, gently tucking my hair behind my ear. "I've just been waiting for you to say the words."

In an instant, his hands came around my waist, lifting me up so that I had to wrap my legs around him. He started walking, aiming for my bedroom.

He kicked the door shut behind him, then crossed to the bed. My ass landed on it with a slight bounce. Now sitting in front of him, he reached behind his back to undo the knot on the apron, quickly pulling it over his head and tossing it to the ground. I didn't hesitate as I shoved his boxers down, his dick springing free.

My hand gripped the base of it as I darted my tongue out to lave up the drop that beaded at the tip.

"Fuck, Sage. I could get off on you doing that alone."

Satisfaction surged through me with the effect I had on him. I was glad I wasn't the only one completely gone at the moment.

My lips wrapped around the head of his dick as I slowly pulled it deeper into my mouth, my movements slow as I took my time with him.

He was gentle as he wrapped his hands in my hair, not to hold me in place, but to make it easier for me to enjoy him without the strands getting in the way.

My hand pumped him in rhythm with my mouth, my tongue flat against the underside of his dick. He cursed, pulling my head back so that my mouth released him. "I can't wait any longer."

"I'm on birth control," I said. "And I haven't had sex in a few years, but I'm clean."

"I'm clean, too—" He angled my head to look up at him as his eyes widened. "Wait, *years*? When you told me about the orgasms before, I assumed you'd still been having sex."

I nodded. "Not since..."

He leaned down, pressing his lips to mine so that I didn't have to say the words. I got lost in him, in his mouth, in the way he released my hair and smoothed his hands over my cheeks, my jaw, my neck.

He pulled back, resting his forehead against mine. "I'll take care of you. You have any second thoughts, or if anything hurts, you tell me, okay?"

I nodded. "Okay."

"And remember, Sage. You're beautiful. Every damn inch of you."

His hands trailed to my thighs, pulling my shorts down so they puddled on the floor. He moved his fingers to my shirt, lifting it up and over, and tossed it to the ground. I fought to keep my arms to the side rather than covering my scar, repeating his words of affirmation over and over in my mind.

His eyes heated as he took in that I wasn't wearing a bra, then brought his hands back to my thighs. He lifted me slightly so that he could move me up the bed, and once he was satisfied with my placement, he laid me back against the comforter, my head resting on the pillow.

"You don't have to be gentle," I told him as he hovered over me.

"Trust me, baby. Gentle will not be in my vocabulary once I'm inside of you."

My thighs wanted to squeeze together to relieve some of the pressure, but Callan reached down, wrapping a hand around my leg. "Spread your legs."

I did, and then he was lining himself up with my pussy. "I can get a condom if you want," he said, his breathing deep and even.

I shook my head. "Please just fuck me, Callan."

The corner of his mouth twitched. "Yes, ma'am."

In an instant, he was easing into me. My breath hitched as the muscles in his arms flexed from where he was holding himself up. With his hands braced on either side of my head, I had the best view of every inch of him. His chest, his stomach, his arms, his face. All of it made me melt into the feel of him.

Once he was fully inside of me, he gave me a minute to adjust, and I wrapped my hands around his arms.

"Breathe, baby," he said, taking a deep breath himself.

I squirmed slightly, wrapping my legs around him, and he took that as his cue to continue. He began thrusting in and out of me, starting slow at first, but then he lost it, pounding into me as my moans got louder, my fingers digging into his skin.

My legs fell to the bed and he pulled out, grabbing my hips to flip me over. He hoisted me up so that my ass was in the air, my chest and face pressed to the bed.

"Fucking hell, Sage. You're perfect."

He smoothed a hand over my ass as he inserted himself back into me and I let out another moan.

"That feel good, baby?"

"Yes," I breathed. *It felt fucking amazing.*

The angle mixed with the fullness of him had my core tightening as soon as he began thrusting again.

My hand fisted in the sheets as I reached between my legs with the other to circle my clit.

His hand gripped my hip. "That's it. Touch yourself for me. Bring yourself to that edge and let go."

As his speed increased, so did my fingers. That blissful sensation built between my legs as he thrust deeper into me. I knew he could feel it, too, because he groaned as it built.

I let the pressure build, the sweetness pooling in my center, and then I did as he said. I let go.

I screamed his name, my voice muffled by the pillow. With my name on his lips, he buried himself as deep as he could go and filled me, collapsing over my body. He held himself up so he didn't crush me as he came down, and I was thankful he didn't move yet.

I'd miss the fullness of him inside me once he was gone.

He kissed the crook of my neck, then moved his lips to my shoulder blade, and placed a final kiss on my spine before pulling out. My hips lowered to the bed as I stayed flat on my belly, and he wrapped an arm around me, laying his head on my back.

"In every sense of the word, you are breathtaking, Sage McKinley." His jaw moved on my back as he spoke, his finger tracing a circle right above the curve of my ass.

"You are, too, Callan Bronson."

He let out a small scoff and I moved, twisting so that I was on my back and his head was now on my stomach. I reached down, cupping his cheeks with my hands so he'd look up at me.

"Not just the physical features. Though, you are great to look at. But your mind, your heart, your empathy for everyone around you. You're so much more than what meets the eye, and I hope you always stay true to that."

He swallowed, then scooted up to press a slow kiss to my lips.

But it wasn't just his lips on mine in that moment. It was the two of us telling one another that words couldn't sum up the feelings we were growing for each other. How it didn't matter if we were laying in this bed or out in the world—we'd be there to bring the other up when they were down.

We'd be what the other needed us to be while being completely ourselves, because me and Callan? We were two souls trying to find another for the longest time, and the universe finally gave us that chance.

It was finally giving us our happily ever after.

30

SAGE

"Thank you for finishing these last night and feeding Pudding her dinner," I said as I stretched the plastic wrap over the top of the glass dish.

"Of course. I wasn't lying when I said I wanted baking lessons," Callan replied.

I let out a snort. "Yeah, yet your instructor fell asleep while they were in the oven."

He set his cup of coffee on the counter and wrapped his arms around my waist from behind. "You needed the sleep."

He was right. After barely getting any the night before, it was nice to feel rested this morning after waking up next to him. The lingering scent of pastry and cinnamon clung to the air when I emerged from the bedroom, and I wished I could wake up to that every morning.

"So, are you doing Avery's party the weekend before or after her birthday?"

I'd gone back and forth on what day to do it because of the fair being the next weekend. Avery would be taking part in it with the horse rescue, so I didn't want her burnt out.

Making sure the edges of the plastic wrap were held down tight, I twisted in his embrace to drape my arms loosely around his neck. Avery's birthday landed on a Friday this year, so we'd have a nice dinner of her choosing that night, but the real celebration would be the next day. "The Saturday after."

"Perfect," he said, sliding his arms back to rest his hands on my hips. "Speaking of weekend plans, would you want to go on a few rides at the fair after the parade?" His cheeks turned the slightest shade of red with the question.

"With you?" I asked.

He frowned. "No. Alone."

I smiled at that. "I'd love to."

Seeing Callan blush over asking me if I'd like to go on a couple of fair rides was one of the cutest things I'd seen him do to date.

I hoped I had plenty more time to see him do a million more cute things just like that.

"I have to get to a lesson if you want to head out," Callan offered.

"Yeah, I guess I should pick up Avery. It's already almost seven." I needed to drop her off at school after she had a cinnamon roll at the Bronsons. I wasn't going to eat all of these, so I figured I'd bring the majority of them to all those hungry cowboys.

Callan's fingers squeezed my hips. "I wish we had time to spare."

My fingers ran through his hair as I scrunched my nose with a smile. "Not today, unfortunately. Later?"

One of his hands released my hip, bringing it up to tap my nose. "Later."

Letting me go, he disappeared into the front entry while I opened the fridge to pull out Avery's lunch I prepared last night before falling asleep. As I turned around, Callan set Avery's backpack on the counter.

The way he thought to grab it, to help me with my morning routine in any way, made my heart skip a beat.

I wanted to get used to this.

"Do you need help with the party set up?" he asked as I slid the lunchbox inside her backpack.

I zipped the bag, then picked it up off the counter. "I don't want to trouble you with it."

He grabbed the backpack from my hand. "No trouble at all. I'd love to help set everything up for her big day."

I pressed my lips together to hide my smile. "You do know there will be a lot of pink, right?"

He nodded.

"And with you at the party, you'll have to wear a party hat. Avery will insist."

"How could anyone say no to a party hat?"

I pictured him standing in the middle of a group of six-year-old girls wearing a pink party hat and glitter face paint, wondering how I got so lucky to find someone like Callan. He was so willing to do anything for my little girl, and if I had to guess, he'd do the same for me.

"How about dinner the night before the party? We can set it all up after Avery goes to bed."

This time, I didn't hide my smile. "That sounds perfect."

***

I slipped through the door to Charlotte and Travis's house with the plate of cinnamon rolls, my belly growling with the urge to eat one. Callan and I had parted ways after a long goodbye out front. We'd driven our separate cars here, and just in that short amount of time, I'd missed him. I wished we could have spent the day together, but he had lessons and I had to take Avery to school and head to work.

"Mama!" Avery exclaimed when she saw me. She hopped off the barstool she was perched on and came running over to me, wrapping her arms around my hips.

"Hey, Aves. Did you have a good night?"

She nodded as Charlotte came over from the kitchen to grab the plate from me. "We colored and played hide-and-seek, and I got to feed the horses dinner."

I bent down, hooking her hair behind her ears so it was out of her face. "Did the horses like their dinner?"

She nodded again, some of her hair coming loose anyway. "They loved it. I even gave Red some treats."

"That sounds fun." I took in her pink polka dot pajamas. "Why don't you go get dressed and then you can eat a cinnamon roll before I take you to school?"

"Okay!" She zipped around me, heading down the hall while she talked about how excited she was to tell her friends all about feeding the horses.

I stood, making my way over to the barstool Avery was sitting in moments before. Charlotte slid a plate in front of me with a warmed-up cinnamon roll.

"Have some breakfast."

"I have a bunch more at home. These are for your family."

She waved me off, setting a fork on the plate in front of me. "They'll eat plenty. Take a minute to have a bite."

I gave in, picking up the fork and digging in. It wasn't often I got to enjoy the flavors that danced on my tongue because more often than not, I was in a rush—unless it was three a.m. and I was having a late night snack when I couldn't sleep.

"Thank you for watching Avery," I said after taking a sip of the coffee she set in front of me.

"Anytime. As a mother myself, I know how hard it can be to have a few minutes alone when you need it."

I set the fork down, wiping the corner of my mouth with a napkin. "How'd you do it with so many kids? Sometimes I can barely handle just one."

She came around the counter to take a seat next to me, facing me on the barstool. "It seems impossible until you're doing it, and then you realize you'd never want anything to be different. The chaos, the stress—it's all worth it for our babies."

"Is it hard? Having all of them doing their own things and not knowing if something could go wrong?" I didn't know how I'd handle it one day when Avery had her first job or a boyfriend, but I only hoped by then that her father was locked away for good.

"That's just what we deal with as mothers. We care so much for our children that it can wreck us, but I wouldn't change being a mother for anything. Even if one of my kids got in a fight for their girl."

My eyes widened slightly. "You know?"

She gave me a sad smile, so many unspoken words floating through her expression. "I notice everything about my kids. Every new scrape, bruise, or shadow in their eyes. Callan doesn't fight for anyone besides the people he loves."

I inhaled deeply, feeling the weight of what she wasn't saying. "Did he tell you what happened?"

"I saw his bruised knuckles and the change in his usual calm demeanor when he was here yesterday. Being a mother, we just know things. And I know when my boys love something. I taught them to give everything their all, and he's doing that for you. You've made him come out of his shell. He never used to go to town unless he had to. He was rarely himself after his ex made him decide between staying at this ranch or running off with her. Ever since, he hasn't been vulnerable, hasn't opened up. But, sweetie—" She reached over, setting her hand on top of mine. "—when he talks about you, I see it in his eyes. See every wall you've broken down without even realizing it."

I blinked away the moisture threatening to build in my eyes and swallowed. "I just don't want to scare him away."

Her soft hand gave mine a squeeze. "Nothing could scare that boy away."

"How do you know?"

"I raised him. Callan doesn't run from the hard things, he hits them head on. He'll take care of you and Avery. It's in his blood."

I slid my hand out from under hers to reach forward and give her a hug. Charlotte was that mom everyone wished they had. She was open to any conversation, always ready to give advice if you needed it. She never judged, and in a world so cruel, that's all anyone really needed.

If there were any in-laws I wanted to go through the rest of my life with, it'd be these ones. The Bronsons welcomed me with open arms and understanding. I didn't have to hide my past from them like I thought. They understood that no one was perfect, and that was just what I needed all along.

Acceptance.

For who I was and where I came from. For being a single mom barely scraping by.

None of the semantics mattered.

Just me and Avery, being loved by the people around us despite our past.

And that's all I've ever wanted.

***

Parking my car out front of Bell Buckle Brews, I headed inside to start my shift. When I put my key into the lock on the door, I found it was already unlocked. I was the only one scheduled to work this morning, so either someone else was here or the closer forgot to lock the door on their way out yesterday.

Inching the door open, I slipped inside carefully to not stir the cowbell. If there was someone in here, I didn't want to alert them to my entrance.

"Sage?"

My heart jumped into my throat as Gemma came out from the back, the door swinging behind her.

"Gemma. What are you doing here?" My hand dropped from where it had flown up to my chest at the scare.

"I wanted to help out," she said hesitantly.

I glanced around the dining area, noting that each table was shining, every chair pushed in perfectly.

"You're not scheduled until the afternoon." I came forward, stopping at the edge of the counter.

"I know. I just... I wanted to talk before you left."

"Hours before?" This wasn't the typical Gemma I'd come to know. She was usually snappy and had no filter whatsoever.

She responded with a nod and stepped aside so I could get past her into the back. I set my wallet and phone in my locker, then got to work getting the ingredients I needed out from the fridge.

Gemma took a few baking sheets out of the bottom cabinet, setting them on the table behind me.

Setting the eggs on the counter, I closed the fridge to face her. "What did you want to talk about?"

She swallowed, wringing her hands together. "I don't hate you."

My brows pulled together.

"If you thought I did. I just wanted you to know that I don't," she clarified.

"I don't think that you hate me." I wasn't sure where she was trying to go with this. And why now? Why bring it all up today? "Gemma, is everything okay?"

Her eyes fell to the ground, and I gave her all the time she needed to conjure up her response. I knew as well as anyone that people could have pain hidden far beneath the surface, and to voice it was to dig up bones that we'd rather stay buried.

"Four years ago, I lost the two people in this world who meant the most to me. A drunk driver took them from me." She paused, her eyes blinking away the tears she tried to hold at bay. "I'll never get what you have, Sage." She finally looked at me, quickly glancing to my stomach before darting back to my face, and I saw it all.

The pain. The reason for her lashing out at me.

"I'm so sorry." But sorry couldn't erase that pain from her past. It wouldn't make any of it better.

"It's alright," she said, sniffling as she wiped a finger under her eyes. "Four years is a long time to cope. I've come to terms with what happened that night. But when you first moved here, shortly after I did, and you'd bring Avery into the cafe sometimes, seeing your little girl made me envious for all the wrong reasons. It wasn't your fault."

"I know," I admitted quietly. Trauma messed with the human brain. It'd find reasons to excuse what happened; pin your anger on others who weren't even involved. "It's not our fault, Gemma."

She nodded, but I could tell she'd been trying to convince herself of that for a long time. I crossed the room, pulling her into a hug.

"It's not our fault," I repeated.

I'd say it a million times over again if I needed to. To engrain it in our brains that the reason we were dealt the hands we got was not because of us.

It wasn't my fault Jason would hit me when he was angry, and it wasn't Gemma's fault that that person decided to drive inebriated.

We were strong enough to get through this.

Gemma pulled back, dropping her arms. "It wasn't your fault either, Sage. Whatever pain you hold, it wasn't inflicted because of you."

My lips pressed together as I nodded. "It wasn't. I know that now."

She glanced at the clock hanging on the wall. "Why don't you go open the store while I get the ovens going?"

"You don't want to head home before your shift?"

She shook her head. "I'm okay staying."

"Alright, well, if you change your mind, I won't mind."

I headed for the door, but paused with my hand resting on it when Gemma said my name. I looked back at her.

"I'm sorry for any trouble I've caused you. It wasn't my intention," she said.

"It's been no trouble at all, Gemma. It's okay."

She gave a closed-lip smile, though it didn't reach her eyes.

Maybe not today, but someday, we'd be okay.

Pain couldn't be the forefront of what we felt forever.

There was more to this life than that. It had just taken me longer than I would have liked to figure that out.

31

SAGE

The combination of tart orange juice played on my tongue with the bubbly pops of champagne. It'd been a long time since I had a mimosa, and I was clearly missing out.

"I'm telling you, that horse is out of his mind," Brandy said after a sip of her own mimosa.

"You don't have to keep trying," Lettie replied as the waitress set the basket of fried pickles down in the middle of the table.

"Do some horses just not want to be ridden?" Oakley asked. She and I were on the same wavelength with the limited horse knowledge.

"Can we get another round of mimosas?" Brandy asked the waitress, who nodded in response, then replied to Oakley. "Some horses are straight assholes, and Lettie seems to pick the best of them."

They'd invited me to a boozy brunch, and I'd almost said no, but Charlotte had popped up out of nowhere when Lettie was asking me at the ranch, offering to watch Avery so I could have a few hours with the girls.

"I like to pride myself with my choices," Lettie retorted.

Brandy downed the last of her mimosa. "I wouldn't get too cocky like that."

"I can try to do it myself," Lettie offered.

Brandy shook her head. "I'll figure it out."

Lettie snagged a fried pickle. "He had a bad past."

"Clearly. It took me weeks to finally get a halter on him after I took the last one off." Brandy set her glass down at the edge of the table for an easier reach when the waitress came back.

"That was your mistake," Lettie said.

Brandy arched a brow. "Are you telling the horse trainer how to train horses?"

Lettie shrugged. "You should let me help you."

A scoff sounded as Brandy picked up her own fried pickle. "And have your brother and Bailey on my ass? No, thanks. I've got it. He just needs more time to warm up, is all."

Lettie nodded as she chewed, all of us digging into the basket. The waitress came back with the mimosas and I finished my other one off to hand her the empty glass. We were on drink number three, but Oakley was going slower than the rest of us because she was our designated driver. She was only allowing herself to have one on top of some food with it.

"So, Sage," Lettie started.

I finished my bite. "Hmm?"

"I know it's pretty informal, but—" She fished something out of her pocket, then set a little pink bow on the table in front of me. "—would you be my bridesmaid?"

A breath of relief passed my lips. "I thought you were going to tell me you were pregnant and having a girl."

Brandy burst out laughing as Oakley giggled. "Lettie can barely take care of herself, let alone a baby," Brandy managed to get out.

The champagne was working its way through us, it seemed.

Lettie lifted her chin. "I take care of myself just fine."

"Need I remind you of when you came back—" Brandy started but was cut off with a yelp passing her lips as I presumed Lettie kicked her under the table.

Lettie had a history of anemia and was quite forgetful, but I was curious what Brandy meant.

"Anyway." Lettie turned her attention back to me. "What do you say?"

I smiled. "I'd love to."

It felt nice to be a part of their group and have this time to hang out with them. I didn't realize how much I missed having girl friends until now.

"Perfect. The wedding is this fall."

Brandy's eyes almost burst out of her head. "This fall? And you're telling us the date now?"

"Well, I don't have a set date yet," Lettie admitted.

"Then how do you know you'll be doing it this fall? Don't you have to book places?" Oakley asked.

Lettie took a large gulp of her drink. "Bailey wanted the fall, and I didn't want to wait another year. We're doing it at the ranch."

My smile widened, the champagne twirling around in my head. "That'll be perfect."

"I hope so. I think we can get everything sorted by then, but I'll need your guys' help."

We all nodded.

"Of course. Anything," I said.

Brandy raised her glass. "To Lettie Cooper."

We all raised our own, clinking them together.

"To Lettie Cooper," we said in unison.

And then we sipped.

***

"How many individual pieces of hay do you think are in a hay bale?" Brandy asked, her words slightly slurred.

Oakley was driving us back to the ranch, where we planned to continue our boozy brunch in the comfort of home. We felt bad that Oakley couldn't indulge as much as she wanted to, but Lennon would pick her up later once he was off work, so she had nothing to worry about once we got to the ranch.

"A fuck ton," Lettie tossed back with a giggle.

"Like how many fuck tons?" Brandy questioned.

I'd stopped after four mimosas, which was probably too many, but Lettie and Brandy both had five. Brandy, I came to learn, was a lightweight, but that clearly did not stop her from indulging.

"Hmm, maybe a thousand?" Lettie replied.

"We could count one," I said, the effects of the champagne making it hard to resist joining in on their debate.

"As much fun as that sounds, I do not feel like counting hay while I'm planning to get buzzed," Oakley said. "The other day, I had to count an entire bag of dog treats because one of the customers didn't believe that there were seventy-two in each bag."

"You should've made *them* count it," Brandy said.

Oakley glanced in the rearview mirror at Brandy in the back-seat. "I wish I would have."

She turned onto the dirt driveway that led to the Bronsons' ranch as Brandy and Lettie went on about different shades of pink for the dresses, somehow getting on the topic of wanting to tie-dye them. Thankfully, we weren't making any final decisions while drunk, because tie-dye did not seem like Lettie's style of choice.

Oakley pulled to a stop and shut off the car. "Uh oh."

"What 'uh oh'?" Brandy asked, looking out the window.

Lettie leaned over Brandy to get a better look outside. "That 'uh oh,'" Lettie answered, pointing in the direction of the barn.

I looked out Oakley's driver window and swore I felt my heart sink. But just as quick as it sank, it started beating fast. Too fast.

I didn't hesitate, opening the passenger door to swing out of the car. Coming around the hood, I beelined it for Callan where he was standing with his back to the barn. Where a woman was standing too close to him, her chest practically touching his.

Any buzz I had fueled my confidence as I approached the two of them. Callan wasn't flirting with her, and he definitely wasn't entertaining whatever it was that she was doing. He looked uncomfortable, shrinking in on himself.

If he didn't have the guts to tell her off, then I would.

"Excuse me," I said, pasting on a sweet tone right along with my clearly fake smile. "Hi." I smoothly squeezed in between them, forcing the woman to take a step back.

Her mouth popped open as irritation coated her features. "We were in the middle of a conversation," she squeaked out, disbelief lacing her tone.

Conversation, my ass.

"You're standing a little too close to my boyfriend. Actually." I paused, lifting a finger. "*Way* too close. And you need to leave."

"*Boyfriend?*" she exclaimed, her voice now rising in pitch.

"Mhmm, so maybe stop harassing him, take the message, and leave him the fuck alone."

Callan's chest was to my back in an instant, both hands on my shoulders.

The woman blinked in shock. "He's my son's instructor."

"Do you corner all your son's teachers like this?" I asked, cocking a brow as I set my hands on my hips.

Callan's fingers dug into my shoulders, gently holding me back like I'd swing at her.

I would.

"This is ridiculous," the woman said, taking another step back. "I'm never bringing my son back here."

I smiled. "Oh, your son is welcome. But you're not."

"What?" she squeaked, as if it was crazy that her son was innocent in this. Like *she* did no wrong.

"Do I need to spell it out for you?" I asked, my tone overly sweet. "Get the fuck off this ranch, and if your son wants to keep coming for lessons, have his father bring him." I gestured to the ring on her finger. "I'm sure he'd love to know the reason why his son might have to quit riding lessons."

Her lips pressed into a thin line, her cheeks red with rage. She turned on her heel, almost losing her balance in the dirt, then yelled for her son. "Christopher!"

"Coming, Mom!" Christopher shouted back, then emerged from the barn shortly after.

They got in their car and peeled out of the drive, and then my eyes landed on the other car, where Oakley, Lettie, and Brandy all had their faces pressed to the glass. They all tossed me a thumbs up and a huge smile.

Callan turned me around, but before I could apologize, he crashed into me with a kiss. His touch was hungry, his lips devouring. Every buzz from the champagne turned into the buzz of him lighting my skin like a match.

"Say it again," he mumbled into my lips as he kept kissing me just as deep.

"Say what?" I questioned, wishing he could take me right here.

"That I'm your boyfriend."

I pulled back, my lips parted.

I guess I had said that.

"Is that— Is that okay?" I asked. I wasn't sure if I stepped over the line by saying that, but all I knew in the moment I said it was that I wanted her to feel shitty for making Callan feel uncomfortable. Then, when I saw the ring on her finger, I didn't feel an ounce of guilt. She deserved the worst for cornering him as if she didn't have a man of her own at home.

"Baby, being your boyfriend is all I want. It's more than okay."

My head swam with the effects of him and the booze, and I couldn't help my smile as I said, "You're my boyfriend."

He smiled right back. "Damn right I am."

His lips met mine again, and I knew behind me that the girls were watching, but I didn't care. I wanted the whole world to know that Callan was mine and I was his.

I didn't know how much time had passed when I pulled away and asked, "Why didn't you tell her to leave you alone?"

He shrugged, but I could tell he knew. "I'm not very good at confronting people."

"What?" He was joking, right? "You punched my ex just last week. I'm pretty sure you're *too* good at confrontation."

He let out a small chuckle. "I can't just punch everyone I don't like, Sage."

This time, I shrugged. "You could."

He frowned, though he was clearly fighting a smile.

"You're damn good at standing up for other people, but you need to put that same amount of effort and care into yourself, too," I told him.

"I know. So do you."

I rolled my eyes. This wasn't about me. "So do it."

His hands found my waist. "Fine."

"Fine," I bit back.

Then we both grinned.

"But what if I want you to stand up for me again?"

I chuckled.

"It was pretty hot. I'll admit it," he said.

"Well, don't get used to it. Next time, maybe I'll be the one throwing punches."

He let out a fake cat growl and I laughed as he pulled me closer to him, sealing our lips together with another kiss.

I got the feeling that life with Callan Bronson was going to be pretty damn sweet.

It was a good thing I had a sweet tooth.

32

CALLAN

After my lessons for the day were complete, I'd waited for Sage to say goodbye to the girls so I could drive her home. She was pretty buzzed by the time seven o'clock came around, so after I drove her and Avery to their house, I'd tucked Sage in first. She'd fallen asleep before Avery could finish brushing her teeth, which didn't surprise me. She and the girls had been laughing and talking the entire day.

After Avery was done getting ready for bed, I'd tucked her in, too. She'd demanded I tell her a bedtime story, so I told her all about how I got my first horse. She was asleep before the midway mark in my story, exhausted from her big day helping my dad on the ranch. She was so eager to learn all of it, her eyes lighting up with just the mere mention of ranch chores.

SCRAPE THE BARREL

Before I met Sage, my head was a dark place. Heading into town always made my heart race with the unknown of who I might get stuck in a conversation with or how long I'd be out. I tried to avoid the trip as often as I could, keeping to the ranch and my house. If I went out, it was with my brothers to the bar for some pool, and then I'd go home. That's how I liked it.

But then I met Sage, and suddenly, going to town wasn't so scary.

My heart would race for an entirely different reason—the anticipation of seeing her.

Watching her face light up when she saw me.

Hearing her laugh at my ridiculous jokes.

And knowing that she felt like my person.

The moment I looked forward to her coming for Avery's lessons or seeing her, even if just for a few minutes, I knew I was down bad for Sage McKinley.

Being into someone like that scared me for the longest time after my ex gave me an ultimatum and left, and while I ultimately chose this ranch, I didn't regret it for a second.

Hard things happened for a reason. I'd always believe that.

All those hard things I endured, they led me straight to Sage.

I'd do it all a thousand times over again if it brought me to where I was today.

***

The next morning, the cowbell above the door dinged as I walked in, and Sage's head popped up from behind the counter.

"Hey," I said.

"I'm about to close if you want to wait for me," she replied, ducking back down behind the counter to continue with what she was doing.

I checked the time on my phone, seeing it was two minutes until closing.

Close enough.

Turning the deadbolt on the door, I flipped the sign to closed.

Her head popped up again with the snick of the lock.

"I could've done that," she said, blowing a stray piece of hair out of her eyes.

I slipped my hands into the pockets of my jeans, cruising through the cafe like I had all the time in the world. With her, I did. Now that I had her, I couldn't imagine a life without her in it.

"It's no problem," I said, glancing at the clean tables. "Already did closing duties?"

She stood, brushing her hands on her apron. "Yeah, I figured I'd try to get out of here as soon as I could to come see you."

One corner of my mouth ticked up as she got to work wiping the crumbs away in the bakery case. "So thoughtful."

I came around the counter, sliding my hands out of my pockets as I walked up behind her. Her ass grazed my jeans as I brushed her hair over her shoulder.

"I'll be done soon," she said, continuing with her task.

"Take your time." My lips brushed her neck as I brought my mouth to her skin. She smelled so sweet after a day here, and I wanted to taste every inch of her.

"Well, I won't be done soon if you're doing that." A blush crawled up her neck, and from this angle, I could see down her shirt.

"I plan for this to take a very, very long time," I said, my voice laced with the severe craving of her.

She paused her wiping, straightening her back so it was flush with my chest. "I'm starting to think you don't mean me cleaning."

My lips twitched as my tongue darted out at the soft skin on her neck. "Catching on."

My hands palmed her waist, sliding down to untie her apron. After it came loose, I lifted it over her head and let it fall to the floor in a heap, then moved my hands to her ass.

"Every second since you called me your boyfriend yesterday, I've been craving you," I admitted. The way she stood up for me and told that woman off, it awoke something in me.

I reached around her front, undoing the button and zipper on her jeans, then tugged them down in a flash, causing her to reach up and grip the top of the bakery case to keep herself steady.

"Callan," she started.

"What, baby?" I continued to pepper her neck with slow kisses.

"There's windows," she said, pointing out the obvious.

My fingers slid into the waistline of her panties, eliciting goosebumps to freckle her skin.

"Windows don't bother me," I told her.

Her breath hitched as my finger ghosted over her clit.

"Unless you want me to stop," I began.

Her fingers curled against the top of the case. "N-no."

I smirked, removing my hand from her panties to slide her shirt off. It took all I had in me not to rip her clothing apart trying to get to her. I needed her, but I didn't want to rush it.

Her shirt landed beside the apron, but her bra stayed on.

"Panties. I want them off."

She reached down, shimmying out of them with ease, tossing them to the floor.

"Hands on the case," I instructed.

Her teeth caught her bottom lip and I grabbed her chin, turning her head to the side so she could see me. "You be nice to that mouth. I may need it later."

She nodded, wetting her lips. I faced her forward again, grabbing her hips to position her ass at the perfect angle, then freed myself from my jeans.

Something about her being so exposed while I was still clothed made this that much hotter. I didn't give a fuck about the windows or the empty streets outside. My entire focus was on Sage and relieving this ache she left in me yesterday.

I dragged the head of my cock between her legs, then let spit fall between us to wet my cock more. Rubbing it to the base, I glided into her with ease, moving to hold her hips in place as I buried deep inside her.

"What a naughty girl, getting fucked in your little cafe."

She let out a small moan as she leaned forward a bit more. I moved inside her, my rhythm slow and torturous. All I wanted was to fill her, to hear her scream as I made her come, but I also didn't want this blissful feeling to end.

I'd fuck her all night if she'd let me.

Reaching up, I grabbed a fistful of her hair, bending her head back slightly. Her breaths quickened as my pace picked up, the sight of me sliding in and out of her fucking beautiful.

What I was doing to her in here was a contrast to the light pink walls and plants spread around the eating area. It was bright and airy in here, and everything I was doing to her in this moment was filthy.

She reached down to rub her clit, keeping one hand on the bakery case. As soon as her fingers started working, her pussy tightened around me.

Her moans filled the empty cafe, mixing with the sound of mine. Our bodies meshed together, every wave of pleasure like fucking ecstasy.

Releasing her hair, I pulled out of her to spin her around, instantly lifting her in my arms. She wrapped her legs around my waist, and I reached between us, sliding back into her. My thrusts were demanding this time, the speed sporadic as her nails dug into the back of my neck.

She gasped out my name as I went deeper, knowing I hit that spot inside of her that made her see stars.

"Yeah, baby?"

But I knew what I was doing.

"Right there, please, fuck—" And then she screamed my name so loud, I thought those windows she was so worried about might break. Her head fell to my shoulder as her body tensed, but I didn't stop.

I didn't want to ever fucking stop.

Her nails dug into my skin even harder, and I knew they'd leave a mark, which I would wear proudly. I wanted everyone in this damn town to know Sage McKinley was mine.

After her orgasm ebbed, I kept her in my arms, my cock still buried inside her, and walked around the counter to the front of the cafe.

"What are you doing?" she asked, lifting her head.

"Staking my claim," I said as I pressed her back to the glass and continued to fuck her.

"Callan, what if someone sees?" Her voice was full of breath, and I got the idea that even if someone did, she wouldn't care. Not with her legs wrapped around me and my dick seated so deep inside her, I didn't think it'd ever come out.

"Let them."

I looked up at her to find her cheeks rosy. She was so fucking beautiful. Every inch of her.

My lips captured hers, my tongue diving between her plump lips.

Our breaths mingled, our tongues dancing together like neither of us could get enough.

Her hand came between us to find her clit again, and it took seconds before she was exploding around me again.

The feel of her pussy tightening on my dick made black dots cross my vision, and then my hands were gripping her thighs as I let go.

Every thought, every movement, halted as pleasure overtook my senses. My orgasm rippled through me as hers continued laying claim to her.

After we caught our breath, I slowly lowered her to the ground, but I didn't move away. My hands cupped her cheeks, angling her head up to mine so I could kiss her again.

I didn't think I could ever get tired of kissing her. Of tasting her. Of being with her.

After I pulled back, she said, "Thankfully for you, no one walked by."

I looked up, scanning the street with my eyes peeled. "I swore I saw someone."

She batted my arm and I laughed.

"No one was out there, don't worry. Almost the entire town is at movie night in the park."

She gasped. "I missed the movie?"

My mom had taken Avery to the park to watch the movie so Sage could join them after, but there was no way she'd make it before the end credits now.

"I'll make it up to you," I told her.

She crossed her arms, then realized she still wasn't wearing any clothes. Dropping her arms, she moved around me, going back behind the counter to start dressing herself. "How?"

"I'll bring enchiladas for Avery's birthday dinner."

She frowned at me as she pulled her jeans up.

"How do I know you make good enchiladas?"

I shrugged. "Guess you'll have to find out."

After getting fully dressed, minus the apron, she walked back around the counter and leaned against it. I stood in front of her, rubbing my hands up and down her sides.

"So is this what being your girlfriend is going to be like?" she asked.

I smirked. "Me having sex with you at your place of work?"

She nodded.

"You could always come have sex with me at mine. There's horse stalls, hay bales—" She shoved my shoulder lightly, her smile stretching her lips.

I kissed her cheek, then moved my lips to graze her ear. "Sometimes I just can't stop thinking about you."

"Sometimes, huh?" she snarked.

"Alright, all the time." I pulled back, looking at her. "Is that a crime?"

"No," she admitted, her smile still wide and beautiful as ever. "It's quite the opposite actually."

"Good. Because I like being able to kiss you whenever, no matter where we are."

She raised a brow. "Just kiss me?"

My smile took on a devilish glint. "Don't tempt me, Sage McKinley."

But something told me she'd be doing that without even trying.

33

CALLAN

The soles of my boots brushed against the jute doormat as I stomped the dirt off. I'd moved all my lessons for this Saturday into the week so I could take that day off for Avery's birthday party. My week was packed because of it, but I wouldn't miss her party or her birthday dinner for anything.

As much as admitting it scared me, I was growing attached to Avery. Her mother and I were already set in stone, but earning that little girl's trust and love was important.

I found my mom in the kitchen prepping pie crusts for Avery's party this weekend. Though there would be cake, Avery had apparently talked her into making three different kinds of pies for her party as well.

"Good day?" Mom asked as she rolled out the dough.

"Been doing lessons back to back since seven a.m., so it's been a day to say the least." Some of the local kids were homeschooled, which made their schedules a bit more flexible. I'd fit them in during the hours I'd typically be helping Dad out with the cows, which meant he'd been alone with Bailey most of the day.

Leaning my hands against the counter, I saw the smile on Mom's face.

"What?"

She shook her head. "You really like them."

I wasn't sure if 'like' covered it anymore.

I reached up to take my hat off, my other hand running through my hair. "I just moved some things around so I could make it this weekend. It's nothing big."

She narrowed her eyes at me, pausing her rolling. "You've never changed your schedule for a woman."

I knew she was referencing my ex and my inability to take on less clients just to spend more time with her. Back then, I hadn't wanted to. But with Sage, it didn't seem all that terrible of an idea.

It was a wonder how feelings could be swayed because of one person.

"It's not just for her. I don't want to disappoint Avery," I told her.

She set the rolling pin on the counter next to the dough and brushed her hands off. "You're not fooling me."

I could feel the blush crawling up my neck. Talking to my mom came easy, but if it was about girls, I couldn't get the words out to anyone. Some part of talking about the person you liked felt vulnerable, like you were giving people the ability to hurt you by opening up that way. And if more people knew about my feelings for Sage, the more official it became. It wouldn't just be between me and her anymore. It'd be public, and I wanted to be one hundred percent sure that was what she wanted.

"You can't avoid things because you think they'll end badly," Mom said. "What if it ends up amazing?"

"I'm not saying it wouldn't." Hell, it already *was* amazing. She'd called me her boyfriend, and while it had come as a bit of a shock in the moment, I didn't want to be anything else.

"But you're not talking about it, and that tells me you're scared."

She knew me too damn well.

"I don't want to mess this up with her and her daughter. They've got their own things going on, and I don't want to overwhelm them with this. I'm happy with whatever Sage wants us to be at the moment, and I'll move at her pace."

Mom stared at me, not a hint of her thoughts showing on her face. "That's what love is, Callan. Going through this life with whatever is thrown at you, together. Their things become yours and vice versa."

I'd already let her problems become my own, and I wanted it that way. Sage didn't deserve to go through any of this alone, and if I had to guess, she felt the same way about me.

"I'll try to open up," I said.

Mom picked up the roller again. "You can take on the world's burdens, but let the world take some of yours, too."

My brows pulled together. "Is there something you're trying to hint at here?"

She drew in a deep breath, looking down at the dough. She studied it for a moment, then said, "Beckham is coming home."

My blood went cold with the thought of what that might mean. "Is he hurt?"

She shook her head, moving her gaze to me again. "No. God, no. He's okay. He's taking a break from rodeo."

"Can he even do that?" I wasn't sure what all the rules were, but he had to be bound by some kind of contract.

She gave an inch of a shrug. "I guess so. He didn't go into much detail, but I'm sure he will when he gets here."

If she said he wasn't hurt, then I believed her, but not knowing the reason he was taking a break worried me all the more.

"When will he be here?" I asked.

"He said he has to wrap some things up, so he's hoping a few weeks."

I nodded, watching as she got back to rolling out the dough. Knowing he'd be home and not risking his life on those broncs should make me feel better, but it did little to comfort me right now.

Setting my hat back on my head, I opened the fridge to pull my enchilada dish out. I'd left it here so I could grab it after my lessons and head straight to Sage's house. A quick glance at the clock told me I didn't have time to shower like I'd planned. More time than I thought had passed since I walked inside.

"I'll see you tomorrow," I said as I walked behind my mom toward the door.

"Drive safe, and tell Avery I said happy birthday."

"Will do."

With the dish in hand, I headed for my truck and fought the urge to call Beckham and ask what was going on. He'd tell us when he was ready, and tonight was about Avery.

I had to learn that I didn't need to carry the weight of everyone's problems on my shoulders all the time. Worrying about everyone else wouldn't ease the anxiety that always sat on my chest like a brick. I couldn't be in control of everything all the time, keeping everyone safe and healthy.

I was finally starting to learn my limits, and though it was going against my instincts to not pick up that phone and call him, it wouldn't be the end of the world.

***

After parking my truck on the street, I walked up the driveway with the enchilada dish in hand, heading for the front door. Sage had texted me earlier to come in when I got here, but when I reached for the handle, it didn't turn.

Frowning, I knocked on the door, then waited. Moments later, the door swung open, and Sage was standing there in an oversized t-shirt and leggings.

Avery was making crash noises somewhere in the house, most likely playing with her toys, as I stepped inside. Sage closed the door behind me, bolting it.

"Everything okay?" I asked, nodding toward the door.

She wrung her hands together, then stopped and wiped them on her shirt. "The oven is preheated if you want to pop those in."

Then she disappeared down the hall.

My brows drew together as I watched her go, but instead of following her, I entered the kitchen to put the dish in the oven.

"Callan!" Avery squealed when she saw me from the living room.

"Aves! Happy birthday!" I set the glass dish on the counter right as she shot around the corner and into my arms. Lifting her under the armpits, I spun her around, then plopped her back on the ground.

"Did you bring gifts?" she asked, the biggest smile on her face.

"I brought enchiladas," I said, taking the covering off the top. Opening the oven door, I slid them in, then turned on a timer.

"That's not a gift," she stated with a frown.

"No? But you love food." I left the plastic wrap on the counter in case we needed to reuse it later.

"Yeah, but I love gifts, too."

I hummed. "I guess I forgot."

Her mouth dropped open on a gasp as a piece of her hair fell over her forehead. "You what?!"

I crouched down in front of her, brushing the hair out of her face. "I'm just kidding, Aves. I'm bringing your gifts for your party so you can show them to everyone."

She huffed a breath of air out of her nose. "But I wanted some today."

"You are. You're getting one gift," I told her.

Her face lit up. "Really?"

"Yep. Enchiladas."

Her smile fell again, but I knew she was faking it. She may not remember, but during one of our lessons, she told me her favorite food was enchiladas because of the sauce.

"What if I told you I put extra sauce on them just for you?"

"What color?" she asked skeptically.

"Red," I answered confidently. Red sauce was far superior than green.

She tried to hide the smile that threatened to show again. Man, she was stubborn, but undoubtedly adorable.

"I may forgive you," she said.

"Good. Can't go through this life without that."

"Without what?"

"You by my side. You ever heard of a sidekick?"

She nodded. "Like superheroes."

"Yep. And I'm just thinking, one day, if you get really good at riding, maybe you can be my sidekick out on the ranch."

She gasped. "Really?"

"Mhmm. But you can't really be that if you don't forgive me sometimes."

"I forgive you all the time!" she said as a way of ensuring she'd get this role.

I chuckled. I really hoped so.

"Why don't you go play with your ponies while I go talk to your mom, and I'll let you know when dinner is ready?"

She wrapped her arms around my waist and I swallowed the lump climbing my throat. I never thought the adoration of a little girl would make me this emotional.

"Thank you for the enchiladas with extra red sauce," Avery said, her voice muffled in my jeans.

"You're welcome, Aves."

She let me go and turned, running back to her toys. I headed out of the kitchen and down the hall to Sage's bedroom. Her door was open, so I slipped inside and closed it slightly behind me, leaving it cracked in case Avery needed us.

Sage was sitting on the edge of the bed, staring down at her phone. I sat next to her and wrapped an arm around her, drawing her in closer to me.

"What's wrong?"

She held the phone out to me and I took it with my other hand, looking at what was on the screen.

> **Unknown:** Did you get the money?

My hand threatened to crush the phone in its grip, but I locked it, setting it on the bed next to me.

"They haven't found him yet," she said, confirming what I already knew.

"They will," I assured her, running a hand up and down her arm.

Sage looked up at me, her eyes slightly glassy. "And if they don't?"

"Then I will."

She straightened. "Callan..."

My arm dropped from around her so I could grab her hand. "I'm not going to let him terrorize you, Sage."

She stood, then slowly began pacing. "I didn't want you in the middle of this." A few more steps. "I'm sorry. I—"

Getting to my feet, I placed myself in front of her so she had to stop. "Sage, look at me."

Her chest was rising and falling with the onslaught of anxiety as it crashed into her like a tidal wave, threatening to bring her under.

Her eyes met mine, and I saw the panic swirling in them.

"You don't need to be scared. I've got you."

"Yes, I do. Avery is vulnerable every day, I'm alone every day, and you can't be there all the time."

I cupped her face, the tips of my fingers buried in her hair. "And you are safe."

She shook her head, the glass in her eyes becoming pools of tears.

"Yes, you are. I don't know what Portland was like, but Bell Buckle sticks together. It's not just the police, it's the community. We all look out for each other, and no one is going to let him put his hands on you or Avery, especially me."

She blinked, a tear spilling over her cheek. My thumb brushed it away, then I pulled her close, wrapping both arms around her and squeezing.

Seeing her panic like this made me want to stop at nothing until I was the one to put her ex six feet under. I didn't know if a jail cell would suffice when he was caught.

"They're going to find him, and he'll be gone for good."

She nodded, her hands fisting in my shirt. I'd never be able to live with myself if something happened to Sage, and knowing this asshole was out there finding joy in tormenting her filled me with a rage I'd never felt before.

The alarm went off on my phone from my back pocket, announcing that the enchiladas were done heating up. Pulling the phone out, I silenced it, then shoved it back in my jeans.

I pressed a kiss to her forehead. "Don't let anyone dim that light of yours."

With a sniffle, she looked at me. "It's hard when you're around."

"Good. It should only shine brighter. And for the people that dim it? You don't need to dwell on them. They're not worth the space in your head if they aren't making your life better."

She blinked away her tears, then grabbed my hand. "How did I get so lucky?"

"I don't know if luck has anything to do with it, baby."

"No?"

I shook my head. "Things happen for a reason, I reckon. And you may be the reason I go to town, or the reason I look forward to getting out of bed now, but I won't hang that up on luck. The world knew I needed someone to pull me out of my head, and it sent me you."

She looked at me for a moment, really *looked* at me, then leaned forward and pressed her lips to mine. It felt like we were made to fit together like this.

Pulling back, I squeezed her hand once. "Ready for some enchiladas?"

She nodded, and I led us out of the room toward the kitchen.

"Is it done?" Avery asked from where she sat in the middle of the living room.

"All ready for a special birthday girl to dig in," I replied as I dropped Sage's hand to grab an oven mit.

"Why don't you go wash your hands and we'll have it all set at the table by the time you get back?" Sage asked.

Avery got up from her spot and her tiny feet padded down the hall to the bathroom.

I pulled the dish out of the oven, closed the door, then switched the knob to off. Sage set some heat-resistant mats on the table, so I placed the dish on top of them as she set plates and utensils out.

"That's a lot of sauce," Sage pointed out as she eyed the enchiladas.

I smirked, coming up behind her as she rounded the table to wrap my arms around her waist. My nose nuzzled her neck as goosebumps crawled up her skin.

"I could give you some special sauce," I mumbled.

Despite her grin, she tried to pry my hands from around her. "Please do not tell me you just compared enchilada sauce to that."

I chuckled, but it was cut short by Avery saying, "That's a big enchilada!" as she came into the dining area.

Sage's cheeks turned a deep shade of red as I unwrapped my arms from around her. I stepped to the side of her, keeping one hand on her lower back, and cleared my throat.

"It's a bunch of enchiladas," I corrected. I wasn't sure if she thought the entire dish was just a single one.

Avery took her seat at the head of the table and I dropped my hand to Sage's ass, giving it a quick pinch before I slid into my own chair.

She pursed her lips, shooting me a glare as she sat down.

"So, Avery. Do you know the cowboy blessing?" I asked.

"No. What's that?"

Sage watched the two of us talk as I said, "Well, it's this saying some people do before dinner." I didn't do this all that often, but with Avery's interest in the ranch, I thought she might like it.

"What's the saying?"

I set my napkin on my lap. "May your belly never grumble, may your heart never ache. May your horse never stumble, may your cinch never break."

Her smile grew as I spoke. "Is that what all cowboys say?"

Sage reached forward to grab the spatula so she could dish Avery up a portion.

"Some of them," I told her.

"Is that what you and my mama are gonna say now?" she asked.

"If I'm here, sure," I replied.

"Aren't you dating my mama?"

The enchilada balanced on the spatula toppled on top of the others as Sage's hand fumbled. "What?" Sage asked, surprised at the question.

"You guys are always touching and doing yucky stuff," Avery said.

I bit my lip to hide my smile as I looked to Sage on this one. I really wasn't sure how to tread on this.

"Well, Aves—" Sage started.

"You don't have to keep it a secret, you know," Avery stated.

Sage gathered herself and finished dishing Avery's food up, then glanced at me before saying, "We're dating."

Avery used her fork to tear a bite of enchilada off instead of cutting it. "Okay."

Sage reached over with her fork and knife, cutting her food for her. "Are you okay with that?"

Avery nodded as she chewed.

I braced myself for more, but nothing happened. No questions, no tears. She just watched her mom cut her food, then dug in once she was done. Sage and I stared at her for a minute, both expecting her to say something, but she didn't.

After a deep inhale, Sage set her fork and knife on the edge of her plate and dished up her own food, then handed me the spatula.

We all ate as Avery told us about all the gifts she hoped to get tomorrow, and as I chewed and drank and listened, it hit me.

They were becoming my family.

And I didn't want it any other way.

34

SAGE

Giggles and conversation flowed through my small backyard as kids ran past mingling parents. Everyone had started arriving early based off Avery's instruction to get here an hour before the invitation stated, which was unbeknownst to me as I opened the door to the first guest a little over forty-five minutes ago.

Callan had helped me set up the decorations last night, so at least that was taken care of, but cookies still needed to be iced, the cake still needed candles, the food hadn't arrived yet, and my helping hands were doing the best they could to offer me assistance with all of it. Pudding was locked in Avery's room down the hall and she was aware that she wasn't supposed to go in there until after the party, yet I couldn't help but glance down that way every few minutes to be sure no one was letting the cat out. The last thing I needed today, on top of everything else, was the cat getting loose again. Thankfully, we'd passed our Food Safety Inspection at the cafe with flying colors, so that was off my shoulders in time for the party.

My hair was thrown in a messy ponytail, matching my stained apron, as I'd been in the middle of the cookies when her first friend arrived.

Some of the parents had stayed, but others had dropped their kid and left, which meant everyone was under my supervision, along with the eyes of whatever other adults were here. Adults including Brandy, Oakley, and Lettie, but I wasn't very confident in their ability to keep things under control because last I'd heard, Brandy was egging someone on to climb the tree in the middle of the backyard.

That was just what I needed—a kid to fall off a branch and end up with a broken arm.

"Is that icing meant for the cookies or you?" Callan's voice filled the air as I used my shoulder to brush a rogue piece of hair out of my face.

I looked down at my apron, then back to the cookie I was currently mutilating with my shaky hands and runny icing. Nothing was going to plan.

"The cookies," I mumbled.

I didn't have time to spare a glance at Callan. Today had to be perfect for Avery.

"Hey," Callan said. The sound of a gift bag crinkling filled my ears as he set his present down. Then he rounded the counter and grabbed the piping bag from me.

"I need to finish these," I told him, but reluctantly let him take the bag anyway. It was sticky and covered in edible glitter.

"They're not going to come out the way you want if you keep rushing," he stated, as if that wasn't obvious.

"People started arriving early," I told him as I grabbed a paper towel off the counter to wipe my hands.

A corner of his mouth tilted down. "Avery's doing, I take it?"

I nodded and silently wished he had been early, too. He seemed to always be calm, keeping everything together when it was so clearly falling apart.

"No one's going to blame you if they're not done right this second."

"I know, but I just want it to be perfect."

He set the piping bag on the counter and grabbed both my hands. "Avery will think today is perfect, regardless of whether every cookie is covered in pink glitter icing or not."

He was right, but it didn't stop me from wanting to get it all done.

I released one of his hands and went to reach for the icing, but he snatched it back. Walking me backwards, he caged me at the counter, and I frowned up at him. "I need to get back to it, Callan."

"Breathe, Sage. You're going a mile a minute right now. You deserve to enjoy the day, too."

I huffed a breath, and he added, "Your little girl is six years old. *Six*. Think of how those years flew by."

I did. I always did. Every day was gone in the blink of an eye, and I wanted all those moments back to treasure them just a little bit more.

"Today will be over before you know it, and all Avery is going to remember is that her mom threw her the best birthday party out of her whole class." He reached up, brushing that damn rogue hair behind my ear. "So enjoy it with me."

I glanced at the mess of the cookies on the counter as Brandy walked in the room from the back sliding door. Callan looked over at her.

"Hey, Brandy. Can you handle this for a minute?" he asked, gesturing to the cookies.

"On it," she said. She was wearing one of the unicorn party hats Avery had picked out for the party, and I would've laughed if I didn't feel like crying at the moment.

"Come with me," Callan said, lacing his fingers with mine.

"Callan, I really need to—"

"Just for a minute."

Sighing, I conceded, letting him guide me down the hall as Brandy got to work on the sugar cookies. In all reality, the kids probably didn't need more sugar, but Avery had insisted. It was one of her favorite cookies.

"What are we doing?" I asked as he led me into my bedroom.

He closed the door behind him, making sure to lock it, then brought me over to the bed.

It dawned on me what his plan was.

"Oh, no. Callan, that's going to take a lot longer than a minute, and—"

"Are you doubting how fast I can make you come?" he asked, arching a brow at me.

"You really think you can do that in a minute?" He was out of his mind.

He took his cowboy hat off, placing it on my head. "Start the timer," he said, releasing my hand to bunch the bottom of my dress up above my thighs.

"My phone is in the kitchen."

"Better start counting, then."

"I'm not going to count," I bit back.

"Then you better take my word for it."

And then this man—this overly-caring, husky, thoughtful man—was on his knees before me. Calloused hands slid my panties down my legs with no restraint, and his head disappeared beneath my sundress. The instant he was out of view, his mouth was on me.

"Holy fuck," I said with more breath than actual words.

He nipped at my clit with his teeth, and my knees almost buckled on the spot. It hadn't even been ten seconds.

His fingers dug into my thighs, and then he slid two digits into me. His tongue flattened against my core as he licked me from my entrance to my clit. He moved at a speed I couldn't handle, my body relaxing and tensing around him all at the same time. His tongue flicked over my clit in rhythm with his fingers, and my thighs were already trembling.

He pulled his fingers out of me, then stood, letting my dress fall back over my thighs. He grabbed my hand to bring me over to the bed.

"What happened to your minute of my time?" I teased.

"Fuck the minute. I want to savor you."

He laid down on the bed, pulling me on top of him, then started to tug me forward.

"What are you—"

"Ride my face, baby. Soak me."

My brows shot up. "Callan—"

"Sage, if you don't sit your pretty little pussy on my face right fucking now, I'll make you beg until I allow you to come, and I'm not letting you leave this room until you fucking do."

I didn't even have time to consider as he hefted me to his shoulders as if I weighed nothing.

I'd let this cowboy manhandle me any day if I had anything to say about it.

My thighs were on either side of his face as my palms laid flat against the headboard. He hiked up the skirt of my dress so that he had easy access, and then the fabric covered his face and what he began doing to my body.

His rough hands slid up the sides of my thighs, coming around to grab my ass in a strong pleasure-inducing grip. He tugged me down, causing me to fall onto him. All of my body weight was pressing my pussy onto his mouth, and the sensation was like nothing I'd ever felt before.

Involuntarily, my hips moved, rubbing my pussy against his mouth. His tongue was out, lapping up every bit of me he could get, and the stubble on his cheeks grated on my thighs.

Every nerve ending lit up inside me like a blazing furnace. My hands wrapped around the top of the headboard, using the leverage to quicken my pace as I rode his face.

Somehow, not being able to see him under my dress made it all the more attractive, knowing he was down there doing the unspeakable to my body and I couldn't see a bit of it.

He pulled my clit into his mouth as I continued moving my hips, and my breath quickened at the pleasure rolling through me.

I tried holding back just to prove him wrong—that it'd be longer than a minute—but I knew he wasn't being literal, and I'd already lost track of time.

Instead of trying to hold it in any longer, I relaxed against him, letting his lips suck my clit in bursts, his tongue flicking over the bundle, and then I fucking exploded.

Every star, every galaxy, bursted behind my eyes as I squeezed them shut and tried to keep quiet. The last thing I needed was someone hearing what was going on in here.

He continued sucking on my clit, and once my thighs relaxed the slightest bit around his face, he moved his tongue to my entrance, licking up every last drop of me. I gathered the skirt of my dress, moving it away so I could slide off of his face.

Once I was straddling his hips again, he smiled up at me. "Baby, it should be illegal to taste that good."

"Probably all the sweets," I joked.

He sat up, placing his hands on my waist as my arms came around his neck. "I don't know what it is, but keep doing it. I want you to ride my face every night."

My fingers slid into his hair. "Every night, huh? You're going to come here that often?"

He shrugged, his hands idly running up and down my sides, the fabric of my dress bunching up with each swipe. "Or you guys could move into my house, and we'd see each other all the time."

My fingers froze in their strokes. "What?"

He blushed, but it felt like all the blood had drained from my own face. "When you're both ready, of course. I don't know when your lease is up here, but we could figure something out. I have the space, the land. It's a little farther from town, but we'd see each other every day."

"Callan—"

"I know. You don't have to decide right now. I just wanted to throw the idea out there." His face fell a bit, but he covered it with a smile.

He wasn't expecting me to answer right now—he'd never put that pressure on me, but I also didn't know how I would tell Avery if I did decide that would be the best move for us.

She'd stay at the same school and nothing would change aside from our house, but then again...everything would change.

Callan and I would be more official than just a title to our relationship. We'd be *living* together.

It shouldn't scare me, but somehow it did.

I hadn't lived with anyone else since Jason, and with how things were going with that right now, I didn't want to bring any more of that drama into his life.

"Sage," he started, giving my hips a small squeeze. "You don't have to decide right now."

"I know. It's just..." How did I even explain that it wasn't him I was nervous about living with? It was merging my life with someone else's again with the risk that it could go south. Callan would never treat me the way Jason did, but it also didn't ease that part of my brain that would always be terrified of the possibility.

His hands came up to cup the sides of my neck. "Get out of that beautiful head of yours, baby. I'm not him."

He was right.

He wasn't him, and my past wasn't my future.

Callan Bronson was safe, caring, and treated me like both the strongest and most delicate flower on the planet.

My head needed to comprehend that not every relationship would end up that way.

It meant more to me than I could ever express that Callan was understanding about my past. Even he didn't let it define me, so I shouldn't either.

"Can I let you know after all of this chaos is over?" I asked.

He nodded. "Of course. I didn't mean to spring it on you right now. It's just been on my mind, but I should have waited."

I shook my head, threading my fingers deeper into his hair to pull his face closer to mine. "It's not that. I just want to talk to Avery about it first, and having that conversation while she's hyped up on sugar probably wouldn't be the best. She'd pack her things tonight if I gave her the option."

The corner of his mouth ticked up. "I guess you're right." He pressed a kiss to my lips, then said, "Ready to go tackle this party?"

"Ready as ever." I got off of him, standing so I could straighten my yellow dress, then looked in the mirror to fix my hair.

"Thanks to me," he sarcastically remarked.

I shot him a joking glare in the mirror. "I would've been fine without it."

In the reflection of the mirror, he cocked a brow in challenge. "Don't make me do it again."

I grabbed for the door handle right as he darted for me. Doing quick work of unlocking the knob, I swung it open right as he got his arms around me.

"Too bad," I said with mock deflation.

"I'll make you pay for that later," he promised.

I silently wished that he would.

"One question before we go back out there."

I turned in his arms as he loosened his hold. "What's that?"

"Avery's gift. I got her a stuffed horse," he started, watching me closely.

"I'm sure she'll love it," I replied, but it sounded more like a question.

"It's not *just* a stuffed horse, though."

My brows drew together in confusion. "Okay…"

"It's a real horse."

My eyes widened. "It's outside?"

He shook his head, his fingers gripping the fabric of my dress. "No, no. I need to go pick it up, but I'll be bringing him to the ranch. I got her a stuffed one that looks just like it, but I wanted to make sure this was okay with you before I gave it to her."

He bought Avery a horse.

This man who had shown up in my life not so long ago bought my daughter an entire horse—her dream that she'd been begging me to get for her for ages.

"Uh, I— Yes?"

He smiled, but the act looked nervous, like he couldn't gauge my reaction clearly. If I had to be honest, I couldn't either.

"You don't have to pay for a dime of it. He's got a place to live and hay to eat, I just didn't want to overstep."

"You're not. It's just…"

"You're shocked."

I nodded, but before I could get another word out, Avery came barreling down the hall toward us. "Mama! I wanna open gifts!"

I turned to her as Callan dropped one of his arms from around my waist. "Okay. Let's go open gifts."

She squealed with her friends behind her, then they all took off toward the living room. I looked back to Callan. "She's going to love it."

"You think so?" His voice was a bit shaky, like he was anxious for our reactions.

"Of course, she is. I know I already do."

"You're not mad?"

I shook my head. "Just in disbelief, is all. I never thought Avery would have the opportunity to have her own horse, and now you're making that come true, and it's just... a lot to take in." Expressing how happy I was over the whole thing was hard to put into words. Obviously, I was surprised, but it was clear he'd fallen for her as quickly as he had with me.

It was my own dream to find someone who loved Avery as much as I did, and if I wasn't sure before, I was now. He loved her like his own.

That's all I ever wanted.

"You tell me if I'm ever too much," he said.

"Hey," I whispered, combing my fingers through his hair and bringing his face slightly closer to mine. "You're never too much." I knew what it felt like to feel like you were taking up too much space and wanted to shrink in on yourself. "You make life a lot more bearable, and I don't think I could ever get tired of you, even if I tried."

A small smile pulled at his mouth. "Right back at you, baby."

"Mama!" Avery called from the other room.

"We better go out there," I said, dropping my arms.

He nodded, intertwining his fingers with mine, and led us down the hall to twelve little girls all gathered around the table full of gifts.

Brandy sidled up next to us and muttered, "Gone a long time, huh?"

My cheeks heated as I elbowed her arm, eliciting a giggle from her. It was at that moment I realized I'd forgotten to put my underwear back on, and my hand instinctively smoothed down the folds of my dress, straightening them out as if everyone could tell.

"Can I open them now?" Avery asked, every pair of eyes on us.

I cleared my throat. "Go ahead," I answered, and she got to work unwrapping the gifts, all of her friends gasping and chatting about each one she opened.

After about seven gifts, she grabbed Callan's, smiling at him after she saw his name on the tag.

She reached into the bag and pulled out the stuffed animal, the fur a dark brown with white socks on each leg near the hooves. It had a little white stripe down the nose, and a black mane and tail.

"I love it! It looks like the horsey I drew," she said, not knowing it would be real in just a matter of days.

Callan had his arm wrapped around me where we stood as he told her, "The real one will be at the ranch next week."

It took her a moment to process what he said, and then her mouth popped open as her eyes turned the size of saucers. "A real live horse?"

He nodded. "You can name it, too."

"Really?" she squealed, her little hands gripping the stuffed animal so tight.

"Anything you want." His smile couldn't have been bigger if it tried, and I got the feeling he didn't just mean that in regards to the name of the horse.

Avery ran over, throwing her arms around him. He hugged her back, and I swore I saw a sheen in his eyes reflecting in the sunlight.

"Thank you," she said, her voice muffled in his shirt.

"Of course, Aves. Happy birthday."

She released him, angling her head back to look up at him. "The best birthday ever."

And when she turned back to her gifts, joining her friends again, I knew, without a doubt, that she was telling the truth.

It didn't make me feel bad in any way that I wasn't able to get her those things.

After all, parenting was supposed to be a joint task, and the fact that she now had a father-like figure to be there for her in ways that I couldn't made my heart threaten to burst with my admiration for him.

After never getting the feeling of being a family with her father, it felt nice to feel it with Callan.

It didn't matter who her dad was—Callan loved her for who *she* was.

And that's all I had ever wanted.

35

SAGE

The afternoon sun beat down on us the following Saturday as we prepared the horses for the Bottom of the Buckle Horse Rescue parade. Callan was supposed to pick Avery's horse up on Thursday, but the seller had an emergency so he had to push it to next week. Thankfully, Avery was looking forward to the parade and fair tonight, so she wasn't too bummed about the delay.

The county fair took place once a year in the next town over, and everyone from the surrounding towns showed up. The community always helped set everything up and volunteered to work booths if they needed extra hands, and the same went for the preparation of the parade.

A few of the ranch horses were here, which would be ridden by Callan and Lennon, and the rescues they brought along would be led by volunteers behind them. Charlotte and another volunteer typically held the banner, but this year, Avery would be doing it with her instead.

Avery had wanted to ride one of the horses, but Charlotte explained to her that it was a bit too risky with the chance that they could spook at something, given it was a busy event.

They only brought the rescue horses that were more used to people and noises, and never the skittish ones. They didn't want to spook them and have a horse running loose. The parade would only be a few minutes anyway, with it being a short walk down the main road through this town, then they'd be loaded back into the trailer to take home.

The awareness the parade brought to the rescue helped a ton, so they always opted to take part in it. Donations would flood in for months after, which made a huge difference in the coverage of medical bills and feed.

I made my way back over to Avery where she was brushing pink glitter paint into the mane of Callan's horse. He'd given her free rein to decorate Ace however she liked, so she took advantage of that and wanted his entire mane and tail to be pink.

"Here you go," I said, setting the plastic hair ties on the stool next to her.

"Can you help me braid his hair?" she asked, her fingers sticky with the paint.

"Of course." I grabbed a hair tie and got to work on the bits she'd already covered in pink. "Are you excited to be in the parade?"

She nodded. "Callan said he's gonna ride on my side."

"Did he?" I asked, my lips quirking up on the sides as I glanced over to where Callan was talking to a volunteer. He was wearing dark brown chaps and his tan cowboy hat, but all I wanted to do was take it all off and have my way with him.

Unfortunately, that'd have to wait until tonight.

He caught me staring and winked, the act instantly igniting a flame inside me.

I turned back to the braid as Avery said, "Yeah. Just wait until he sees Ace."

I was sure Callan would flaunt this horse around even more with the work Avery did on him. A little girly makeover wouldn't scare him away.

"He's going to love it."

There were people floating around everywhere, everyone helping each other out as they got ready. There were a few other nonprofits in the parade, but they were in various spots around the dirt parking lot getting ready with their own banners and volunteers.

Bottom of the Buckle was the only horse rescue in the county, but others were raising funds for other organizations.

All of the rides at the fair were already put together. Off of the main street, behind the small businesses, was a large grass lot that they'd set it up in every year. People could watch the parade, then hop on over to the fair to enjoy the rest of the night.

Avery and I had never come before. My anxiety was always too high at crowded events like this, but something about having Callan here, along with the entire Bronson family, made it a little more bearable. I wasn't constantly looking over my shoulder, despite Jason still being on the run. With a community like this, no one would let anything happen to us.

I had to believe we were safe, because the longer I told myself we weren't, we'd keep isolating ourselves and miss out on everything due to fear.

It was time I stopped letting that fear run our lives.

Beside me, a hand came up to pat Ace's neck, and I instantly knew who it was.

"Parade is starting soon," Callan said, watching me as my fingers worked the coarse hairs of Ace's mane.

"Almost done!" Avery said down by his tail.

"You still don't want to join us?" Callan asked.

I glanced at him as I continued braiding. "I want to watch you guys from the side. I'm hoping to get a few pictures."

He nodded and pulled a cookie out of his pocket. Ace instantly moved to take it from him, his big lips grabbing for it in the palm of Callan's hand as he held it out for him. "Need help with anything before the parade starts?"

"I have an extra ribbon I don't know what to do with," Avery said, fishing through her pocket to then hold it up with pink fingertips.

Callan eyed the light pink ribbon, approaching her. "I think I know just the place." He reached up to remove his hat, then crouched to prop it on his knee. Grabbing the piece of ribbon from Avery, he looped it through the band around his hat, tying it into a delicate bow. "How's that?"

"It'll match Ace so good!" Avery replied, elated.

"Avery, you ready?" Charlotte asked as she walked by with the banner rolled in her arms.

Avery quickly ran the remnants of paint on her fingers through the tip of Ace's tail, then spun to follow after Charlotte. "Ready!"

Callan stood, placing his cowboy hat back on his head as I watched her scurry off. She wiped her sticky hands on her jeans as Charlotte explained what her task was. She was so attentive to everything she said, her passion for this evident in her demeanor.

Looking at my work, I considered it good enough. I hadn't braided his entire mane, but half would have to suffice.

"She worked very hard," I told Callan as he surveyed his horse.

He nodded. "I'm suddenly feeling like my chaps should have confetti and sparkles on them."

"I can call Avery back, have her do that for you real quick."

He grinned, pulling me in for a kiss, then said, "Maybe next year."

"You'll have to take care of it yourself next year. I'm sure she'll be too busy decorating her own horse." Saying those words would take some getting used to. Even though Avery had been asking every day since her party when she was going to meet her horse, it still felt foreign on my tongue.

Stepping to the side, I gave Callan space so he could set his boot in the stirrup and heft himself up into the saddle.

He looked down at me, the pink ribbon shifting on his hat. "See you when it's done?"

I nodded. "I'll be waiting."

I set a hand on his leg, reaching up on my tip toes as he bent down to press his lips to mine. Every kiss with Callan was a reminder that our lives were only getting better from this point forward, together.

I readjusted his cowboy hat on his head before he straightened in the saddle.

"See you in a few," he said with a grin, then eased Ace into a walk so he could get to the head of the group. They were already lined up in the formation Charlotte had instructed them to stand in, so his mom gave him a playful side eye as he found his spot.

I took a quick picture of everyone lined up, with Callan and Ace standing just behind the banner Avery was holding. Her little hands were gripped tight on the material to keep it steady, and then they all started walking down the street behind the firefighter group ahead of them. Callan was a step late, caught up in staring back at me with a smile on his face.

In a crowd full of people, his eyes were glued on me.

"That's love," Lettie said, coming to stand beside me.

"What?" I asked, watching the next group start lining up behind them.

"The way he looks at you."

I shook my head. "We just recently made things official. He couldn't."

Lettie was quiet until I looked at her.

"My brother has always hidden his feelings with kindness, never letting anyone past those walls he has reinforced in his head. In the past, he was made to believe he couldn't be vulnerable without being controlled, yet he opened up for you after all those years of keeping to himself."

My teeth gnawed at the inside of my cheek. "I'm not following." Not because I didn't know what she was saying, I just didn't know if my brain was ready to hear it.

"You're his light at the end of the tunnel, Sage. You and Avery. I didn't think he'd ever let his feelings show for anyone, but then he found you. Don't be like me and push that person away because the timeline doesn't line up. Life is never going to be perfect enough to let someone in. You have to work to make it happen."

It wasn't that I was pushing him away, especially now. But I understood what she was telling me. Callan wasn't someone I'd ever take for granted, and I quickly figured that out shortly after we met.

"I won't," I promised her. Lettie looked out for her brothers like they looked out for her, and I loved that about the Bronsons. Not many families were as close as they were, and it filled my heart thinking one day, Avery and I might be a part of that.

Some days, it felt like we already were.

Lettie and I watched in silence as they made their way to the end of the street, then circled back. The entire time, Avery had the biggest smile on her face, and halfway back to us, Callan leaned over to place his hat on her head. She beamed up at him, the hat clearly way too big for her with the way it bobbed.

Things were so perfect right now, regardless of what was going on in the background.

All my mind could focus on was those two and the way they completed me.

We were happy.

36

CALLAN

Reed and our dad worked to get everything packed and loaded up so they could head back to the ranch with the horses. Most of the crowd had dispersed, heading over to the fair right behind all the buildings. The short walk was convenient, which was why they always did the same events in the same town each year.

Avery had helped my dad with his side of things, her little hand always moving to adjust my hat on her head. I'd have to get her one of her own if she wanted to be a cowgirl, but for the time being, mine would suffice.

"Did you have fun?" Sage asked, finding me in the cluster of people.

"Not as much fun as Avery," I replied. "Did you?"

She nodded as she slipped her hands into the pockets of her sundress. "You looked very cute up there."

Heat rose in my cheeks. "I did, did I?"

Another nod. "Bit distracting, if you ask me."

My arm snaked around her, bringing her close. "Is that so?"

Our noses were almost touching now as she fought a smile.

"Do you not like when I distract you?" I teased. Little did she know, she distracted me from any anxious thoughts that might've crept their way into my mind before. With Sage, I felt somewhat unstoppable.

"Depends how you're doing it."

"Mama!" Avery said, skipping over to us with a hand on my hat, holding it in place.

Sage didn't move away as she looked down at Avery.

"You looked so good out there!" Sage exclaimed.

Avery's little feet jumped up and down in place. "It was so much fun! Can I go on rides now?"

Before Sage could reply, my mom came up beside Avery. "Why don't I take her on some?"

"Are you sure?" Sage asked.

My mom nodded, then looked at Avery. "Can't go on any rides with Callan's big ol' hat like that."

As if it dawned on Avery that the hat was too big, she took it off, handing it back to me.

"I want a hat," she said with a small pout as I took it.

"I'll get you one. You can pick it out and everything," I told her.

Her eyes lit up as Charlotte reached out to grab her hand. "Yay!"

"What do you say?" Sage asked.

"Thank you," Avery answered, aiming it at me.

"You're welcome. Now go have fun. We'll see you in a little."

Charlotte and Avery disappeared as they headed over to the rides, leaving me and Sage alone.

"Do you want to go over there?" I asked. She fit in the crook of my arm like she was made to be there.

"You really want to go on rides?" she questioned, like she couldn't believe that a twenty-eight-year-old man could ever want such a thing. To be fair, I was deathly afraid of them, but I'd do anything if it made her happy. Plus, how hard could it be to shove that fear aside if it meant I got to see that beautiful smile light up her face?

"As if I wasn't the one to ask if you'd go on them with me." My hand slipped lower on her back, toward the curve of her ass under her pink-and-white plaid sundress. "Unless you had other plans?"

Pink tinged the apples of her cheeks as she pivoted, setting her hands on my chest. "What if I do?"

"Yeah?" My voice lowered so only she could hear me. "Does your plan include me hiking this pretty little dress up and making a mess of you?" My hands fisted in the fabric, the material rising ever so slightly up her thighs.

"It may," she said, her words laced with satin.

"That what you want, baby? Me to bring you over to my truck and have you ride my cock until your screams fill the cab?"

She swallowed, her throat bobbing. "Yes."

I dropped her dress and grabbed her hand, leading her over to where my truck was parked in the back of one of the parking lots. My windows were tinted, so the chances of someone seeing us were slim, but even if they did, all I needed was her panties moved aside, so she'd be covered.

I made quick work of removing my chaps once we got to the truck, tossing them in the bed before pulling the handle on the passenger door. I got in, then helped her into the cab. She maneuvered her legs around my thighs as I closed the door and locked it from the inside.

She set a hand on the seat behind me as I quickly unzipped my jeans, freeing my cock. Then I grabbed my hat, tossing it on the driver's seat.

"Are you sure we should do this?" she asked, even as she hiked her dress up her thighs.

"We don't have to if you don't feel comfortable."

Her teeth bit into her bottom lip as I reached up to brush a strand of hair behind her ears from where it was dangling in her face.

"I want to," she admitted.

My hands immediately tangled in her hair, pulling her face down to mine. Our lips met, the kiss slow and full of breath.

Reaching up under the fabric of her dress, I pushed her panties to the side to expose her slick center. I internally cursed at how wet she was, loving that her body responded to mine so easily.

After lining my cock up with her entrance, I grabbed her hips as her hands found my shoulders. I lowered her down onto me, her lips parting in a gasp, causing our kiss to break.

Once she was fully seated on me, a moan escaped her. I wanted to hear her make that sound all fucking night.

She slowly began rocking her hips, lifting herself to the tip of my cock and then burying it deep inside her again. With her on my lap, her breasts were so damn close to my face, and all I wanted was a taste.

Reaching up, I pulled a side of her dress down along with her bra so that her tit was out. My lips wrapped around the peaked nipple, my tongue instantly darting out to flick at it. Her hands tangled in my hair, keeping my face close to her as she let out another breathy moan.

My hand gripped her breast as my other stayed on her hip, moving with the pace she set. She was in control, riding me like she could do this all fucking night. Having her vulnerable for me like this in her cute little sundress made my cock impossibly harder.

Releasing her tit, I moved my mouth up her chest to her neck, relishing in the feel of her soft skin under my lips.

Her hand reached down between us, moving her dress out of the way so she could rub her clit.

I took my time kissing her neck, then moved back over her chest to her breast again, sucking the bud back into my mouth.

Her breath hitched, then her thighs tightened, and my name passed her lips as her entire core shook around me. Her pussy gripped my cock so tight, I saw stars, and then I came along with her.

My mouth popped off her tit as I groaned, my hand that was on her waist moving to grab her ass as she continued to milk every last ounce from me.

As her orgasm ebbed, she stayed seated on me, her forehead resting on my shoulder as she caught her breath.

"You should wear this dress more often," I said. The sight of her coming apart in it was my fucking undoing.

She let out a small chuckle. "You like it?"

"I fucking love it."

I felt her smile before she lifted her head to look at me. "I love you."

I froze, unable to even blink. "You—" I cleared my throat. "You love me?" Maybe I'd heard her wrong.

She nodded, her bottom lip disappearing as she worried it with her teeth.

"Me?"

She nodded again. "Yes, you. There's no one else in this truck."

"You're sure?"

"Should I not?"

I quickly shook my head. "No. No, you should, because I love you, too."

Her mouth slowly pulled into a smile before she crashed her mouth to mine in a kiss that stole every thought, breath, and feeling straight from me.

She pulled away, asking, "It's not too soon, right?"

"We're living on our own timeline, baby. If it's right, it's right."

She looked so damn beautiful sitting on me with her rosy cheeks and mussed up hair, her dress still hiked up her thighs with my cock still inside her.

"I like that," she said.

My mouth quirked up. "Me, too."

She smiled as I fixed her dress back over her breast, situated myself back in my pants, then reached for the locks. I opened the door and helped her out, making sure her dress was tugged down so she was decent.

Once we were both out of the truck, we headed toward the rides and booths where the screams of children filled the air as they were flown around on swings and metal contraptions that looked far too rickety to trust.

"Do you still want to go on some rides?" I asked Sage as we walked, her hand folded in mine.

"Do you?" With a glance her way, I noticed she was eyeing me with a grin on her face.

"What's so funny?"

She shook her head. "You look a bit worried."

I gestured to the chaos ahead of us as we walked under the lit up arch. "Are *you* not worried about these metal death machines?"

"You ride horses," she said, as if that made me indestructible.

"And your point is? Horses don't fly in the air at high rates of speed and spin you around with mere screws holding your seat together."

She threw her head back, letting out a laugh that could've put the sun and all its glory to shame.

"They're not far off. In fact, I bet more people have been hurt on horses than on carnival rides."

I scoffed as a group of kids ran past us, giggling amongst each other. "I highly doubt that."

"How about we play it safe and just do the Ferris wheel?"

I looked ahead of us to where her line of sight was trained, then looked up, and up, and up... "How is that playing it safe, exactly?"

She laughed again, her hair slipping over her shoulders and down her back. She was blinding in her beauty. I was so entranced by every inch of her.

"Come on," she said, picking up her pace to get a spot in line. I trailed right behind her, seeing the smiles on everyone's faces around us.

Though we did the parade every year, I never stayed for the fair. I'd help my mom with the rescue portion and head home to drink a beer and go to sleep. It was a tradition I'd fallen into seamlessly.

Being here with her, though, made me realize there wasn't a damn place on this floating rock I'd rather be than holding hands with Sage McKinley at the county fair.

"After this, do you want to get some funnel cake?" she asked as we stepped up to the stairs, third back in line.

"I've never had it."

Her jaw dropped dramatically low. "You've never had funnel cake?"

"Nope."

"It's amazing."

"I'm sure it's not as amazing as your baking."

"Listen, I may be a good baker, but nothing beats a fresh funnel cake at the fair."

I smiled. I couldn't help it. "I'll put that to the test after our ride, then."

We climbed the three stairs to the metal platform and they let us through after I handed them two of the tickets Bailey had given me earlier. He'd snuck in early to buy a shit ton of tickets before the lines got long and gave each of us a handful of them.

Letting Sage go ahead of me, she slid onto the seat, the entire cart swinging with her movement. I eyed it warily, and she let out a snort. "Come on." She patted the seat beside her.

Reaching a hand out to steady the contraption, I sat. The guy who took our tickets dropped a metal bar across our laps, the tiny knob at the end clicking into place, and then we were moving.

"You trust that with your life?" I asked, staring at the little knob where it knocked around in the lock.

She squeezed my thigh, scooting closer to me. "No, but I trust you with my life."

I shook my head as I set my hand on hers. "I wouldn't. Not up here."

A small laugh escaped her. "I thought you could fly?" she teased.

"Only on the back of a thousand-pound animal."

She looked out at the fair below us, people walking every which way, lights lit up in an array of colors. "I bet it does feel like flying when you get to a certain speed."

I nodded. "Helps clear my mind when I need it most."

She turned her gaze to me then, her eyes reflecting the lights below. "What do you need to clear your mind from?"

I shrugged, wrapping my fingers around hers. "Life, I guess."

"You can talk to me, Callan. Just because I have my own issues doesn't mean you can't talk to me about yours."

She was right. It went both ways. It wasn't that I was under the impression that I couldn't open up to her, but when other people had things going on in their lives, it felt so burdening to unload my own problems. Because of that, they stayed bottled inside.

"Before you, I rarely went to town unless I had to," I told her.

She nodded, but she already knew that, so she waited for me to continue.

"When my ex gave me the ultimatum that I'd have to choose between her and the ranch, it gave me this outlook on life that I wish I never saw."

Just the thought of saying this out loud made my pulse quicken.

"She made me believe we were living this fairytale life, like I really could have it all and things would be fine. But that day, it all switched. A full one-eighty, if you will. It broke that trust I'd built that things could all work out. I could get the girl, the house, the job I always wanted, and be happy. She tore that dreamland away faster than I could blink, and I knew it couldn't be her. Who gives that kind of choice to the person they love, right?"

Sage sat silently, our seat swinging slightly as we continued going in circles.

"It turns out that even if you give your whole heart to someone, it doesn't mean they'll take care of it, regardless of the words they say. And I should've seen the signs. I really should have. But I didn't. I was blind because I thought what we had was love and it so clearly wasn't. And being blindsided by that, it proved to me that I really didn't know anyone at all. I may see the image they try to portray, but that's all it is. An image. A perception of who they are that they want to show, but one day, that disappears. Their true self comes out, and it can either be the most beautiful thing or the ugliest."

I inhaled deeply through my nose, not taking my eyes off the metal bar strapped across us.

"Seeing that side from someone I thought I loved ruined my perception of the other people around me. Like maybe one day, they'd change, too. So I stopped entertaining friendships and stayed home, only hanging out with my brothers or Bailey." I looked at her then, her rapt attention focused solely on me. "I pushed everyone away to protect my heart. And you, Sage? You spilled that coffee on me on a real shitty day, but I didn't think for a second how much you inconvenienced me that day, only that you made me slow down while I was somewhere out of my comfort zone and I *felt*. I saw you and I wanted to feel again. To stop caring so much about what others might do to me, or how my family was doing, and finally fucking feel something for someone without the fear of it ruining me. Because when I saw you, I didn't think for a split second that you could ever ruin me. That look in your eye that day, the fear on your face when you spilled that drink on me, I knew someone put that there in you, too. You were hurt by someone, and maybe not in the same way I was hurt, but hurt people know hurt people."

She sat on that, letting my words sink in. I'd kept it all in for so long, I didn't know how to say any of it without it sounding messy, but she didn't need me to spell it out simply or sugarcoat my feelings.

She sympathized, but most important of all, she understood.

I didn't fall in love with Sage McKinley slowly. Every moment with her added up to me plunging off the cliff, and my heart was swimming in affection for her. I fell for her hard and all at once, and I didn't want it to happen any other way. Things happened for a reason, and Sage and I? We were damn good together. Our reasons were our past, and before I met her, I was just scraping the bottom of the barrel when she swooped in and showed me how great life could really be.

I'm just glad fate let us end up in the presence of each other.

Before she could open her mouth, the ride swung to a stop at the bottom and the ticket man lifted the bar across our laps. I intertwined my fingers with hers, the two of us standing from the seat, and walked down the three steps to the yellow grass. Only a few feet away, she turned and threw her arms around me, her cheek resting against my chest. The beat of my heart pulsed against her with the knowledge that I just spilled every transgression to her on a fucking Ferris wheel.

My arms wrapped around her, holding her tight to me.

"Thank you," she murmured.

I let out a disbelieving chuckle. "For what?"

"For sharing that with me."

My throat worked around the emotion that suddenly clogged it.

Her head lifted off my chest and she looked up at me. "I love you."

"I love you, baby. For a million years."

"A million years," she repeated, her lips a caress around the words.

This was love.

37

SAGE

The sugary funnel cake we'd inhaled after our Ferris wheel ride sat heavy in my stomach as if I had chugged a gallon of milk along with it. I felt bloated, my dress feeling a bit too tight as we walked through the rows of booths.

"Hey, Cal!" Bailey shouted from somewhere behind us.

We turned to find him and Lettie by the goldfish booth. We headed over to them as Lettie attempted to toss a ping pong ball into the little bowls of water in the center.

"Do you two *really* need another pet?" Callan joked.

I took a sip of lemonade as Lettie's ball bounced off the rim of the glass.

"Lettie would take the whole damn bucket of fish home and raise an aquarium full of 'em if I let her," Bailey said.

"We'd treat them better than any other random person coming through," Lettie tossed over her shoulder.

"I'm sure you'd give them five course meals and paint their fins," Callan teased. Lettie shot him a glare before focusing her attention back on the ball.

"Avery looked real cute in the parade," Bailey told me.

I smiled. "She really did. It was the highlight of the year for her, I'm sure."

"Where's she at?" Lettie asked after missing another throw.

"With Charlotte. Speaking of." I turned to Callan. "I should probably go check on her."

"I'll come with," Callan offered.

"It's okay. I'll come back after I make sure she's not raiding the cotton candy stand. I'll be quick."

He looked like he wanted to push, but then he let it go, thinking better of it. His hand slipped into his jeans, pulling out his wallet, and he handed me some cash. "Give this to Avery for some more tickets."

"You don't have to—"

"I want her to have fun," he said, and I knew he was being genuine. There was no ill intent behind giving me the money.

"Okay." I grabbed the cash from him, then he leaned in for a quick kiss.

"I'll wait for you here."

The fair wasn't too big, so even if he moved for some reason, I was sure it'd be easy to find him again. "I'll be back."

Heading away from the booths in the direction of the lit up rides, I meandered through the crowds of people. A couple shoulders bumped into mine despite my attempts to avoid them.

As I rounded the corner booth, the field opened up a bit before it turned into a few rows of food trucks and metal storage containers. The lights from the rides and spot lights dimmed slightly over here, shadows cast over the flattened yellow grass. Behind me, a balloon popped, causing me to jump.

My hand covered my racing heart as I paused, taking a steadying breath. As Avery and I didn't go many places like this, the sounds were a bit overwhelming at times, but nothing I couldn't handle. It was just a balloon.

Seeing a small alley I could cut through to get over to the rides, I turned in that direction. It was a narrow pathway between two storage containers, but it was the only opening not blocked by food truck doors or garbage cans. About five feet from the alley, I stopped in my tracks as my gaze landed on the man from the bar.

He stood an equal distance away from the opening, staring threatening daggers at me as children and parents walked by in every direction. Blissful chaos ensued around us as every breath, every beat of my heart, narrowed in on the man, blurring the rest of the world out as panic settled into the marrow of my bones.

There had to be only one reason he was here—the same reason he was at the cafe and the bar—and this time, I had no one to pull me out.

The familiar squeeze of my shrinking lungs penetrated my thoughts, and the urge to flee coursed through my veins. I didn't ignore my mind screaming at me to go the other way. I spun on my heel, nearly barreling into a group of teenagers passing around a giant corn dog.

"Excuse me," I muttered, the words barely audible as I maneuvered around them. My heart beat faster than a herd of wild horses galloping across flatlands, and my breaths came in short pants. My feet stumbled over one another as I looked back over my shoulder to find the man storming toward me with a mask of calm that did nothing to settle the terror washing through me like a wave.

Callan was too far away for me to get to him, and if the man figured out I was going to him, I was sure he'd quicken his pace in moments. Under the glow of the rides and food trucks, I could see the faint traces of a black eye lingering from the night at the bar when Beckham sent his fist swinging. I swung my head around, my eyes darting in every direction to find a pair of familiar eyes—whether they belonged to Callan or one of his brothers. I wouldn't involve the girls in this, even if I found one of them first. The man had already made it clear he didn't have boundaries, and I had no idea what his intentions were tonight.

"Oh, Sage," the man sang behind me, and my lungs seized as my stomach spun in on itself as his voice stuck out over the crowd. "There's no point in running this time."

I picked up the pace, brushing past people in a whir. But one glance over my shoulder told me he was doing the same, and gaining fast.

My eyes landed on the opening to the rides, but the hesitation to turn that way was one second too long as his hand clamped around my wrist. With his punishing grip, pinpricks of pain shot up my arm, making my attempt to pull away futile.

He yanked me toward him, pressing his lips to the side of my head as if this was some act of affection to any watching eyes. "Wouldn't want to make a scene, would you?" he mumbled into my hair.

A shiver broke out over my body with the multiple points of contact he had on me. I wanted him off. Off. *Off.*

"I don't know what you want from me." My pitch was high, my voice shaking as my fist gripped the cash still wadded in my hand.

He wrapped an arm around my shoulders, letting go of my wrist as he kept me close. His hand on my upper arm was bruising as he squeezed it. "I want a lot from you, sweetheart, but unfortunately, you're strictly off-limits."

My body shook harder at his words. I knew he didn't mean that because of Callan, which meant Jason was here, and he'd clearly staked his claim.

"Come on," he said, strict command behind his words despite the relaxed image he tried to put on for any prying eyes around us. Everyone was so distracted with the fair, though, that

I doubted anyone would catch on to what was really happening between us.

"Please don't do this," I begged as he steered us back in the direction of the food trucks. "H-he's a bad man. Whatever he's paying you, I can double it. Please."

"He had my back for years. I'm not about to betray him for some bitch like you."

I glanced up at the guy to see if I recognized him, but still, no recollection hit besides the two interactions I'd had with him prior to right now. Were they friends in prison, and now he was helping him out?

"Whatever he's told you—"

"Is the truth," he filled in, tightening his hold around my shoulders. I had no choice but to press into his side. "Women like you always manage to get away unscathed while us men suffer. Same fucking shit with my ex. I'm not letting the same happen to him."

My fingers felt stiff as my body wanted nothing but to freeze and fold in on itself. This man hated women to begin with, and after the stories Jason probably spun to him, I had no hope there was any getting out of this.

He steered me past the alley I was originally going to cut through, heading to another about fifteen feet down the way. As soon as we were in the opening, he dropped his arm and shoved my back. I tripped, holding a hand out to the wall to catch myself.

The buzz of the generators filled my ears as I righted myself, but as soon as I looked up, all the noise drowned out as the pounding in my chest beat a rhythm I had no chance of escaping. My eyes narrowed in on the familiar smirk in front of me.

Before I could blink, I was shoved up against the metal, my head snapping back with a clang. On impulse, my hand released the money Callan had given me, the bills falling to the ground.

"It's not all of it, but I'll take it," his deep, scratchy voice said.

In the shadowed alley, I focused in on Jason directly in front of me.

And my heart sank.

38

CALLAN

The goldfish in the bag Lettie held swam around in the few inches of water the worker gave her.

"What about Goldie?" Lettie said, offering up what had to be the fortieth name suggestion.

"How about we give it to Avery?" Bailey was not a fan of keeping the goldfish, regardless of him egging her on as she played.

"Already giving her a horse," I told him. "I don't think Sage needs a fish on top of that."

Bailey held his hands in front of him like he was weighing the two options. "Goldfish, horse. I think the fish wins out on the easy factor."

"I want to keep it," Lettie complained. "They're not that hard to take care of."

"Lettie, you can barely take care of yourself. Now you want to add a fish to your to-do list?" Bailey questioned.

He had a point.

"I promise to take my iron pills every day," she pleaded.

Bailey scoffed. "That's not up for argument."

"Oh, come on!" Lettie whined.

"I'm going to go find Sage," I interrupted. I loved hanging out with the two of them, but listening to them argue over a goldfish was not how I wanted to spend the rest of my night.

"Take me with you?" Bailey muttered jokingly to me, which earned him a frown from Lettie.

"You signed up for this," I told him.

Lettie turned her scowl at me now.

I parted ways from them as they went back to their bickering, heading in the direction of the rides. It hadn't been too long since Sage went looking for Avery, so I hoped she wouldn't already be on her way back.

Weaving through the crowds of people, I made my way past all the food trucks and booths, rounding the corner to where it opened to a less crowded part of the fair. The rides were a decent amount of space apart from each other, making it easier to look for Sage and Avery.

After passing the bumper cars, I spotted my mom standing at the fence blocking off the funhouse.

"Hey," I said, coming up beside her.

She glanced at me before turning back to the ride, her eyes focused on the bridge going across the second story. "You having fun, sweetie?"

"I am," I admitted with a grin. "Is Sage in there with Aves?"

Charlotte shook her head. "Just Avery and one of her friends she found running around earlier. They've been bouncing from ride to ride all night."

I turned around, scanning the crowd for Sage. "Did Sage find you a few minutes ago?"

"I haven't seen her since the parade. Was she supposed to come find us?" my mom asked.

Behind me, a tiny voice yelled down, "Charlotte! Look!"

I twisted back to face the funhouse as my mom smiled and waved up at Avery and her friend, who were both looking down at her from the bridge.

"I see you!" my mom shouted back.

I grinned up at Avery, whose smile widened when she saw me standing there, then she and her friend were off again.

"She was, but she may have gotten caught up talking to someone. I'm going to go look for her. Text me if she finds you?"

"I'll keep you updated if she does."

"Thank you for watching Avery. We really appreciate it."

My mom looked at me. "I'm happy to give you guys the alone time you need. Plus, Avery is like a breath of fresh air compared to you and your siblings."

I smiled, shaking my head. "I'm sure she is."

Heading further into the section with the rides, I kept an eye out for Sage. I wouldn't miss her with her plaid dress on, but the more I looked, the more the worry set in. The fair wasn't massive, so she couldn't be far.

So where was she?

Picking up my pace, I hurried past groups of people. Before I knew it, I was circling back toward the food trucks with no Sage in sight.

My inability to find her in a crowd full of people shouldn't concern me this much, but with her ex still out there somewhere, the worst crept in, enveloping my mind.

I shouldn't have let her walk away alone. I should have gone with her, no matter that she felt safe here.

Protected by the crowd or not, I wouldn't let anything happen to her.

She was safe.

She was just caught up somewhere and I hadn't found her yet.

But as much as my thoughts tried to soothe me, the worst kept creeping in.

What if she wasn't?

What if he found her?

I just had to hope I got to her first.

39

Sage

"What the fuck, Jason?"

He grabbed the cash in a flash, shoving it deep into his pocket with his other hand still on my arm in a bruising grip. "Where's the money, Sage?"

I tried to keep the tremble out of my voice, but failed. "I'm not giving you any money."

He shook me once, hard, as the man who brought me over here stood at the edge of the alley like some kind of guard dog. "Then where's my daughter?"

I reached up to remove his hand, but he caught it before I could grab his wrist. His squeeze was punishing, and I was surprised none of my fingers snapped in his grip. I tugged, tears springing to my eyes. "Let me go," I gritted out.

He clicked his tongue, holding me like it was nothing. He was always good at that. Treating me like I was nothing more than a bird's feather on the wind, inconveniencing him.

"It's either money or the girl."

"The *girl*?" I exclaimed, exasperated. "She's my *life*, Jason. You don't even love her!"

In a flash, he dropped my hand and pain bloomed in my cheek as he slapped me, my head snapping to the side. My cheek and jaw stung, more tears puddling in my eyes.

"I'll get child support if I have her," he said, as if that was at all appealing to hear.

"Not if you kidnap her," I seethed, though it came out more as a whisper. Raising my voice with him never got me anywhere. It only made it worse. But he was bringing Avery into this, and my heart couldn't handle that.

His grip on my upper arm somehow became harder, cutting off the circulation. "Then give me what I want."

"How did you expect me to give you money if you made me lose my job?"

"You'd move back to Portland and get a job that paid more than that shitty coffee shop." It wasn't confirmed before that he was the one who made the call to Erica, but now I was certain.

"You really think I'd move back with *you*?" He'd lost his mind. Though, I wasn't sure if he'd had it to begin with.

"You wouldn't have a choice. I should drag your ass back there tonight. But I can't do that without any money."

"I don't have money on me." Did he expect me to hold thousands of dollars in my dress?

As if he needed proof, his gaze roamed over me, taking in my outfit. The hand he'd slapped me with dropped, patting down my sides, then went for my skirt.

No fucking way.

"Get off of me!" I shoved at his shoulders with all the force I could muster, despite his hold on me.

He brought me forward only to shove me hard against the storage container, my head snapping back again. My skull rattled, tiny black dots blooming across the corners of my vision. He continued moving his hand down, fisting his fingers in my skirt, lifting it.

I did all I could not to cry. He was checking me for money.

That's what I told myself.

That was all he was doing.

My head lolled back against the metal as I closed my eyes, trying to avoid thinking about the pain in my head and arm. I couldn't take it anymore. If I quit the fight, I wouldn't get it as bad.

That was how it worked all those years I suffered his wrath.

But before my dress could lift any higher than my thigh, his hand released me with a tug, and my eyes shot open at the sound of a scuffle.

I blinked away the haze to see Callan swinging a fist into Jason's cheek right before he fell to the ground. I spun my head toward a shout at the end of the alley to find Lennon shoving the other man up against the storage container, his forearm pressed firm to the man's throat.

Callan went down with Jason in front of me, sending punch after punch into his jaw. Jason tried to fight back, but Callan was too fast. People were crowding the end of the alley, gasps and shouts being thrown about as Lennon held the man firm. He was shouting something at him, but Lennon wasn't giving in to the bait as he kept an eye on both him and Callan.

Three officers shuffled down the passageway, a fourth grabbing the stranger from Lennon so he could release his hold. One of the officers heading our way shouted at Callan to stop. After another punch that sent Jason's head snapping to the side, Callan wiped his mouth on his arm and stood, his eyes instantly finding me.

I hadn't realized I was breathing so heavily as the panic set in further.

"Baby," Callan murmured, stepping over Jason's leg to wrap his arms around me. He led us out of the alley, the crowd parting for us to get through. Once in the opening, he moved his hands to my cheeks, looking over every inch of me. "Are you hurt?"

My eyes felt heavy, lagging to keep up with his movements. "My head."

His gaze snapped to mine, surveying my face. His eyes landed on my cheek, which I guessed was red from where Jason had slapped me.

My hand came up to touch the back of my head and I winced once my fingers found the little knot.

He moved my hand away gently. "Did he hit your head?"

"Against the storage unit." I didn't mention that it was twice.

His eyes narrowed as he studied my face, most likely looking for some sort of sign that I had a concussion.

"Is she okay?" an officer asked behind me.

I turned, quickly wishing I hadn't moved so fast as my head swam. Callan steadied me as I swayed on my feet. Between the adrenaline and the pain, I wanted to curl up in a ball and disappear. There was too much going on. Too many noises, lights, people.

"Possibly concussed," Callan told him. "Do you have an EMT on site?"

The officer nodded. "I'll bring you to them."

Behind the officer, the other two emerged with Jason in cuffs, his face bruised and bloody. I averted my eyes, focusing on the officer as he began walking toward the end of the row littered with food trucks.

I kept my gaze downcast as people watched us pass. They weren't being nosy, they were just concerned about what had happened, but I still couldn't bear to look. Having issues arise publicly in Portland was bearable, but in a small community like this, it felt wrong, like I was the one disrupting their lives. Everyone was so peaceful, and I brought Jason here, tainting the beauty of it all.

With Callan's hand in mine, his thumb brushed my skin in a soothing stroke. All I wanted was to go home and wish tonight never happened.

"You're safe now," he whispered to me, inching closer as we walked.

I nodded once, not looking up from the ground with the fear that the panic would set in again if I took in the busyness of the fair.

I felt safe next to Callan, knowing he had found me, and I had him thinking of me enough to go looking.

If he hadn't, I didn't know what Jason would've done. How far he would have gone.

The officer brought us over to an ambulance that was parked a few dozen feet from the fair, and I sat on the back step, letting the EMT check me over. He confirmed it was a mild concussion, but that I should be fine. He also looked over my cheek for swelling, and made sure my hand or arm wasn't broken.

In just a few minutes, Jason had inflicted so much pain, and after a lifetime of it, I was so tired.

Callan thanked the EMT as I stood. He brought me a couple feet away, then lifted my chin gently so I'd look at him.

"None of this was your fault, okay?"

I nodded once.

"Baby, talk to me."

I opened my mouth to speak, but a rock of emotion instantly lodged itself in my throat, and the tears fell. Callan gathered me in his arms, holding me tight to his chest while remaining wary of the parts of me that hurt.

But it wasn't just the physical that pained me.

It was over now, but all of the past, it hit me at once. My tears soaked his shirt as his hand rubbed my back soothingly.

"I need Avery," I managed to get out through a sob.

He nodded, pulling back and wiping my tears with his thumbs.

Of course I wanted Callan in this moment, to hold and comfort me, but I wanted to make sure Avery was safe. I needed to see it for myself.

After all the years of worrying that Jason might drag her into this, even while he was in prison, I needed that reassurance.

He was so close to her, so able to take her and leave forever.

I needed my little girl.

Callan led us through the groups of giggling children and adults milling about. As we broke through the throng of people, I spotted Avery and instantly broke into another sob.

I tried to hide it from Avery when I was worried or panicked, but I couldn't. Not this time.

She was safe and unharmed. Untouched by the man who had done too much damage for far too long.

"Aves," I gasped out, and she ran to me, worry etched into her features.

I kneeled as her arms came around me, and I held her tight. Children needed their parents, but they never told you how much a parent needed their child, too.

"Mama," she mumbled into my shirt. "Callan found you."

Through the tears, I looked up to him, finding him watching us with a love in his eyes I didn't think was possible.

"He did, baby girl. He did."

40

CALLAN

After giving our statements to the police, I drove Sage and Avery to my house. Though Jason and the man that was working with him were arrested, I couldn't bear to have either of them out of my sight tonight, or possibly for the rest of forever.

Sage had gathered herself rather quickly after seeing that Avery was unharmed and safe, but I could tell she was still shaken up.

I wasn't sure what Jason was attempting to do when I found them in that narrow pathway, but I wasn't going to wait a moment longer to find out. Sage had looked so defeated, her head tilted back against the storage container while Jason lifted her skirt.

If I had been one second later...

I killed the engine, my hands gripped so tight on the steering wheel I thought it might break into pieces. The memory of seeing that man from the bar standing at the opening to the alley like he was making sure no one went down that way instantly made alarm bells ring. Thankfully, Lennon had been in line for a corn dog for Oakley when I saw him. Otherwise, I would've gone in completely alone.

Hell, I'd walk through fire if it meant Sage came out unscathed.

"I can carry her inside," I said to Sage as she sat in the silence.

She turned around in her seat to see that Avery was asleep.

"Sorry," she said as I unbuckled the seat belt.

"Don't be. It was a long night." I got out, coming around the hood of my truck to Avery's door. I gently unbuckled her, then picked her up. Her head flopped against my shoulder. She was out.

Sage got out and closed both the doors, then followed me up to the house. I fished the keys out of my pocket, unlocking the door to let us in. Sage bolted it behind me as I headed down the hall to one of the guest bedrooms.

Maybe one day it could be Avery's room.

I peeled back the sheets, then eased her onto the bed, cradling the back of her head as I laid her on the pillow.

My fingers brushed some of the hair off her forehead as my other hand covered her with the blanket. She looked so similar to her mom, down to those little hairs that always dangled in their faces.

I wondered if, one day when we had kids, they'd look just like Sage, or if they would be a perfect blend of us both.

Tiptoeing out of the room, I eased the door shut, being careful that the knob didn't make a loud click.

Heading back down the hallway, I found Sage in the kitchen, putting a kettle on the stove. "Tea?" she asked.

I came up behind her, turning her around so she was facing me. "I'll make it."

"Okay," she said, her green eyes sparkling up at me with something so deep, so raw, that I wanted to hold her close for the rest of my life to ensure she'd never feel the way she did tonight again. "Thank you."

"It's only tea, baby."

She shook her head. "For stepping in. You've never hesitated when the moment calls for it, and I think that's always been a problem of mine."

"Hesitation?" I asked.

She nodded.

"That's not a flaw, Sage. It's a reaction ingrained into you because of the consequences that happen when you don't. But you never have to hesitate around me. Lay it all out, the good, the bad. All of it. You want to get mad at me? Get mad. You want to cry? Sob like there's no tomorrow. But, baby, never hold it in. Not with me."

The words were what she needed to hear, and what I needed to say.

"I've been in your shoes, maybe not verbatim, but with thinking that I had to think before I reacted, to filter myself to appease someone else. We don't have to do that, not with each other," I told her.

"Your ex?" she asked, bringing it up for the first time.

I nodded. "You and I are both soft people, Sage, but there's nothing wrong with being soft. The world tries to make it seem like we have to be hard, have our guard up at all times, but that's not right. It shouldn't be. I'm just happy you're alright, and that he's gone for good."

"Me, too," she agreed. "Already, it feels nice not having to look over my shoulder or worry that he might show up."

My hands rested on her hips. "I'll be looking over your shoulder for you. No more doing it alone."

Her lips lifted in a slight smile. "No more doing it alone," she repeated.

I pressed a kiss to her forehead. "I love you."

"For a million years," she murmured.

I had my girls, the house, the job.

It was all I had ever wanted.

Happiness presented itself to me in the form of these two women, and I wouldn't have asked for it any other way.

41

Callan

The bay stood quietly where he was tied to the fence. I did my best to stick a sparkly pink bow on his back, but it wasn't staying very well, so anytime he shifted, it slid right off.

I called to Brandy where she was in the round pen working on desensitizing a colt.

"What's up?" she called back.

"Got a minute?"

Her spurs clanged as she walked across the pen, proceeding to hop the fence and come over to me. She looked at the bow. "Trouble?"

"How do I make this thing stick to him?" She had to have some kind of idea.

"One sec," she said before disappearing into the barn. A minute later, she came out with a tube. "Plaiting wax."

"What?"

"You know, to keep the plaits secure."

I stared at her blankly.

She sighed before stepping in front of me to lay a glob of it on the horse's back, then pressed the bow into the gooey substance. "There. It'll stick."

"Thanks." Looking closer, I eyed the bow, and as the horse shifted to his other leg, it didn't slide off.

"Mhm," she mumbled, disappearing into the barn with the tube to put it away.

I'd picked the horse up the following Thursday after the fair as scheduled. I'd spent every day with Sage since the incident. Today was the first day we were away from each other for longer than a few minutes. She'd been updated a few days ago that Jason was being transferred back to the Oregon State Penitentiary, where he'd be charged for violating probation, breaking a restraining order, and attempting assault. His friend, Derek, would be going right along with him for all sorts of charges I couldn't keep track of.

It wouldn't keep them locked away for forever, but it was a start.

I turned to the sound of tires coming up the driveway, but instead of Sage's SUV appearing, it was Beckham's truck.

Leaving the horse tied to the fence, I made my way over to Beckham as he shifted into park and turned off the engine.

"Long time no see," I said as he got out.

He pulled his duffel bag out of the back seat, then closed the rear door.

"Need any help?" I offered.

He shook his head. "This is it."

I eyed the bag. "That's all your belongings?" If he was taking a break from the rodeo circuit, I expected him to have a lot more than that.

"Yep," he clipped as he passed me, aiming for the house. "Got some stuff in a storage unit, but as for clothes, this is it."

"Are you doing okay?" I asked, not bothering to follow after him. I had to be out here when Sage and Avery arrived.

He paused, looking over his shoulder at me. "Just want to visit my family, Cal. Don't look too far into it."

The old me would've pressed further until he spilled it all, but the new me acknowledged that regardless of my concern, he'd open up when he wanted to. It didn't have to be to me, though I'd be there for him if he wanted to talk.

"That horse for Avery?" he asked, lifting his chin in the direction of the gelding.

I nodded.

"She's going to love him." He faced forward, heading up the porch steps and into the house.

Behind me, a car came up the driveway, and once I turned, I saw it was Sage's vehicle. I willed the worry I felt for Beckham away as I walked across the driveway to meet them near the barn. As soon as the car was off, Avery was out and running for the horse.

"Boots!" Avery squealed as she approached him from the side.

The horse turned his head to look at her, letting out a snort as she reached up to run a hand along his snout.

"He looks just like the picture," Sage acknowledged, coming up beside me. "How'd you do that?"

"Took a lot of searching. When I saw his ad, it was like it was too good to be true. Went out to ride him, and I just knew he was the one for her."

"Well, you've sure made her dreams come true," she said, wrapping an arm around my back.

"I figured adding this guy to our family would make her happy."

Avery scratched at Boots' neck, his upper lip stretching into the air as he craned his neck.

Sage nuzzled closer into me, and I wrapped an arm around her shoulders, my fingers trailing up and down her bare skin.

"You know," she started, pure bliss shining in her tone, "we'll be adding another member in about seven months."

My movements froze. I looked down at her, finding her smiling up at me, then glanced at her stomach before searching her eyes for the confirmation. "A baby?"

She nodded, the smile taking up every inch of her beautiful face. "A baby."

My arm immediately slipped from her shoulders, my hand coming to her belly. I couldn't help the tears that sprang to my eyes.

"So I thought, maybe, I could take you up on that offer to move in."

I laughed through the tears that threatened to spill. "I thought you'd never say the words."

"Don't cry, or I'll cry." But she already had a sheen to her eyes as well.

"Avery's going to have a little sibling," I said, looking down at her belly where my hand was pressed against it.

"She is."

Sage joined me in staring at her belly, absolute joy taking over every thought in my mind.

"She's going to love them," Sage said.

"For a million years," I whispered, and brought my lips to hers.

Avery and this baby were already my entire world, Sage my universe, and that was all I needed.

Words couldn't express how much that meant to me.

How much they meant to me.

We were a family.

Epilogue

Sage

Two weeks later...

"I'm honestly surprised it's still alive," Oakley said before taking a sip of her lemonade.

"Or that Bailey let you keep it," I added.

Lettie kicked her feet up on the chair next to her. "What can I say? I'm a pro at this mom thing."

Oakley snorted. "Mother to a goldfish."

"It's a title I wear with honor," Lettie announced proudly, her chin held high in the air.

Stay-at-home mother of two and part-time baker would be the official title I held soon, and I was nervous as all get-out to tell my friends. We were just waiting for Brandy to show up, and then I could spill.

Callan and I had made the decision for me to quit my job at Bell Buckle Brews so I could be home with Avery and enjoy my pregnancy without the added stress. When the baby was born, I'd be able to stay home with them, too. On the side, I'd be taking on orders for baked goods from people around Bell Buckle. Charlotte and Lettie had already declared that I'd be catering every Bottom of the Buckle event, which I'd had no problem agreeing to. Lettie had also asked me to make her wedding cake, which would be nerve-wracking in itself, but I was up for the challenge.

Avery and I were slowly moving into Callan's house, waiting to move the larger items until my lease was up in a couple months. Avery chose her room—the one she slept in the night of the fair. The baby would get the other one.

It felt surreal even thinking those words.

Our baby.

"Where is Brandy anyway?" Oakley asked, changing the topic.

Lettie shrugged. "Probably with some guy she met at the fair."

"You think?" I didn't peg Brandy to be the dating around type of girl.

"If she's not, we need to set her up on a blind date," Oakley said.

Lettie's eyes popped wide, pointing at Oakley. "That is a brilliant idea."

"But with who?" I couldn't even begin to guess Brandy's type.

Behind me, the front door opened, Callan appearing as he closed it. "Hey, guys."

"Hey," Lettie and Oakley said in unison.

He walked up behind me where I sat in the end chair at the dining table, wrapping a single arm around my shoulders as he pressed a kiss to the top of my head. My hands instinctively wrapped around his forearm.

"I got your stuff," he murmured against my hair.

"Thank you."

"What stuff?" Lettie asked, eyeing the plastic bag in his other hand.

"Pickles and peanut butter." It was currently the only thing I was craving aside from cheesy noodles, both of which I needed in abundance.

Lettie scrunched her nose in disgust as Oakley sent me a smile. From that look alone, I could tell that she knew. Lettie, on the other hand, was oblivious.

"Sounds like literal barf in my mouth," Lettie said.

I shrugged. "Not everyone likes it."

"Does anyone?" she questioned.

"Some women," Oakley answered, doing her best to hide her knowing grin.

Callan dropped his arm, heading for the kitchen to put the items away.

"So, Cal, we're trying to set Brandy up on a blind date," Lettie said from her seat, looking over her shoulder at him.

He chuckled. "Good luck with that."

Lettie crossed her arms. "I think she'd love it."

He raised his eyebrows as he stuffed the peanut butter jar in the pantry. "I'm sure."

"Do you have anyone we could set her up with?" I asked.

Callan closed the pantry door, moving to stand at the counter, crossing his own arms in thought.

There was a tense silence as he pondered who he could offer up, but instead of telling us the name that came to mind, he said, "I know just the guy."

"Who?" Lettie asked, her voice rising in pitch at her excitement.

The front door opened and shut, then Brandy walked into the room. "Who, what?"

"Oh, nothing," Lettie said before pursing her lips shut. It'd be hard for her to keep it a secret.

"Are those pickles?" Brandy asked, ignoring Lettie's obvious, sad attempt at keeping a poker face.

"They are," Callan confirmed.

Brandy moved toward the kitchen instead of the empty chair at the table. "Can I have one?"

"Do you want to fight a pregnant woman for them?" he teased.

Oakley couldn't have smiled bigger if she tried as Brandy swung toward me, her eyes and mouth wide as could be.

Lettie's brows drew together. "No one's pregnant, Cal." She faced the table, taking in everyone's reactions. She looked back and forth between all of us before staring at me. "Are you pregnant?"

I nodded, unable to hide my grin any longer.

"Oh my God!" Lettie squealed as Brandy and Oakley rushed to wrap their arms around me. "That's why he got that nasty food!"

I laughed, feeling a few tears slip down my cheeks as Lettie joined the hug. "It's not nasty."

"Okay, I'll let the weird food slide, but Sage! You're pregnant!" Lettie shrieked.

Oakley let go, standing beside my chair now. "I'm so happy for you."

I looked up at her between Brandy and Lettie's embrace. "Thank you."

I glanced over at Callan, who mouthed, "I'm sorry."

I shook my head as my smile widened. I didn't care how it came out, just that everyone finally knew. Travis and Charlotte were having the hardest time keeping it a secret, so they'd offered to watch Avery today so I could tell everyone.

"We all are!" Brandy said, letting go at the same time as Lettie.

Lettie gleamed down at me. "If you guys are anything to show, it's going to be the cutest baby on the planet, right next to Avery."

"Damn right," Callan agreed before disappearing into our room to give us some girl time. We got lost in conversation about the baby shower, the due date, the gender reveal. All of it.

I sat around the table with my friends, the man I loved just a room away, and my daughter spending time with her grandparents.

Life couldn't be any more perfect if it tried.

THE END

Acknowledgements

My biggest thank you will always be to you—the reader. Without you, I wouldn't be able to do what I love. I'm forever grateful for your support, and giving me the ability to keep telling these stories.

Alex. My forever love. Thank you for all your support and crazy ideas for my manuscripts. I will always be grateful for you cheering me on and giving me the daily words of encouragement that I need. I love you.

My baby, Colter. I'll always put you in my acknowledgements, buddy. I would have never pursued my dreams had I not found the confidence you instilled in me that I could do anything. The sky is the limit, baby, and we're going all the way.

Thank you to my beta readers. I'm truly so thankful for all the feedback you give, and all the input you offer. You help to make these stories what they are, and I value all of your opinions and thoughts.

To my editor and best friend, Bobbi. As always, thank you for putting up with my mistakes and loving these stories as hard as I do. I hope I gave your sweet angel baby daddy Callan the love story he deserves—I'm sad to say he ends up with Sage, but maybe in another life, you two were meant to be.

My cover designer, Ali Clemons. Thank you times a million for putting up with my millions of revisions. It's truly a process, and you make the whole thing so enjoyable.

Kate. I always have to thank you. It's just a thing now. You listen to my hundreds of voice memos of me simply ranting and stressing, and for your listening ear alone, you keep me sane. Our friendship is a plus. No, I'm kidding. Dipping my toes into the author career has been so much less daunting because of you, and I can't express how grateful I am for this community bringing us together.

Rose—thank you for helping with so much of the backend stuff. You make my job easier, despite my crazy desires to add more stress to my shoulders, and I'm so dang appreciative of everything you do for me.

And all the moms out there—whether single or not—this book is for you. Since having my son, I found the love I hold in my heart has never been bigger. Our babies are our world, and I hope you found some solace in the pages of this book. Sage was a small way for me to get my insecurities out, and in her character, I found a sense of peace. Writing her was healing, in a way. In the end, it doesn't matter how our baby came into this world. Just that they're in it, and they're ours to love and hold forever. We are strong, resilient, and do our best every day. Never doubt your place on this planet, and the next time you look in the mirror, don't beat yourself up. We're beautiful, no matter what.

Last but not least, my ARC readers. You hype the heck out of my books, and always make release day so dang special. I'm not kidding when I say I cry over your edits. You may not feel like it, but you make a difference. I appreciate the heck out of all of you.

ABOUT THE AUTHOR

Karley Brenna lives in a small town in the middle of nowhere out west with her fiancé, son, and herd of pets. Her hobbies include writing, reading countless books heavy on romance, and listening to country music for hours. If she's not at home, she's either at a bookstore or getting lost in the hills on horseback. To stay up to date with Karley's future projects, follow her on social media @authorkarleybrenna.

Printed in Great Britain
by Amazon